"Is there somebody out there who wants to kill you?"

Mandy asked.

Ransom's face was suddenly inscrutable. "Not that I know of. I've been out of action for a long time, Mandy. Does it make a difference?"

She regarded him steadily. "No," she said finally. "I hate to think that anybody might want to hurt you. But right now I wouldn't care if you were an inmate on death row." And that was downright terrifying.

"Now tell me something," he said. "Are you sure about this? Because, by God, if you're not, I'll understand. What I won't understand is if you regret this."

She drew a deep breath, then exhaled slowly. "I think we've both got plenty of scars. I'm not looking to collect any more, and I'm not looking to inflict any."

"What were you doing yesterday, Amanda Lynn?" Ransom asked softly.

"Waiting."

"And what will you be doing tomorrow?"

"Living."

He smiled then, a gentle, warm smile. "I intend to see to it."

Dear Reader,

There's so much excitement going on this month that I hardly know where to begin. First of all, you've no doubt noticed that instead of the four Silhouette Intimate Moments novels you usually see, this month there are six. That increase—an increase you'll see every month from now on—is a direct result of your enthusiasm for this line, an enthusiasm you've demonstrated by your support right where it counts: at the bookstore or by your membership in our reader service. So from me—and all our authors—to you, *thank you!* And here's to the future, a future filled with more great reading here at Silhouette Intimate Moments.

And speaking of great reading, how about this month's author lineup? Heather Graham Pozzessere, Barbara Faith, Linda Turner, Rachel Lee and Peggy Webb, making her Intimate Moments debut. And I haven't even mentioned Linda Howard yet, but she's here, too, with *Mackenzie's Mission,* one of the most-requested books of all time. For all of you who asked, for all of you who've waited as eagerly as I have, here is Joe "Breed" Mackenzie's story. This is a man to die for (though not literally, of course), to sigh for, cry for and—since he's a pilot—fly for. And he's all yours as of now, so don't let him pass you by. And in honor of our increase to six books, and because Joe and some of the other heroes I have in store for you are so special, we've decided to inaugurate a special program as part of the line: American Heroes. Every month one especially strong and sexy hero is going to be highlighted for you within the line, and believe me, you won't want to miss his story!

Finally, I hope you've noticed our bold new cover design. We think it captures the sense of excitement that has always been the hallmark of Silhouette Intimate Moments, and I hope you do, too.

In the months to come, expect only the best from us. With authors like Kathleen Eagle, Emilie Richards, Dallas Schulze and Kathleen Korbel coming your way, how can the future be anything but bright?

Leslie Wainger
Senior Editor and Editorial Coordinator

EXILE'S
END

Rachel
Lee

Silhouette®
INTIMATE MOMENTS®

Published by Silhouette Books New York
America's Publisher of Contemporary Romance

SILHOUETTE BOOKS
300 East 42nd St., New York, N.Y. 10017

EXILE'S END

ISBN: 0-373-07449-2

First Silhouette Books printing September 1992

Books by Rachel Lee

Silhouette Intimate Moments

An Officer and a Gentleman #370
Serious Risks #394
Defying Gravity #430
*Exile's End #449

*Conard County series

RACHEL LEE

wrote her first play in the third grade for a school assembly, and by the age of twelve, she was hooked on writing. She's lived all over the United States, on both the East and West coasts, and now resides in Texas with her husband and two teenage children.

Having held jobs as a waitress, real-estate agent, optician and military wife—"Yes, that's a job!"—she uses these, as well as her natural flair for creativity, to write stories that are undeniably romantic. "After all, life is the biggest romantic adventure of all—and if you're open and aware, the most marvelous things are just waiting to be discovered."

To Rob, who daily fights dragons.
With love.

Prologue

In the shadowed room, a man lay unconscious on the blue sheets of a hospital bed. An IV catheter ran into his left arm. A suction tube ran up into the bandages that covered his face, then disappeared into a hole where a nostril must be. Both his legs were elevated and splinted from hip to toe with stainless steel bars, and bandaged on thigh and shin. His left arm showed scars from recent surgery, paper thin and red.

He had already been through a number of operations, and there were more to come.

The only light in the room came from a baseboard night-light, which provided just enough illumination to guide a nurse's steps to the bed. In the corner farthest from the small light there was a darker shadow, a shadow with substance. If the man in the bed awakened with clear senses, he might, just might, notice the watcher in the shadows. But he would not awaken. Not yet.

It would be easy to kill him right now. So easy. A little potassium solution injected into the intravenous tube would bring a quick cardiac arrest. Or it would be pitifully easy to smother him with a pillow. Chances were, after all the man in the bed had been through, everyone would assume he had

*merely been too weak to withstand the rigors of surgery. He
had, after all, been through a lot. The thought was pleas-
ing. Yes, he'd been through a lot. Four god-awful, endless
years of hell. Why was he still alive?*

But killing him now would be too swift, too *easy. He
needed to suffer. He needed to know it was coming. He had
to twist and turn like an insect trying to escape the spider's
web.*

The squeak of rubber soles warned the watcher of a
nurse's approach. As the nurse stepped into the room, she
immediately spied the watcher and hesitated.

"You shouldn't be here," she scolded gently. "It's well
past visiting hours."

"I had to come."

The nurse nodded, trying for a pleasant smile. "He'll be
all right. Really. He's remarkably strong. Why don't you
come back in the morning?"

The watcher gave one last look at the bed, at the golden
hair that identified the patient despite the bandages. *Your
face will be different, but I'll know you. Wherever you go,
I'll find you and stalk you. You're going to learn exactly
what it's like to be hunted. As I am hunted because of you.*

The nurse bent over the bed and checked the tubes. Then
she took the man's pulse. When she looked up, she saw that
the watcher had gone.

"I must be losing my marbles," she muttered under her
breath, "but that character was *creepy.*"

And right there and then, she decided to keep a closer eye
on this patient. It was the visitor's eyes, she thought, and,
remembering them, she shivered faintly. Nobody should
have eyes like that.

Chapter 1

He came walking up the dusty drive with a long-legged stride that betrayed a slight, curious hesitation. Amanda Grant saw him while she was weeding her flower bed, and she sat back on her heels, shading her eyes against the bright Wyoming sun. At times like this, she thought, living alone practically in the middle of nowhere seemed like a dumb thing to be doing.

He wasn't dressed the way most people in Conard County preferred. He wore a green army-style fatigue jacket and no hat at all, not a Stetson or even a baseball cap. His hair seemed to flame like burning gold in the bright morning sun. As he got closer she could see that the hair was a little too long, and that he had a full beard, as well.

A stray, she thought. She often saw them along the roads, mostly in the summer, not usually when the first nip of fall was in the air. Homeless, jobless, always on the move. Lost.

Feeling uneasy, she stood and wondered if she should go inside and get the shotgun from the cabinet. The next ranch house was five miles away as the crow flew.

Yes, a stray. He carried a huge duffel, and a knapsack was visible now, slung over one shoulder. Jeans. Black boots. He was getting closer, and she was standing there dithering like an idiot about what to do. Get the gun, she ordered herself. Stand on the porch like some kind of paranoid idiot with the gun and let him know you're ready for anything. Turning, she took a step toward the house.

"Mrs. Grant?"

He was still a hundred yards away as he called her name. Uncertainly, she turned.

"Mrs. Grant, Sheriff Tate sent me."

She seriously doubted any strange, dangerous drifter would have used an opening line like that. She waited uneasily. The stranger came to a halt some distance away, giving her room to run. It was a reassuring gesture, and she relaxed a little more.

"My name's Ransom Laird," he told her. "Sheriff Tate said you were looking for a hired hand. Said you needed the barn roofed." As he spoke, he dropped the duffel and knapsack to the ground. "I'll work for room and board and fifty dollars a week."

It sounded too good to be true. Most of the hired hands in the area wanted twice that or more in cash every week.

One corner of his mouth curved upward in a faint smile. "Why don't you go call the sheriff and check my references? Then we can talk."

Mandy watched Ransom Laird from the kitchen window as she dialed the Conard County Sheriff's Office. He stood with his hands on his hips, head thrown back, face to the sun. Like a man who couldn't quite believe the beauty of the day. She liked that.

"Yeah, I know him," Nathan Tate said, his voice a gravelly growl. "Known him twenty years, Mandy. He was in my unit in Vietnam, and we kept in touch over the years. He's going through a bad spell, and I thought maybe you two could help each other out. He's okay. You can trust him."

"What kind of bad spell, Nate?"

"That's for him to tell, if he wants."

Mandy smiled into the receiver. In this underpopulated area of Wyoming, Nathan Tate was one of the few people who never indulged in the Conard County passion for gossip. "I should have known better than to ask," she said, and heard Nate's gravelly laugh.

"Well," he said, "if I told you about him, you'd have to wonder what I'd said about you. Now you don't have to wonder."

"That's a point."

"You coming into town tomorrow, sweet face?"

"Yes, it's grocery day." Nate called her funny little names sometimes, but he meant nothing by it. He was the happily married father of six daughters, and he took a brotherly interest in Mandy because her husband had been one of his deputies. John Grant had died in the line of duty four years ago.

"Don't forget to stop by the office for coffee, babe."

"Will do."

She stood by the phone for a few minutes longer, watching Ransom Laird sniff the breeze and soak up the sun. Come to think of it, he did look a little thinner than he ought to. What kind of bad spell?

When she stepped outside again, he turned at once, as if he could feel her presence. She hadn't made a sound.

"Okay?" he said, giving her that half smile again.

"Okay," she said gravely. "Room and board and fifty bucks a week for as long as it's agreeable to us both. Your cabin is on the other side of the barn. There should be enough wood stacked beside the cabin to keep you warm when it cools down tonight, but if there isn't you can find more in the woodshed by the other end of the house. You'll have running water over there, but no hot water, so you can shower here in the bathroom off the kitchen. There's a hot water heater in the barn. If you want to install it in the cabin, you can have hot water there, too. Up to you." John had bought that water heater for the cabin just two days before he got killed.

"Fair enough." He bent to pick up his duffel and knapsack.

"Breakfast is at seven, lunch at one, dinner at six."

She watched him walk south toward the barn and cabin. Except for a very slight hesitation, he walked easily, as if he'd walked an awful lot of miles and had learned how to do it with a minimum of effort. She wondered what his eyes looked like. He hadn't yet gotten close enough for her to see. Then, with a tired sort of sigh, she returned to her weeding. The dry breezes of Conard County were desiccating her, she thought suddenly. All the moisturizers in the world couldn't help her shriveled soul.

Less than an hour later Ransom Laird was on the barn roof. Fatigue jacket abandoned, he walked the gambrel roof with the surefootedness of a cat, pausing often to bend and study a rotted area. Behind the barn he'd found the roofing supplies and plenty of one-inch plywood, enough to sheet the roof before laying the new shingles. It was a job that had needed doing for quite some time, but evidently Mandy Grant hadn't been able to afford it until just lately.

The shingling was a job one man could do, but getting the plywood up would be tough. It would need ingenuity and an extra pair of hands. He wondered how tough Mrs. Grant was.

Inside the barn he studied beams and rafters. The damage appeared to be limited to the roof. The rest of the structure was sound enough. In a corner, under a tarpaulin, he found gallons of red exterior paint. So, painting was next on the agenda. He also found a forty-gallon hot water heater, still in its shipping carton, and enough tools to indicate that the late Mr. Grant had been a hobbyist as well as a handyman.

Suddenly a clanging noise reached him from the distance. Glancing at his nondescript, battered but accurate watch, he saw that it was one o'clock. She was calling him to lunch.

The back door was open, so he stepped in without knocking and found himself in a bright, friendly kitchen. It was a big room, big enough to hold a table that would seat twelve, and it spoke of better times, times when this had been a thriving ranch and big families had lived here. It was so empty now that the ticking of a clock in the next room was audible. At the moment, though, it was full of the delicious aromas of soup and coffee. Two places had been set, far apart, with bowls of chicken soup. Next to one place, his, he supposed, was a plate of sandwiches.

"Take a seat," Mandy said. She stood near the stove, her jeans and sweatshirt covered by a bibbed apron. She pointed to the place with the sandwiches.

He smiled faintly, holding up his hands. "Need to wash first," he said.

She colored then, embarrassed by her oversight, and Ransom became unexpectedly aware that behind that grim, cool exterior lurked a woman. Her auburn hair was bound in an unflattering knot on the back of her head, her figure was completely concealed by the huge sweatshirt and apron, but she was a woman. A woman with sad brown eyes. A woman with soft lips drawn into an unnaturally tight line. A woman.

He turned abruptly in the direction she indicated and found the bathroom. He didn't need this. He didn't want this. He stepped on that small, flickering flame of awareness as ruthlessly as he would have crushed vermin.

His hair, Mandy thought, *was* like molten gold. It looked as if it had just been poured from a crucible, then finely veined with silver. He was older than she had thought at first. He would have to be, to have been in Vietnam with Nate. Outside in the sun, he had looked to be around her age, about thirty. Now, up close, she knew he was at least forty. There was silver in his hair and in his beard. There were deep creases fanning away from his eyes. Blue eyes. Eyes the color of the Conard County sky. Eyes that had looked utterly empty except for one brief flare of something as he looked at her. That flare disturbed her.

Narrow hips, she noticed as he turned to walk away. Narrow, flat hips. Long legs. Broad shoulders. He was tall, but not too tall. Compact. Lean. Pared to the essentials. She'd never liked that body type. John had been a little stocky, with just enough softness to him to make him huggable. This guy looked too hard to be human. He looked as if he didn't understand the meaning of indulgence. He looked as if he were unforgiving of himself.

So why was her heart racing suddenly? Why did she suddenly feel warm and weak? Too much sun in the garden, she assured herself. Too much sun, and not one damn other thing.

Taking her seat, she waited for him. Some manners couldn't be ignored, even with hired help.

John. His memory sighed through her mind like the warm, dry Wyoming breeze. The pain was long since gone, leaving only a constant, steady sorrow. John's bright brown eyes, smiling as he walked through the door after a shift, reaching for a beer with one hand and Mandy with the other. His hands. His warm, gentle hands, feeling her belly, feeling the child he would never see, the child that had been stillborn the day John was buried. The girl child he had wanted to name Mary after his mother. Both of them slept now under a cottonwood.

Looking down, Mandy realized her hands were clasped tightly over her stomach, as if to hold in the ache. John had been a man to grow old beside. Life with him had been a gentle, warm, easy flow, a natural progression of days.

"You okay?" The voice was deep, faintly husky.

Mandy looked up into eyes that weren't brown, into a face that hinted at things that were neither natural nor easy nor warm. A face chiseled by extremes and harshness.

"Stomach ache?" Ransom asked.

Mandy shook her head, making an effort to unclasp her hands. "Memories," she said shortly. "Sometimes I remember."

"Yeah." The husky voice was suddenly softer. "Me too."

He pulled out his chair and sat, waiting. Mandy picked up her spoon, and he followed suit.

"I'll need help with that plywood," Ransom said after a moment. "I can get it up there with the pulley, but it'll take at least two people, and it'd be easier with three."

"My neighbor said he'd lend me a couple of his hands to help with that. When do you want to start?"

"Whenever we can get the help."

We. How easily he linked them together. She didn't know if she liked it. But maybe that was how he looked at things.

Maybe he was accustomed to team efforts. She was accustomed, after four years, to solitary ones.

"I'll call Tom after lunch."

"I found the water heater," he continued between mouthfuls of soup. "I was thinking. How old is the water heater in the house here?"

Mandy had to think. "At least six years," she said. "It was here when I married John."

"Then maybe we ought to put the new one in here and move the old one out to the cabin. It might save you some money."

She was surprised by his thoughtfulness. She hadn't expected it. "Makes sense."

Again he gave her that faint smile. "I'll get on it this afternoon. I saw paint in the barn, so I'm assuming you want the barn painted, too?"

"If the weather holds."

"The house could use a coat, too."

"Yes." She looked down at her bowl. "Mr. Laird."

"Ransom. Or Laird. Just skip the mister."

"Ransom," she said, trying it out. "Okay. Look, this isn't a working ranch. It hasn't been one in a long time. John went to work for the Sheriff's Department to pay off the debts his folks left. When ... when John died, his life insurance paid off everything that was left. Except for taxes, utilities and food, I haven't got any expenses. That's the only reason I've been able to keep the place."

"You don't work?"

"I work. I'm a writer. It doesn't make me wealthy. It took me a long time to save the money to buy the roofing supplies. Whether I can paint the house is going to depend on my next royalty check. I need help around here. I can't keep up with it all. That's obvious. You've got a job as long as you want it. But major projects are going to be rare."

"Okay." He pushed aside his soup bowl and reached for the sandwiches.

"Coffee?"

"I'll get it, Mrs. Grant. Well, if that's the way it's gotta be, then fifty bucks a week is too much."

She looked up, astonished. "To keep you hanging around here for what needs doing, it's not too much. Everybody else wants more."

He shrugged. "I don't have any needs. No, let me put that another way. I need a place to sleep, some work to keep me busy and enough cash to keep clothes on my back. I don't go for expensive women, I don't spend Friday nights boozing it up, and I don't even have a truck to put gas into. What I need at this stage in my life is solitude and plenty of thinking time. Make it twenty bucks a week and we've got a deal."

"That's ridiculous. I can't agree to that."

"Sure you can. All you have to do is say yes."

"I won't."

Again he shrugged, reaching for the coffee mug by the plate. Rising, he crossed the kitchen to fill it. "Have it your way," he said presently. "The soup was good. It's been a long time since I had any home cooking."

"Have some more."

"Thanks, but I'm full. I haven't had a chance to work up an appetite yet." He returned to the table, sitting back with his legs loosely crossed. "Were you and your husband planning to work the ranch?"

She hesitated. It had been a long time since anybody had mentioned John in her presence, and here this stranger was talking about him as if it were perfectly natural. Well, it *was* natural. John had lived. He'd been a real human being. He had dreamed and planned, and burying him didn't erase that forever.

"We talked about it. It would have been an awful lot of risky debt, though, and John was happy with the department."

He nodded slowly. "This isn't the world's best climate for farming or ranching."

"No," she agreed. "One bad winter could have wiped us out." Rising, she cleared her place and poured herself some coffee. "We wanted to keep the land. For our children." There was a slight catch in her voice, but it leveled out. "It's like owning a piece of the future."

"What do you write?"

She turned, pulling herself out of memory with an effort. Living alone, she was accustomed to drifting into her own thoughts. "Science fiction. Fantasy."

He smiled suddenly, more than a half smile, and for a moment his eyes didn't look empty. "Great. My favorite stuff. Do you use your own name or a pen name?"

"My maiden name. A. L. Tierney."

He straightened. "I know your stuff. I've read all your books." He looked surprised and pleased. "I've got your latest in my duffel right now. You'll have to autograph it for me."

A smile cracked the bleakness of her face. She was aware, suddenly, of every muscle in her cheeks stretching into the unaccustomed expression. "I'm flattered," she said.

The fan of lines by his eyes deepened. "You ought to be. I'm a picky reader. I'm also a cheap reader. Yours are about the only books I buy in hardcover."

He had thawed her a little with his attempt to cut his own wages, but he thawed her even more with that remark. She knew she had fans—she received the nicest letters from them and treasured every one—but this was the first time she'd met one face-to-face.

"Are you working on something now?" he asked.

"Sort of. It's just starting to gel."

"Maybe you'll let me take a peek at it if I'm a good boy."

There was something very boyish in his hard face at that moment, something genuinely eager and interested, and she melted a little more.

"Maybe," she said. "Maybe."

He nodded. "Thanks. Guess I'd better get to work on the water heater."

"And I'd better call Tom," she said, recalled to the reason he was here. "It might be a couple of days before he can free somebody up."

Ransom shrugged. "There's plenty to keep me busy around here. It's been a while since you had a handyman, hasn't it?"

Mandy nodded. "A while."

"Well, I can paint the trim on the barn while we wait for help."

We, she thought as she watched him walk across the hard ground toward the barn. How easily he said it, as if it were a life-long habit. As if being alone were an unnatural state for him. It was the opposite for her. Except for her marriage, she had been alone all her life. During that all-too-brief period of happiness, *we* had been a word to cherish, a warm, lovely, magical sound. It had never come naturally to her tongue. It had always sent a thrill coursing through her, had always been spoken in a slightly reverent voice.

Mandy's mother had given her up for adoption at birth. Her adoptive parents had died in an auto accident when she was only three, leaving her no legacy but her name: Amanda Lynn Tierney. A lonely, solitary child, she had grown up in a long series of foster homes, escaping finally on a scholarship to the University of Wyoming.

There, in Laramie at the rodeo, she had met John. He was in town for the week and swore that from the minute he set eyes on her sitting in the bleachers, he was head over heels. She was much slower. It had taken John fully three years to overcome her defenses, to unlock the barriers around her heart. Weekend after weekend he drove to Laramie, then to Casper after she graduated, to woo her. Little by little the cold, reserved young English teacher melted. And then, one frosty winter morning, she had opened her eyes to realize that her soul no longer lived only on the pages of the book she was secretly writing. It lived, too, in John's presence, in his smile and gentle eyes, in the tender touch of his lips and hands. Without another moment's hesitation, she had picked up the phone and dialed him at home.

"I love you," she had said when he answered. They were married a week later.

She realized suddenly that she was still standing at the kitchen window, and that steady tears were rolling down her cheeks and dampening the front of her apron. She hadn't cried since they laid little Mary in the ground beside John. That had been the last time. The barriers had slammed into place again right after that. Once again her soul existed only within the pages of her books.

Drawing a deep, shaky breath, she lifted the hem of the apron and wiped her face. She had to call Tom about getting some help with the roof. Then she would wash the lunch dishes and go write for a while. She had a crying need to write. It was the only satisfaction she found in her life.

A funny little lady, Ransom thought as he wrestled the water heater onto a handcart he'd found and repaired. Her books were musical, taking leaping, soaring flights of fancy, full of descriptions that heightened the senses, full of adventure and daring. He never in a million years would have believed that A. L. Tierney could be a closed up, locked up, frozen widow. He'd guessed the writer must be a woman; there was more sensitivity in those books than most men were comfortable with exposing. But this woman? This lost lonely soul in the barren reaches of a desolate western state?

He found himself shaking his head and grinned slightly behind his beard. Well, it was far more interesting to think about Mandy Grant's problems than his own.

He got the heater onto the cart finally and paused for a couple of minutes to wipe the sweat off his forehead and catch his breath. Damn, but he was more out of shape than he'd thought. Evidently it took more than a few months to come back from years of confinement and poor diet.

Well, they'd told him it would be a while. He was just so damned impatient these days. He'd missed so much, lost so much.

The sun felt good on his face. Throwing back his head, he closed his eyes and let the heat beat on his skin, feeling the tingle in every cell. And the air. So fresh, smelling of sage and not one damned other thing. No stinking bodies, no human excrement, no rotting flesh. Just clean, fresh air and sunshine.

"Ransom—"

Mandy came around the corner of the barn and halted dead in her tracks.

He was standing with his head thrown back, face turned
up to the sun, shaggy, molten gold hair scraping his bare
shoulders. He'd cast aside his shirt and Mandy couldn't
suppress a gasp. His shoulders were broad, but his skin was
too pale, as if he hadn't seen the sun in a long, long time.
And there were scars. Angry scars on his back as if—as if—

She couldn't complete the thought. It was too awful.
Rooted, she couldn't move, could only stare. He'd been
sick, she thought. Very sick. Muscle stood out leanly on
him, as if it had been maintained by hard labor on a near-
starvation diet. His waist was too narrow. Too impossibly
narrow.

Suddenly blue eyes the color of the Conard County sky
looked into hers. Empty eyes. She couldn't speak. Nor, it
seemed, could he.

Suddenly he moved, stepping back swiftly into the shadows of the barn. Mandy turned, running as fast as she could
back to the house. When she got there, she leaned against
the kitchen counter, gasping. What had been done to him?
And by whom? And Lord, he must be so humiliated by the
way she had stared at him, as if he were some kind of freak.

"Mrs. Grant?"

He stood at the kitchen door, shirt buttoned, tails hanging out.

"Mrs. Grant?"

When she didn't answer, he stepped into the kitchen.

"You okay?" he asked in that deep, oddly husky voice.

She managed a nod, trying to catch her breath enough to
tell him she was sorry, so sorry....

"I'm sorry," he said quietly. "I shouldn't have had my
shirt off. It won't happen again. I'm sorry I upset you. The
sun just felt so good—"

And suddenly she rounded on him, rage filling her with
white heat. "Don't apologize," she snapped. "If you want
to walk around with your shirt off, then you can damn well
do it! You can sunbathe in the nude for all I care! Just don't
apologize. I'm the one who should apologize. I shouldn't—
I never would have—I was just so surprised! I'm the one
who's sorry. Now forget it."

He stood staring at her, hands clenching and unclenching at his sides. After a full minute he cleared his throat. "I guess I should warn you that my legs are in kind of the same mess."

She closed her eyes. "How?" she whispered. "Who?"

"I can't tell you that," he said quietly. "I'm very sorry you were upset. I really am. I'll go get that water heater now." He paused, hand on the screen door. "Did you come out to tell me something?"

She managed to open her eyes to meet his gaze steadily. "Tom'll be sending over some help the day after tomorrow. If anything, you'll probably have more help than you want."

"Mighty neighborly," he remarked.

"Tom's a good guy. John, my husband, saved his son's life a long time ago. He's been trying for years to do something for me. Guess it's time I let him. He'll feel better."

Ransom smiled faintly. "That he will. I'm sort of like that myself. Now I owe you one."

"Me?" She blinked. "You don't owe me a thing."

"Sure I do. You just treated me like a human being." With a nod, he stepped out.

Well, of all the odd things to say! Once again she found herself standing at the kitchen window, watching him stride away toward the barn. He looked, she found herself thinking, like a guy who ought to be a hero in a fantasy novel. A mysterious man with a mysterious past, a man who had clearly suffered unbelievable horrors.

Molten gold hair threaded with silver. A lost king? Or maybe just an old soldier who'd opposed evil forces . . .

Hardly aware of what she was doing, she wandered into her office, spinning a character in her mind as she turned on her computer and pulled up her chair. Lost love. There had to be lost love, too.

Ransom found her there later in the afternoon. He'd been working on the hot water heater in the kitchen and had simply followed the rapid tapping of computer keys to the office. Standing in the doorway, he allowed himself to snoop a little. Her back was to him as she typed rapidly at the keyboard. On the walls were wild and wonderful fantasy posters and drawings, many of them autographed. Books filled two large bookcases and spilled onto the floor in random heaps. Brawny-chested warriors and scantily clad women stared back at him from the covers. The haphazard confusion showed a vitality lacking in the rest of the house, and it pleased him somehow.

Quietly, he rapped on the door frame. "Mrs. Grant?"

"Just a sec," she said, tilting her head to one side. She typed for another couple of moments and then sat back as the computer drive whirred, saving what she'd just written.

"Okay," she said, turning in her chair with a faint smile. "Sorry to make you wait."

"Sorry to interrupt genius at work, but I figured you'd want the hot water back on before supper, and I need a hand. Do you mind?"

"Not at all." She stood up immediately and followed him to the kitchen.

"I've got to shove the heater into the closet," he explained, "but I can't see the connections when I do it. The fit's too tight. So if you could give me directions?"

"Sure."

He gripped the heater and shoved while she peered into the small closet.

"Another eight to ten inches," she said when he paused, "and just an inch to the left."

"Okay."

He shoved again, wiggling the heater slightly to the left, and cursed as his knuckles scraped the side of the closet.

"Ransom? Are you okay?"

"Just scraped my knuckles." He gave her a small grin through his beard. "Did you ever know a man who didn't curse when he was doing something like this?"

She felt herself smiling back. "No, I guess not."

"So ignore it." He paused, wiping his brow on his sleeve. "Damn, but I wear out easy these days."

"So take a break," she suggested.

"That's more than my ego can take. Come on, where are we now?"

"Two inches back, and maybe a half to the right."

"The right? Figures I'd go too far. Okay, lady, get your nose out of the way. It looks better straight. And cue me as I push this time."

Two minutes later the heater was in place and Ransom was muttering some colorful curses as he struggled with his big hands in the small space to tighten the connections.

"My hands are smaller," Mandy suggested.

"But I'm the hired hand." He bared his teeth as he gave a last, hard twist. "There! Now the gas."

He stretched out on his back, twisting his head at an angle, and reached for the gas fittings. "You've got propane, right?"

"Right."

There was some clanking and banging, a few more swear words, and it was done. He sat up, looking pleased and pale all at once. "Matches?"

She watched him while he lit the pilot, thinking he looked exhausted.

"Ransom?"

"Yo."

"Why don't you knock off for today?" she suggested. "It's almost four anyway, and you look beat."

He turned his head slowly as the gas burner whooshed on. "Did you hire a hand or are you running a convalescent home?"

She couldn't help it; she smiled ruefully. "A little bit of both, from the look of it." And then, in the endless pause before he answered, she tensed, wondering if he was offended. Probably, she decided uneasily.

He astonished her. "Guess so," he said finally. "From the look of it." And he smiled. "Tell you what. You go back to your writing, and I'll cook dinner. I used to be a pretty good cook, and I wouldn't mind trying my hand at it. Okay by you?"

"Sure, if you promise not to get blood in everything." She pointed to his knuckles. Blood was oozing down his fingers.

He sighed and stood up. "Looks like I'm not old enough to be on my own."

"I'll get the first-aid kit," she said.

"It just needs some soap and water."

"Yeah, but this is a convalescent home, remember?"

His surprisingly deep, husky laugh followed her down the hall. She brought the kit back and left him with it. She figured that she would be pushing him too far if she tried to help. A man who'd been through whatever he had was bound to have a lot of invisible scars, too, and making him feel helpless probably wouldn't be welcomed at all.

Back at her computer, in the minutes before she picked up the thread of her story again, she was surprised to realize that the two of them had gone through a couple of potentially emotional crises today. And they'd only just met this morning—and he was just the hired hand.

Biting her lip, she stared blindly at the computer screen. She had felt things today, she realized uneasily. For the first time in four years, she had felt something for somebody besides herself.

Ransom was feeling uneasy, too. It had been a long time since he'd made so much ordinary contact with another human being. She'd even made him laugh, and he hadn't laughed in years.

He set only one place at the kitchen table and called her when dinner was ready. Then he took his own plate and headed back to his cabin. He needed space, lots of space. At this point he still wasn't sure if the events of the last few years hadn't warped him into something unnatural. By himself, in the clean air and open spaces, he could almost believe himself cleansed and whole.

The cabin consisted of one room, comfortable enough for a man or a couple. He looked forward to building fires in the wood stove and cozying up on cold winter nights. He longed to feel the cold again. At the moment, however, he wasn't ready to be confined, even in coziness. He dragged an old wood rocker onto the covered porch and sat with his plate on his lap. The barn concealed him from the view of Mandy's kitchen windows, but over the edge of the gambrel roof he could see the upstairs windows of the house. His privacy was incomplete.

The day was beginning to blend into evening, the autumn chill creeping back into the air. He imagined that some sunsets would be spectacular from here. This one, however, promised to be a quiet fading. The evening star in the west and the moon in the east were both brightening. The sense of space and freedom was a welcome relief.

After his return, they'd kept him in the hospital for three months, putting steel rods in his legs so he could walk again, breaking and resetting his twisted arm. They'd even given him a new nose and cheekbone. The parasites that had ravaged him for so long had almost proved too tough, but the doctors had finally whipped them. Physically he was clean again, and nearly whole. It was his mind he worried about now. His mind and soul.

While they had him confined, trapped by casts and traction on his legs, they'd sicced a psychiatrist on him. First the guy had told him what he could expect in terms of post-traumatic stress and emotional recovery. He'd laid it out like some kind of unalterable plan of operation, and it was a bleak prospect. Then he tried to get Ransom to talk about it. Beyond hours of official debriefing, Ransom had never said a word about what happened, and not even in debriefing had he mentioned how he felt about it. Somewhere, somehow, during his descent into hell, he had severed all feelings. They were in there somewhere, he figured, and sometimes he thought that if he ever started feeling again it was going to be like a nuclear explosion, leaving him burnt to a cinder. He hoped nobody else got singed by it.

But today he had laughed, really laughed. And he had been touched by a small, grim woman's concern for him. Feelings. Normal, ordinary feelings. He wondered if it was a good sign or a worrisome one. Perhaps he could just keep the last few years entombed forever and pick up where he'd left off, ordinary and normal.

"Ransom?"

It was the persistent Mrs. Grant, coming hesitantly across the hard ground. Lately he'd been annoyed any time his solitude was interrupted. He didn't feel annoyed now, however. Surprisingly, the corners of his mouth were stretching into a smile she couldn't see in the twilight.

"Nice evening," he remarked.

"Yes." She hesitated, halting fifteen feet from where he sat. "I just got back from the mailbox," she said.

"Did you walk? I didn't hear a car."

"I always walk. It's about the only exercise I get."

He waited, sensing there was a purpose to her intrusion.

"Um—I got my new book in today. It's not in the stores yet, but my publisher always sends copies as soon as it's off the press. I brought one for you, if you want it."

Damn, she was touching him again, and he was liking it. Some frozen corner of him thawed by a degree or two.

"Thank you," he said, and there was a surprising amount of warmth in his voice, so much that it caught them both by surprise. Rising, he stepped off the porch and accepted the hardcover volume from her. "This is really great," he said, trying to read the title in the failing light. "Really great. Did you autograph it for me?"

She flushed and was grateful the dusk concealed it. "I thought I'd better ask what you wanted me to say."

"Anything you like. You're the writer."

"Um..." She bit her lip. "Let me take it back to the house for a minute. I need some light and a pen."

He could have provided both in the cabin, but he sensed that would make her uncomfortable. Picking up his dishes, he followed her back to the house. In the bright light, the world took on a more normal cast. He washed his dishes at the sink while she sat at the table, chewing thoughtfully on a pen. After a while, she opened the book to the flyleaf and wrote swiftly.

"There," she said, closing the cover emphatically and handing the book back. "Please don't read it now."

So he carried it back to the cabin and there, by the light of a small lamp, opened it to the inscription. Her handwriting was elegant, perfectly formed.

"To Ransom Laird," she had written. "Wounded warriors rise to fight another day, and lost kings return to rule. Parted lovers meet again, and dreams really do come true. Amanda Lynn Tierney."

He sat for a long time staring at the words. She had tried to tell him something without being too obvious. The words, almost banal, skirted something that wasn't at all banal. Funny, he thought. Mrs. Mandy Grant, with her tight lips and sad eyes, couldn't have written that. Mrs. Grant had no faith in such things. A. L. Tierney, on the other hand, had an abundance of it.

Chapter 2

"Morning, Nate," Mandy said as she stepped into the sheriff's dusty, crowded office. She never called him Nate without wondering at the parents who had long ago named him. Nathan Tate wasn't a bad name, but being called Nate Tate had surely caused him some grief in childhood.

"Morning, Mandy." He was a burly man with a permanently sunburned face. Without apology, he was sinking steadily into the softness of middle age. "Is Ransom working out okay?" he asked as he poured coffee into two chipped mugs and handed her one.

"Fine. Thanks for sending him. Tom Preston is sending over a couple of his men tomorrow to help get the plywood on the barn roof."

"Tom would have done the whole damn job for you, sweet face."

"I know. I couldn't let him."

"John saved his kid's life."

"John was just doing his job, Nate. That's how he always saw it."

"Yeah." Nate looked down at his cup. "That's why everybody liked him, Mandy. He never got full of himself. I could use another dozen like him." Sighing, he looked up with a rueful smile. "I'm sure you do enough grieving, babe. You don't need to listen to me. So Ransom is okay?"

Mandy smiled. "He's just fine. I'm glad you sent him. I even think I like him." She bit her lip and then asked, "Nate, what happened to him? I saw his back yesterday."

"His back?"

"It looks as if—as if he'd been whipped, or beaten." She could hardly get the words out. Everything inside her clenched unpleasantly at the memory of his scars.

His mouth tightened, and for an instant his eyes turned as bleak as a winter prairie. "I didn't know. Mandy, you know I don't gossip."

"Yeah." She sighed and sipped her coffee, knowing Nate wouldn't tell her any more. "He's not real well, whatever happened."

"He's convalescing. I know that much."

"I know that much, too." She saw the grimness in Nate's expression. Clearly, she had shocked him with her remark about Ransom's back. Maybe he didn't know much about what had happened to his friend.

"Whatever he's been doing since Nam," Nate said slowly, "it's hush-hush."

Mandy looked up. "Classified?"

"Yep. That's why neither of us will ever know what happened to him."

"Oh." She'd suspected something like that from the way Ransom had said he couldn't tell her who had done this to him. Possibilities flitted through her head, but she probably couldn't begin to imagine the many hush-hush things people could be involved in. There must be all sorts of federal agencies that employed people in such tasks. The Drug Enforcement Agency. The CIA. The Treasury, with its customs agents, and alcohol, tobacco and firearms people.

Nate leaned forward suddenly, appearing to have reached some kind of decision. "I'll tell you a little more, doll. You're the only other person in this county who doesn't gossip. Besides, you may run up hard against some of the fallout from it, since you'll see so much of him.

"Ransom married about five years back. He fell for some girl in Washington. He wrote and told me all about her, and mentioned that he was planning to get out of the business and settle down and raise a family. Just one more mission, he said. Said he was going to bring his wife out this way after the baby was born."

Mandy set her cup down. "What happened?" Instinctively, she knew it wasn't going to be pleasant.

"Ransom didn't come back from the mission. His wife sent me his personal effects about a month after he vanished, said they'd mean more to me than her. I called her to see if there was anything I could do to help her with the baby. She told me she'd aborted it and was divorcing Ransom."

"My God!"

"I don't know where he was or what happened, except that he must have been some kind of prisoner all those years. And it sure wasn't finished when he got home."

"I guess not." She knew the pain of losing a baby you never had the chance to hold. She couldn't begin to imagine how it would feel to know your baby had been deliberately killed. "How long has he been back?"

Nate shrugged. "I'm not sure. He called me for the first time in April. Said he was stuck in the hospital and that they were piecing him back together. That's when I made him promise he'd come for a visit. I expected him to be a guest for a week or two, Mandy. I didn't expect him to come hiking into town like he did, looking for work. To tell you the truth, this isn't the Ransom I used to know. That guy was driven, aggressive. I always figured he'd wind up the top dog in some big agency."

"He probably just needs a breather, Nate," Mandy said reassuringly. "I mean, whatever he's been through must have been terrible, and then to come home and find out he didn't have a wife or a child—"

"Yeah." Nate turned toward the window and sipped his coffee. "One of my buddies was a POW in Nam. It took him a while to get his feet under him when he got back. By the time he got it together, he was divorced. Four years is a long time. A man can be changed forever in a lot less time than that. And it can take a hell of a long time for him to find himself again."

A hell of a long time, Mandy thought. Especially if you had been a prisoner and had been mistreated.

They talked for a while longer in a general way about the weather, the upcoming Harvest Dance, the approaching county elections. Nate was standing unopposed as usual, but the county commissioner seats were being hotly contested.

"Marge has got her raspberry preserves put up again," Nate told Mandy as he walked her to the door. Marge was his wife of twenty-four years. "Said she put aside the jars you asked her for last spring."

"Guess I'll stop by and get them on the way home. See you in a couple of weeks."

At the door he smiled down at her, touching her shoulder. "You need anything at all, you just holler."

"Thanks, Nate." Standing on tiptoe, she brushed a friendly kiss on his cheek, then stepped out into the sunshine.

She had taken only two steps along the sidewalk when she had the overwhelming feeling that someone was watching her. She turned immediately, expecting to see Nate or one of her other acquaintances, but among the many people walking on the street, she recognized no one.

Turning toward her truck again, she came face-to-face with Micah Parish, the man who had replaced John as deputy. He was an enigma, a half-breed who wore his black hair to his shoulders despite local prejudices, and who seldom had anything to say. All anyone knew about him was that he was a career military man who had served with Nate in Southeast Asia. And that he was a good, if taciturn, deputy.

"Morning, Miz Grant," he said politely, touching the brim of his Stetson hat.

"Good morning, Deputy." Mandy hesitated, suddenly aware that in the last four years she and Micah Parish had passed many of these aloof greetings, but had never exchanged anything more. Perhaps he felt she resented his taking John's place. Perhaps, unconsciously, she had. Suddenly it seemed important to let him know that any resentment on her part was gone. "Maybe you should call me Mandy," she suggested with a tentative smile. "Four years seems like an awful long time to go on being so formal with one another."

Micah Parish smiled even less frequently than he spoke, but just now one corner of his mouth hitched upward and made him look a little less remote, a little less chilly. "Reckon I'll give it a try, Mandy. If you call me Micah."

Satisfied, she smiled broadly, bid him good day and headed for her truck. First she would go to Marge Tate's for the raspberry preserves, and then she would go to the supermarket. It sure was a pleasant morning.

This time when she felt the back of her neck prickle, she ignored it. Micah Parish was probably watching her walk away.

"Nate," the woman had called the uniformed man who had come out of the building with her a few minutes ago, unwittingly identifying Ransom's friend. The woman was of no significance beyond pointing out the sheriff, nor was the deputy with whom she had just spoken. The sheriff was the one to watch. Sooner or later Ransom would turn up here, because Nathan Tate was an old friend. It was pleasant waiting here on the sun-drenched street, so pleasant that patience was easy to come by.

Two hours later Mandy was pulling up to the house with enough groceries to feed her and Ransom for a couple of weeks and a dozen jars of raspberry preserves on the seat beside her. Just as she was braking at the back door, something under the hood exploded loudly and white smoke billowed everywhere.

"Damn!" she swore, pounding her hand on the steering wheel. Just what she needed.

Suddenly the truck's door flew open and strong arms seized her, pulling her from the seat and carrying her free of the clouds of smoke.

"Mandy! Are you okay?"

She looked up into Ransom's concerned face as they emerged into the brilliant noon sunlight. This was absurd, she thought. He was carrying her as if she weighed nothing at all, like a hero out of one of her books.

"I'm fine," she said drily. "The truck's not. I think that was my radiator."

She watched as his concern was transformed into embarrassment. He had reacted like a man accustomed to life-threatening situations. It had never occurred to her that she might be in danger. It had never occurred to him that she might not be. She didn't have the heart to embarrass him further by asking him to set her down, so she simply waited.

And had time to realize that he smelled good: musky, soapy, masculine. And that his chest was hard, and regardless of whatever he'd been through, his muscles were like steel just now, holding her effortlessly. And his mouth, largely unnoticed because of his beard, was firm and well-shaped. She stared at it, her gaze fixated. Time seemed to stand still.

Slowly he slackened his hold and let her feet slide to the ground. Mandy was aware of every single hard contour of his body as her legs slid downward against him. Too thin, she thought, but every inch a man.

"Sorry about that," he said with a faintly sheepish smile.

"Don't be." Carefully she stepped away. "I always wondered what it would be like to have somebody come dashing to my rescue and carry me away to safety. Now I know."

"Silly, huh?"

A smile caught the corners of her mouth, softening her whole face. "Only because it was a radiator and not a bomb. The effect was the same." Turning, she looked at her still-steaming truck. "Double damn!" she said in exasperation.

"Your only transportation?"

"Yeah."

He put his hands on his hips. "I'll look at it when it cools off, Mrs. Grant. I used to be a passable mechanic."

"Mandy," she said. "Call me Mandy. Guess I'd better get the groceries in before everything thaws." *Used to be,* she thought. She wondered how many *used to's* there were in his life.

Mandy spent a singularly unproductive afternoon. Waking from a long sleep, she thought uneasily when she realized she was back at the kitchen window for the fifth time, staring out at Ransom as he worked under the hood of her truck. Never in her life had she been so conscious of a man's physical attributes or her own sexuality as she was right now.

Funny, she thought, leaning against the counter, staring frankly at the way Ransom's buttocks stretched the worn denim of his jeans as he bent over. All these years she'd believed that she was either undersexed or that sex was overrated. With John it had been a comfortable, warm, affectionate experience, and with his death she thought she'd buried her meager desires. Suddenly her desires were very much alive and not at all meager.

Now, here she was staring at Ransom as if he were a pinup. That was something she'd thought only men did, but here she was looking him over like . . . She flushed and left that thought incomplete. Instead she wondered what his skin would feel like under her hands.

Shrugging, feeling like a silly kid, she shoved her hands in her jeans pockets and went outside. Drawn, like the moth to a flame. The uncomfortable thought crossed her mind and then vanished as Ransom looked up from beneath the truck hood and smiled.

"You blew a radiator hose," he said. "No big deal. The explosion was a backfire."

"Not the radiator?"

"Nope, just a coincidence. The carburetor needs some work, but I can do that. It'll cost you maybe seven bucks for a new hose. I can jury-rig it until you can get to town."

The afternoon was warm, and perspiration plastered his shirt to his back. He would have taken it off if she hadn't been there. The thought made her even more uneasy. It reminded her of the scars. The suffering.

"That's a relief," she managed to say. "I was figuring two or three hundred dollars."

He straightened, wiping his hands on a rag. His blue eyes settled on her, growing thoughtful as they passed over her face. "Did you see Nate in town?"

She nodded, feeling herself color faintly.

"How much did he tell you?"

Her eyes widened. Apparently this man didn't miss a detail.

He shrugged, giving her a lopsided smile, as if to say it didn't matter. "He doesn't gossip. Much. But I figure you're bound to be curious, and he's bound to be concerned, and between the two, there's going to be some talk."

He tucked the rag into his back pocket and paused, looking out over the prairie toward the blue line of the western mountains. "Beautiful country," he said. "Nate doesn't know much, but he's always been good at putting two and two together. It's why he's a good cop." Slowly his eyes came back to her face. "I guess we both spent the last four years in prison."

A soft gasp escaped her. It was true, she realized. But not exactly. She hadn't been living in a prison but inside a fortress. And she wanted to stay there, so what was she doing out here, talking to this man who kept making her feel things?

"So," he said softly, "what were you thinking when you were standing at the kitchen window?"

For the second time that afternoon, time stood still. Mandy didn't even breathe. And then, hardly believing what she was doing, she reached for his shirt. It was unbuttoned, exposing a chest covered with fine golden hair. Carefully, she pushed it off his shoulders. He was holding his breath, too, she realized. He was rigid, taut, motionless. When she had pushed it to his elbows, she walked around behind him. Still he didn't move a muscle. He might have been made of stone.

She made herself look at the crosshatch of scars as she pulled his shirt the rest of the way off. She was sure he must feel her eyes on his back as if her gaze were fire. Then, freeing him of the shirt, she balled it up and hurled it across the yard.

The muscles of his back jerked sharply, but he didn't move. Reaching up, she laid her palms flat against his shoulders, lightly, soothingly.

"I told you," she said quietly, "that you didn't have to wear your shirt. Enjoy the sun, Ransom. You haven't had any in a long time."

Turning, she walked back to the house.

He didn't show up for dinner that evening. It was just as well, Mandy thought. She still couldn't believe what she'd done, and she didn't know how she was going to look him in the eye. Any way you looked at it, taking a man's shirt off was a blatant invitation, no matter how it was intended. And she wasn't sure herself just how she *had* intended it. She had felt possessed.

In fact, to come right down to it, she didn't know what was happening to her. Waking from a long sleep, she had thought earlier, and it was the best description she could think of. That or recovering from paralysis. It was as if something compelled her to reach out to Ransom. First the book and then that little scene this afternoon. Maybe she just recognized a kindred spirit, a fellow paralytic. But that didn't explain the swift rush of sexual feeling she'd had.

Damn, she thought, and buried herself in her office. Damn, damn, damn. John had awakened her once with his slow, gentle persistence, but it had been nothing like this. This was fast, somehow out of control. Dangerous. She couldn't let this happen. Somehow, she had to get a grip on herself before she got hurt.

"Mandy?"

She was sitting in the near dark, a small desk lamp illuminating the computer keyboard, the light from the display casting an amber glow on her face. She swiveled her chair quickly and saw Ransom standing in the doorway, a shadow.

"Ransom!" The exclamation escaped her. Something coiled inside her, a tension she didn't know how to name. She'd never felt it before.

"I knocked," he said. "You didn't hear. I knew you were in here. I saw you through the window when I came walking up."

She managed a nod. If her mouth got any drier it would stick shut forever.

He took one step into the room. "I got to thinking about—hell, I just wanted to tell you to forget it. I figured you were maybe worrying about it...."

He couldn't find the words to explain, but she understood anyway. He was telling her not to be embarrassed, that it was okay. He had understood how she would be feeling. It amazed her, his sensitivity.

"I thought you were mad," she admitted, her voice little better than a croak. "It was...it was..." She couldn't find the words, either.

"It's okay," he said. "I understand. I understood. I didn't come for dinner because—I wasn't mad, Mandy."

"Okay," she said. Words were so inadequate sometimes, she found herself thinking. A traitorous thought for a wordsmith, but she and Ransom were both communicating more with what they weren't saying. "Thanks for telling me." She managed a brief, brittle laugh. "I *was* worrying."

"I figured. I feel like I kind of know you. Because of your books, I guess." He paused, edged a little closer. "I was...I was *touched*. I haven't been touched in a hell of a long time."

"Me either." Understanding somehow that it was not easy for him to admit such a thing, that it made him feel exposed, she felt she owed him similar honesty—especially since he was forcing himself to admit his feelings in order to ease her embarrassment.

"I know." He sighed. "Anyhow, I didn't take it wrong, so don't worry."

She drew a deep breath, cleared her throat. "Have a seat. If you want." Now, she thought, was her chance to make sure he hadn't misunderstood *anything*, despite his assurances.

He looked around in the dark and picked out the easy chair. John had often sat there in the evenings when Mandy got carried away with her writing. She didn't mind Ransom sitting there.

"I'll tell you a little story," she said slowly. "If you want to hear it."

"I do, but only if it begins with 'Once upon a time.' "

She smiled at that. She liked the way he thought, the way he defused the moment.

"Okay. Once upon a time there was a princess born to a queen who was fleeing from her enemies. The queen couldn't keep the baby princess, so she gave her up to a nice rancher and his wife, who promised to cherish the princess forever and gave her a new name to protect her from the queen's enemies. The nice couple kept the princess safe and loved for a few years, and then they were killed by an awful dragon. So the little princess was passed from family to family in the community. Nobody ever wanted her for very long, because she was an odd child with odd fancies of being a lost princess. And the princess never knew who she really was. She only *believed*."

Ransom drew a long breath. "Poor little princess," he said softly.

"She didn't feel poor, precisely. But she felt very, very lonely, as if something were missing, as if she didn't really belong. And she learned very rapidly not to care, because every time she cared, she lost the people she cared for. And always, always, she had the conviction she was someone else. You see?"

"Yes."

"So she grew up with her head filled with fairy tales. She created worlds where people didn't go away forever, where she could be herself, her real self, and people loved her. All of which made her even odder. She became a teacher eventually, because she loved words, but there was always a sense of waiting, as if at any moment her own people would discover her and claim her.

"One day, at a great tournament, a knight saw her and fell in love with her. The princess found him to be all that was gentle and kind and honorable, but she was afraid to care for him, because she was convinced, you see, that every time she cared for someone, an evil wizard cast a spell to take that person away from her. It was the only explanation. The princess tried to tell herself it wasn't true, that it was just a silly fancy, but there wasn't any other possible explanation.''

''I can see why she felt that way,'' Ransom said, very softly.

Mandy shrugged a little. ''Well, the knight was persistent. He wooed the princess for three years, and one morning the princess woke up and discovered it was already too late. She cared. It had happened when she wasn't looking. So she rode off to the knight's castle, and her days were filled with warmth and happiness. And then the evil wizard found out about her happiness and her knight and her unborn baby, and he cast a spell on them all.''

Ransom drew a sharp breath, but he said nothing.

''The princess vowed she would never care again. It made her an even odder person, I can tell you. But still, inside her, was the belief that someday, somewhere, she would be found by those who would love her and protect her from the wizard. Someone would recognize her eventually, someone who would know how to defeat the evil wizard.''

She paused, turning to stare at the computer screen, where amber words glowed at her.

''One day a warrior came walking up to the nearly deserted castle. He was battered, nearly broken. He'd fought a great many evil wizards, and the marks were all over him. The princess saw him and knew immediately that he had suffered as much as she had had and more. He gave her a little courage, and the princess cared. Just a little. Not enough to draw the evil wizard's attention, mind you. She wouldn't risk that. The warrior had suffered enough, and so had she. But she cared just that little and wanted very badly to heal the warrior so far as her small herbs and potions might help. She wasn't quite sure how to do that, but she offered him shelter and tried to let him know his wounds touched her. That she understood he wasn't a battered, beaten warrior, but that he was in reality a lost king who would eventually come into his own. And being the odd person she was because of her odd life and her odd notions, she went about it in a rather odd way.''

Holding her breath, Mandy looked back at him, grateful that the dim light made it almost impossible for either of them to read the other's face.

"The warrior," she continued, "had a kind heart and put up with the princess's odd ways. Unfortunately, I can't tell you how the tale ends yet."

"I can tell you the next paragraph," Ransom said quietly.

"You can?"

"Sure. I happen to know the warrior." He pushed himself out of the easy chair and caused her to gasp by kneeling right in front of her.

"The warrior was touched," he said. "Touched more deeply than he had been in years. It moved him that the princess who had lost so much still had enough compassion to care about his wounds. He was wary of the evil wizard, though, so instead of taking a warrior's vow to protect the castle forever, he simply took the princess's hand in his." As he spoke, Ransom took both of her hands. "And he told her that as far as he was able, he would help her out. And he sealed the promise not by swearing fealty, but by asking for the princess's colors to carry on his lance. This was a small thing, and wouldn't attract the wizard's notice."

And as he spoke, he leaned forward and touched his soft, warm lips to hers. Just a touch. Just enough to waken a sleeping heart to a half-sleeping state.

"And then the warrior got quickly to his feet, because he hadn't carried a princess's colors in a long time, and he wasn't really sure he was quite up to it yet, and he bade the princess good night and went out to the stable to sleep with his horse, determined to do nothing that might hurt the princess."

He leaned forward again, kissing her a little more firmly, yet demanding nothing. His lips moved warmly against hers. Then he stood up.

"Goodnight, Mandy."

She sat in the dark long after he left, realizing he had just returned the gesture she had made in the yard that afternoon. They had laid soothing hands on one another's scars.

Four of Tom Preston's men arrived at seven-thirty the following morning to begin roofing the barn. By eight the yard was full of hammering, banging, swearing and joking. Convalescent or not, Ransom worked and joked as hard as anybody. When the men trailed into the kitchen for lunch, a huge meal of roast beef, potatoes and apple pie that Mandy had slaved over all morning, she noticed he was pale and his hands trembled. There wasn't a thing she could do or say about it, however. Taking a cup of coffee, she slipped away to her office, leaving the men to enjoy their meal without a woman hovering over them.

At five, with a roar of pickup engines, Preston's men left, and silence returned to the ranch. The barn roof was completely sheeted with plywood and tar paper, and packages of shingles had been distributed at neat intervals. From here on out, Ransom could finish the job alone.

He stood with his hands on his hips, his legs splayed, staring up at the roof. It had been a devil of a long time since he had felt such a sense of accomplishment and satisfaction. He could easily get addicted to living like this, he realized: hard physical labor with visible results, open spaces, neighborly people.

"Ransom? You want some coffee or a beer?"

Turning, he saw Mandy poking her head out the back door. "In a minute," he called back. "I want to clean up first." And what a luxury that still was to him, to be able to step into a hot shower and clean clothes. One thing for damn sure: he'd learned to appreciate the small things.

Half an hour later he stepped into the kitchen, hair still damp, and accepted a beer from Mandy, who was putting together a meal of hot beef sandwiches from the lunch leftovers. She stole a glance at him from the corner of her eye.

"You kind of pushed it today, didn't you?" she remarked.

He leaned back, crossing his legs loosely at the ankles. Behind his beard, the corners of his mouth quirked. "I'm still upright," he replied.

"I'm not paying you enough to kill yourself with over-work."

"No danger of that." He sipped his beer. "You're new to this hired help business, aren't you?"

"What do you mean?"

"You treat me like a guest. Or a friend. I can almost feel the guilt radiating from you when I work. Ease up, Mandy. I'm doing what I want to, and I'm happy with the arrange-ment. And you aren't underpaying me."

With a fork she lifted slices of beef from the simmering gravy and laid them on bread. He was right, she supposed. She was uneasy with the situation, and that was stupid. She was, after all, paying him exactly what he'd wanted for the job.

"You looked worn-out at lunch," she said. "I know it's none of my business, but I was worried about it." She put the steaming, gravy-drenched sandwiches on the table. "Just promise me you'll break when you need to. Then I won't have to worry, and I'll leave you alone."

He let her see the smile he was feeling. "I promise. I *do* have some common sense."

Mandy sat across from him, not nearly so far away as at the first meal they had shared. "Broccoli?" she offered, passing the plate. "John always said I was a natural mother hen and that I worried far too much. He used to tease me about whether I was born this way or if it was teaching that did it to me. He never did make up his mind. And I'm still a mother hen." She looked up with a small smile. "I'll try to curb the impulse."

"You'll get over it when you realize I'm practically inde-structible," he said wryly. "Even *I'm* a little surprised at how durable I am."

Her eyes dropped. He wondered how those eyes would look soft and warm with longing. "I bet," she said after a moment. "*Very* durable, from what I can tell."

"There, you see?" he said, gently teasing. "I don't claim to leap tall buildings or be faster than a speeding bullet. I just hold up. I'm like that old pair of jeans you can never throw away because they just won't wear out no matter what you do. They look like hell and you can't wear 'em to town, but you can crawl on concrete in 'em and they just won't tear."

A chuckle escaped her. "I get the picture. I'll shut up."

He shook his head slowly, catching her eye. "I don't want you to shut up. I don't mind your mother-henning. It's sort of nice, actually. But every time you do, I'm going to look at you and say, 'old blue jeans.'"

She laughed outright, and her sad brown eyes sparkled for the first time since he'd met her. She was pretty, he thought suddenly. He hadn't noticed it before. Quietly pretty. And he had the sudden conviction that she had the potential to be beautiful. Not all the time; not like an actress or a model. Just sometimes, at very special moments. It required some effort to return his attention to his plate. No, he told himself, he didn't need this. Not at this stage of his life.

"If you keep feeding me this way, Mandy, I'm going to be back up to my fighting weight in no time."

Her gaze was drawn to him again. His fighting weight. Ten pounds heavier? Twenty? She couldn't imagine him any other way than he was right now, missing gauntness only by a hairbreadth. Her palms suddenly burned with the memory of how his skin had felt beneath them. Smooth. Warm. Boy, did she have it bad!

"How about you?" he asked conversationally. "Is your new story coming together?"

"I think so. A little at a time, at any rate."

"What's this one about?"

Hesitantly at first, then with increasing confidence as he displayed interest and asked questions, she talked about her ideas. As she spoke, they grew clearer in her mind, and almost before she knew it, the entire story was falling into place.

They finished dinner and washed the dishes together, still talking about her book. As naturally as if they did it every day, they took coffee into her office. Ransom sat in the easy chair. Mandy perched on her steno chair and put her feet up on the edge of a desk drawer.

And still she talked. A dam had broken; words rushed forth. This was A. L. Tierney, Ransom realized, the woman who existed behind Mandy Grant's defenses. She emerged as if from a chrysalis, hands moving descriptively, eyes shining. She was caught up in the excitement of her vision, brought to life by a fantasy. Released momentarily from the evil wizard's spell, she dared to share herself.

"I like it," he said when she at last fell silent, head cocked thoughtfully as she considered her newborn story. "How long does it take you to write the book once it comes together?"

"A few months for the first draft. That's the easy part. Rewrites are the killer."

He was a little amazed. He couldn't imagine that writing the first draft of one of her wonderful books could be easy. But that, he supposed, was the difference between a writer and a nonwriter.

"Your books were the first ones I asked for when I could read again," he said suddenly, instinctively understanding what it would mean to her. "I'd read *Talespinner* when it first came out, and I loved it. So when they asked me what I wanted to read when I was recovering, you were the first author I thought of." He saw her face soften perceptibly. He wished she could look soft like that all the time.

"John never read it," she remarked. "He was tickled for me, but he wasn't much of a reader."

"So you couldn't talk your stories over with him?"

"Not really. He encouraged me, and he was proud of what I did, but it wasn't something we shared." She sounded factual about it, not sad or disturbed. "More coffee, Ransom? I think I want some."

He followed her to the kitchen, and while she made a fresh pot, he stepped out onto the porch. The night sky was beautiful, scattered with bigger, brighter stars than he'd even seen.

"Mandy? Come on out. The sky's beautiful. I wish I had a telescope."

"I have one somewhere," she said, coming to the screen door. "Maybe it's in the attic. I'll look for it tomorrow."

The springs groaned as she pushed the door open and came to stand beside him at the rail. The night air had grown chilly, and she wrapped her arms around herself as a shiver took her.

"Here," Ransom said. He stepped behind her and drew her back against his chest, covering her arms with the warmth of his own. For an instant she resisted; then he felt her relax and lean back against him.

He was so warm, she thought, and it felt so good to be held again, even casually. She had nearly forgotten how good it felt to have arms around her. Somehow she just plain couldn't heed her mind's warnings that this was dangerous. It was only for a couple of minutes, after all. Surely she was entitled to be held for just a couple of minutes. What harm could it do?

His voice was a low, husky rumble just above her head. "Thank you," he said.

"For what?"

"This. Night after night I went to sleep imagining myself standing free under the stars, holding . . . holding a lovely woman."

"Your wife," she said softly. For some reason her heart squeezed.

He sighed. "Damn Nate. Yeah. Only as time dragged on, I knew it wouldn't be her. I knew she wouldn't stick it out for long. Certainly not that long."

"I'm sorry, Ransom."

"I'm not. Not after what she did."

Mandy said nothing, uncertain whether he would be upset if he learned she knew about his child.

His arms tightened fractionally. "I knew it was over. I knew it for a long, long time. So I replaced her."

"With whom?"

"Whom?" He chuckled softly. "Your English degree is showing, A. L. Tierney. Nobody real. A dream. A fantasy.

A sweet, sweet fantasy. My priorities got turned around. Nothing I used to think was important seems important now. And things I didn't think much about have become very important.''

"I can see how that might happen," she said when she sensed he expected a response. "It would be weird if you weren't affected."

"So they tell me. They also tell me I'll have nightmares for years and all kinds of hang-ups. So far I haven't even had a dream, let alone a nightmare. I think I got nightmared-out a long time ago."

"Maybe."

"But I didn't get dreamt-out. Funny, but the dreams are starting to come again. Not sleep dreams. Life dreams."

"Then you'll be okay, Ransom."

"Like old blue jeans," he said.

Mandy smiled into the dark. "Like old blue jeans," she agreed.

"You, too," he said. "You're old blue jeans, too."

"I'm afraid I have a few holes."

"Nah. Faded a little bit here and there, maybe. So am I. But not worn out, Ms. Tierney. Not worn out."

She noticed his use of her maiden name and wondered if he had somehow sensed the dichotomy that was so much a part of her nature. Again his arms tightened, just a fraction more, but responding to the implied invitation, she let her head fall back against his shoulder, and together they watched the stars.

"Nice," he said a while later.

"The stars are really bright tonight," she agreed.

"I meant you, Mandy. Holding you. It's nice. It feels just the way I hoped it would all those years."

She caught her breath. "Ransom?" Suddenly, she had to know, even if it meant flirting with danger.

"Yeah?"

"Was that your whole fantasy?"

"No. But I have no intention of asking you to fulfill a dream, so relax." He paused. "However, it's been a hell of a long time since I held a woman, and I'm either going to have to let you go or kiss you."

Her heart started to hammer so hard that she felt almost breathless. She knew he would let her step away right now if she made the slightest move. She also knew that if she stayed where she was, he was going to kiss her. All her self-protective instincts were suddenly muffled, distant. A warm, hazy heat filled her. "I'm a great believer in dreams coming true." *Liar*, said that small, objective voice in her mind that never shut up. You believe in dreams in your books, but not in life. Not in life.

Slowly, very slowly, he took her shoulders and turned her to face him. "Are you?" he asked, his husky voice soft.

"I believe in warriors and princesses and lost kings, don't I?" Her voice was hardly more than a whisper.

"And evil wizards," he reminded her gently.

Holding her breath she raised her eyes. His face was a pale blur in the little bit of light from the stars.

"And evil wizards," she admitted. "But maybe there's a talisman—"

"No talisman," he said almost grimly as his arms closed around her and drew her carefully against his steely length. "No talisman. Just hope."

He lowered his head and touched her mouth with his. His beard was surprisingly soft, silky, his mouth warm and gentle. Aching for the caress, she let her head fall back and let her arms find their way around his waist. A too thin waist, but it hardly mattered suddenly as his heat and strength filled her senses. His tongue found hers with a surety that seemed to proclaim that he already knew her this way from another time, another place, that he knew exactly how she liked to be kissed, how she liked to be cradled. There were no false starts, no tentative movements. It was knowing. It was right.

Mandy felt safe. Security washed through her, along with the rising tide of pleasure he elicited in her. His arms sheltered her so securely that all thoughts of evil wizards and spells vanished. She clung, hands creeping up his back to his shoulders, crossing ridges of scar tissue that could be felt even through his shirt, crossing them gently like a familiar, cherished landscape. One hand found his silky molten-gold hair, sliding into it. He fit her perfectly, she thought dreamily. Not too tall or too short. Just right.

"Mandy." One of his arms held her shoulders; the other was wrapped around her waist. He held her tightly, pressing his cheek to hers. "Sweet Mandy," he sighed, and rocked her gently side to side. He made no effort to conceal the need she had aroused in him, but simply waited for it to pass away into tenderness.

"Ransom?"

He could hardly hear her, even in the silent night. "Yes?"

"That was absolutely the nicest kiss anybody's ever given me."

His embrace was suddenly almost fierce, and the softest of chuckles escaped him. "For me, too, Mandy. We'll have to try it again sometime."

"Definitely."

As he released her, she stepped back, and he could see the softness of her face. He hoped suddenly that no evil wizards were watching.

"Have you ever felt," she asked, "that you've lived before?"

"Often," he acknowledged.

She cocked her head, regarding him steadily. "Then maybe I'm not crazy."

"Crazy?"

"I feel as if we go back a long way. A very long way. I hope the karma's not bad." She reached up suddenly, touching his cheek with gentle fingers. "Thank you. Sweet dreams. You deserve them."

The screen door slapped closed behind her, and then the kitchen light went out. She hadn't locked him out, he realized. She hadn't barred the door against him. Hell, she hadn't even closed it. That was an awful lot of trust for a scared princess to be showing in a wounded warrior who'd walked into her castle just three short days ago.

Smiling, he opened the screen door and pulled the inner door shut before he turned and headed back to his cabin. Every time he thought he had her pegged, she turned around and surprised him again.

Chapter 3

Mandy hardly saw Ransom over the next week. He spent long hours on the roof laying shingles and took his meals with her in quick silence, never lingering for a cup of coffee afterward. He was filling out rapidly, she noticed, growing sturdier by the day, and the sun was returning the color to his face and torso. As for his withdrawal, she was at once relieved and disappointed. They'd moved too swiftly, she felt, strangers who had somehow touched one another too deeply for their brief acquaintance. Perversely, however, she missed his easy companionship. After four years of solitude, the brief taste of friendship had left her hungry for more. And that was why his withdrawal relieved her. Surely she had learned that caring only meant pain. Surely she didn't need to learn that all over again.

On Sunday she walked over to his cabin to ask if he wanted to go to church with her. As she rounded the barn, she saw him cutting across the fields and heading out into the open spaces. He needed a horse, she thought. For that matter, so did she. She'd sold the horses after John's death because there just didn't seem to be any point in all the work and expense when she was sure she would never want to ride again.

On the way to church, she considered the idea and felt herself smiling. They definitely needed horses. Loners both, they needed to be able to gallop off away from everything. A warrior especially needed a horse. She felt bubbles of laughter rising in her throughout the service, and afterward a couple of people remarked on her high spirits, wanting to know if something nice had happened.

Nothing had, she thought, driving home. Nothing had happened except that incredibly, wonderfully, she was simply glad to be alive. The autumn days were perfect—dry, clear, with just a hint of crispness in the air to make an invigorating contrast to the sun's warmth. Her marigolds still bloomed riotously around the house, but the first frost was fast approaching. Now, she thought, now was the perfect time to saddle up and ride out to see the last wildflowers, the last green leaves, the last lovely blaze of dying summer.

So she called Tom Preston. She thanked him again for his help with the roof and assured him that Ransom was handling the shingles just fine on his own.

"Actually, Tom, I have another favor to ask, if you don't mind."

He chuckled. "I been waiting a long time to do you a few favors, gal. Fire away."

"I've decided I want horses again. I don't know a thing about judging horseflesh, though, or tack, for that matter. I was hoping you could advise me."

"I'd be delighted, Mandy. What kind of horses do you have in mind?"

"A nice, gentle lady's mount for me, and something suitable for Ransom to ride fence on."

"Fence, huh? You thinking about starting a herd?"

Mandy blinked. She *was*, she realized. "I guess I am," she said after a moment. "John and I used to talk about it a lot." On long winter evenings when dreams were spun out of the gossamer of love and hope. So much, so incredibly much, had been lost. She closed her eyes momentarily against remembered pain.

"John would have made a great rancher, Mandy. It was in his blood." Tom's voice had softened a shade, just a shade, as if he'd guessed the direction of her thoughts.

"Well, I don't know if it's in mine." Her voice was steady, hiding, as she had always hidden, the depths of her feelings. "I have all winter to think about it. In the meantime, I thought I'd have Ransom take a look at the fence and see how much I need to do. Then I'll have to figure out if I can afford it."

"Some things are never affordable," Tom said drily. "You just have to afford them anyhow."

She smiled, and some corner of her mind noted that it was getting easier to do that. Just a little easier. "But I don't *have* to, Tom. I'm not into it yet. As it is, I never mind it if a neighbor's cattle stray into my grazing land. I'm not sure they'll feel the same if mine do the straying because I haven't mended my fences."

He laughed. "Good point. Well, if you want horses, I can send over a couple today. Tack, too. If you like the looks of them, you can have the kit and caboodle for a song."

"Tom, I can't—"

"Sure you can. I was trying to sell off a few head anyhow. Never ceases to amaze me how much a horse can eat over a winter. And the kids don't come home like they used to, Mandy. I just plain don't need to keep 'em hanging around eating their heads off."

"Fair market value, Tom. I insist."

"Mandy, you wouldn't know fair market value if it stood up and bit you on the nose. Tell you what. I promise to give you a deal that's fair to us both. You want me to have Jim bring them over?"

Ransom hiked back into the barnyard that afternoon feeling better than he had in a while. He'd walked long enough and hard enough to stretch every muscle in his body and to beat back his private demons with weariness. It occurred to him that he owed Mandy an apology for his withdrawal over the past week. He'd kissed the woman, after all, and then had pulled back so far into his private hell that she must be wondering if she'd somehow disgusted him.

As he rounded the corner of the barn, he found Jim Preston, Tom's oldest son, off-loading a gray horse from a trailer. Mandy stood a few feet away, holding a chestnut horse by its halter. She was laughing. She was actually laughing, with her head thrown back and locks of auburn hair falling loose from her habitual bun. Ransom came to a dead halt, unable to believe the transformation in her.

And then Jim Preston laughed, too, as the horse he was leading sidled and bumped him. Ransom saw the gentle way Preston looked at Mandy. Was that the way the wind blew? Shoving his hands into his jeans pockets, he sauntered up to them.

"Ransom, look!" Mandy's eyes were bright as she saw him. "Aren't they beautiful?"

"Beautiful," he agreed, a smile briefly softening the bleakness of his blue eyes. "You two going for a ride?"

Something flickered quickly over Mandy's smiling face, so quickly he couldn't interpret it. He was left with the impression that she was somehow disappointed, but before he could weigh the feeling, Jim spoke.

"Not me, Ransom. You. And what's more, you get to muck out their stalls every morning. It's two less for me to tend to." He smiled at Mandy. "Let's get them saddled and you can try them out, Mandy. If you like them, I've got the bill of sale right here."

Sale? She was buying horses? Ransom stared openly, watching the way she stroked the chestnut's nose. Damn, she looked so happy!

"You're getting horses?" he asked.

She smiled and nodded. "This beauty's for me. I hope you know how to ride, because you're going to spend an awful lot of time on that gray's back."

Ransom turned to look at the gray gelding. Good, deep chest, sturdy legs. A durable beast, like himself. "I am, am I?"

"Fences need mending," Jim said, grinning. "Help me saddle 'em, Ransom. I'll show you how."

But Ransom surprised them both by hefting the chestnut's saddle and readying the mare for Mandy as competently as if he'd been doing it for years.

"Right now," Jim drawled to Mandy, "I'd lay odds he knows how to ride, too."

She laughed. "I'll tell you something I've learned already. Jim, there's nothing Ransom doesn't know how to do."

Ransom's blue eyes flashed a sudden smile at her over the horse's back. "I'm just a great pretender. Come on, Mandy. Mount up so I can check the cinch and adjust the stirrups."

He gave her a little boost with his hands, and then she was in the saddle for the first time in years. She was almost too impatient to wait while Ransom fiddled with the stirrups. Finally he stepped back, and she cantered out of the yard, laughter trailing behind her.

"You better saddle up the gray and go after her," Jim said to Ransom. "Looks like she won't be back for a while. Here's the bill of sale. Tell her Dad'll stop by later." He started to turn away as Ransom tucked the folded paper in his breast pocket, but he turned back.

"Ransom?"

Ransom looked over at him.

"That little lady hasn't laughed in better than four years. A lot of us would be obliged if you'd see to it she stays happy."

"Fond of her?"

Jim smiled faintly. "A lot of us were real fond of John, and she made John real happy." He looked past Ransom to where Mandy was riding slowly. "She came to church smiling this morning. It'd be nice if she kept smiling."

"Am I being warned?"

Jim grinned suddenly and stuck out his hand. "Hell, no," he said, shaking Ransom's hand firmly. "Just asking you to keep a friendly eye on her. We've all fretted about her being alone out here. There's wildcats out there, Ransom. All kinds. Reckon you know that as well as anybody. Maybe better. And Mandy's about as naive as they come."

It was true, Ransom thought as he saddled the gray and Jim drove away. Her defenses had sheltered her, and she was naive in some ways. But there were other ways in which she wasn't at all naive. In his opinion, Mandy didn't need nearly as much protecting as Jim Preston seemed to think.

He caught up with her about a quarter of a mile from the house.

"You *do* know how to ride." She smiled as he pulled up beside her. "I'll keep the mare for sure. What do you think about the gray?"

"Strong and healthy, and his mouth hasn't been abused."

"Jim says he's a trained cow pony. That may come in useful. Guess I'll go back and tell Jim I'm keeping them both."

"Jim left. Said his dad would come by later. Here's the bill of sale."

Mandy took the folded paper from him and looped her reins around her arm so she could open it. "Eight hundred dollars! He must be joking! The tack must be worth four hundred!"

"It's used," he pointed out.

"So? It's been well-cared for. And these horses are young."

"A gelding," Ransom said. "You can't breed this pair."

"Still—"

"Mandy, something tells me you can argue yourself blue in the face and Tom Preston still won't accept a penny more. In fact, I'm willing to bet it's galling him to take even that much."

She released an exasperated breath and stuffed the bill of sale in her breast pocket. "I can't let him do this. It's not right."

"Fine. Take the horses back. And while you're at it, slap his face so he gets the message."

She turned her head sharply and found him looking grimly ahead. "What do you mean?"

"The man wants to do something for you. Why the hell don't you just let him? In fact, why don't you try putting yourself in his shoes for a minute? You're the writer. Use your imagination."

They rode on slowly, neither of them speaking. Mandy's pleasure in the day had vanished. First Tom gave her the horses at too low a price, and now Ransom was annoyed with her. And what right did he have to be angry at her, anyway?

Plenty, she admitted glumly. She was the one who had put their relationship on a more personal footing than employer and employee.

From the corner of his eye, Ransom watched the expressions play over her face. She wasn't laughing any longer, and he felt like a royal cad. And then she surprised him yet again.

"You're right," she said with a rueful smile. "I'm looking a very kind and generous gift horse in the mouth."

"It's hard sometimes to accept things from people," he said after a moment. "There was a time when I would have reacted the way you just did."

"But not anymore?" Unconsciously she leaned toward him in her saddle, hoping to learn more about him.

"No. Where I was the past few years, none of us would have survived without one another. You come to realize that no one is completely independent. And you also realize that it's our willingness to help one another that makes humanity special. Or at least some of us." Some of us are just masquerading as human. Some of us aren't human at all.

She looked down thoughtfully. After a while she said, "You amaze me, Ransom."

"Why?"

"You're not at all bitter."

He laughed then, a harsh, jarring sound. "Oh, I'm bitter, all right. Very bitter about some things. Just not about everything."

Not knowing how to respond, she chose silence, leaving it to him to decide if they would converse and what about. She was contradictorily eager to hear more and terrified of what he might say. In her books she often painted visions of evil, but she suspected they weren't nearly as terrible as the evil that real men could do to one another.

Eventually he spoke. "How come you decided to buy horses?"

"Because it's autumn, because the day is perfect, because every castle should have a couple of horses in the stable for peculiar princesses and stray warriors. Because I need to ride like this. Because you probably need it, too. Because my fences need work after all this time. And because I'm thinking about starting a herd. If I can afford it. A small start. No debt."

"A herd. How small?"

"I'll have to see what I can afford and whether I can afford the loss if I fall flat on my nose. What I know about cattle ranching you could probably write on the head of a pin with a ballpoint pen."

He smiled at that, turning his head to look fully at her. "I know something about it."

She drew rein, twisting in her saddle to look at him. "Tell me," she demanded. "What do you know, and how?"

"I was raised on a cattle ranch in Montana. About the time I went off to college, my dad was ready to throw in the towel. Cattle ranching's not an easy thing to do, especially when the winters are harsh. He lost the ranch eventually."

Mandy nodded and sighed.

"Sheep, on the other hand," he said slowly, "might be a better idea. Wool's back in fashion, for one thing. You can shear the suckers every spring and not have to replenish the herd every time you make a little money. Beef prices stink these days."

She half smiled. "Not in the supermarket."

"The rancher gets little enough of that."

"Sheep," she repeated thoughtfully. "I'd probably be the laughingstock of the county."

"Who cares? The only thing is, your neighbors'll want to lynch you if the sheep stray. They crop the grass so close that the cows can't graze after them."

"That's the point of a fence."

She was considering the idea, he could tell.

"Ransom?"

"Yo."

"If I get into this, are you going to stick around and help me out, or am I going to find myself with a herd and no advice?"

"How do you know my advice is any good?"

Her brown eyes met his fully. "It's just this absolutely crazy feeling I get about you."

"What feeling?"

"That you don't shoot off your mouth when you don't know what you're talking about."

"You haven't known me very long," he reminded her.

"I've known you forever," she said, and then rosy color bloomed deeply in her cheeks. Touching her heels to the mare's side, she took off across the wide open Wyoming spaces. He took off after her, enjoying every minute of the chase. It had been a hell of a long time since he'd galloped wild and free across open ground.

The chestnut had quarter horse in her somewhere, Ransom thought as he urged his own mount all out. The cow pony, on the other hand, had more endurance but less speed. When he at last caught up with Mandy, she had dismounted beneath a cottonwood beside a stream.

"John and Mary are buried beneath a cottonwood," she said as he reined to a halt beside her.

"Mary?"

"Our baby." Her back was to him. He couldn't see her face, but she sounded calm, reflective. With a creak of leather, he dismounted, wrapping the gray's reins around a bush. A well-trained horse would stay anywhere you dropped its reins. He didn't know about these two yet.

He walked up behind Mandy, taking the reins of the chestnut from her slack hand and looping them around another bush. Standing a foot behind Mandy, he said, "What happened?"

"She was stillborn. They didn't know why. The hospital wanted to take care of it, but I couldn't let them. John had wanted her so badly. She's buried beside him." She turned slowly, and although her face was calm, wet trails of tear ran down both cheeks. "She was born the day he was buried. I like to think John has his daughter."

"I'm sure he does." Very carefully, he drew her into the circle of his arms and gently pressed her head onto his shoulder. "Poor little princess," he whispered.

An unsteady sigh escaped her, and she gave in to the comfort of being held. It amazed her that Ransom could feel compassion for her after what he'd been through. He was an amazing man.

"I sometimes think," she said presently, "that life is a passion play we write for ourselves. Life after life we come back to learn, to experience. And in the perspective of eternity, it doesn't much matter whether you experience joy or sorrow, only that you taste it all, learn from it all." Again she sighed. "And I ask myself sometimes why the devil I wrote this script. It hasn't been a heck of a lot of fun."

"Maybe," he said softly, "you saved the fun for last."

"Do I sound crazy? Am I crazy?"

His arms tightened around her, and he battled an urge to pull the pins from her hair and discover the fully glory of those shiny, confined locks. "You don't sound crazy, Mandy. People ask those questions all the time. Your answer sounds more reasonable than most."

"How do you explain what happened to you? What do you tell yourself? What did you say to yourself all those years?"

"Somebody set me up." His voice was suddenly harsh. "That's reason enough."

She shivered against him. "You were betrayed?"

"Exactly."

"By a colleague?"

"And a friend."

She tilted her head back, looking up at him, ignoring the fact that his hold on her had become almost painful. This man had courage, she thought. So much courage. If only she could understand how he remained strong and compassionate in the face of such things, she might be stronger herself. "How do you cope with that?"

"What are you after? Cope with what? That people are imperfect? That a friend sold me out? I was in a position to be sold out because of choices I'd made over the years. I knew all along that I had a dangerous job. Betrayal was just one facet of a filthy business. I wasn't shocked to find myself the victim of something I'd seen happen to others. Human nature being what it is, I was just a random target."

"Random target? Do you believe that much in chance?"

She felt him draw a slow, deep breath. Gathering her courage, she met his gaze.

"When I look at you," he said, his blue eyes intense, his voice low, "I don't believe in chance at all. There's no way on earth I can believe chance led me to you."

His blue eyes came closer. His breath warmed her lips. Weakened by sorrow, tired of her isolation, Mandy gave up her internal battle and closed her eyes, offering herself to his kiss. His perfect, so right kiss. Their lips met, touched, caressed—and retreated.

"I'm riding a wild bull," he whispered, tasting the corners of her mouth. "Sometimes it's all I can do to hang on."

"I know." She understood. Somehow, she understood. She could almost feel it in the air around them, a coalescing wildness like a building tempest. Things were sliding rapidly out of control for her. For him.

He answered her with another kiss, this one deeper, searching. So knowing, she thought hazily. His mouth and tongue were so knowing, evoking feelings not even John had elicited. His arms molded her to him, every contour of their bodies fitting perfectly, and his burgeoning hunger pressed against her shamelessly. There was no shame, not for either of them.

"You feel so right, so good," he whispered, trailing his mouth across her soft cheek. And he gave in to his need, raising a hand to pull the pins from her hair.

"I'm riding that bull, too, Ransom," she said as her hair cascaded down her back, the pins falling carelessly into the grass. His fingers slid into the silky waterfall, combing it gently.

"Hold me, Mandy. Please."

Her hands slid from his chest, one rising to wrap around his neck, the other sliding under his arm around his back. She held him tightly, yearning to comfort him as he had comforted her. Now tenderness seemed to crystallize in the air around them as they kissed yet again, holding at bay the hunger of their bodies, cocooning them against wants and needs and longings—holding at bay the approaching storm. It was enough to hold and be held, to kiss and comfort. One by one her hand traced the ridges of his back, and her gentle touch was like balm to him.

They rode back to the house side by side. Only when they dismounted in the yard did Ransom break the soothing silence between them.

"A couple of battered old warriors," he said softly and brushed the lightest of kisses on the top of her head. "I'll see to the horses."

In the kitchen Mandy started making a dinner she more than half expected Ransom would never show up to eat. It was too late in the day to prepare the elaborate Sunday meal she had planned, so she made thick cold roast beef sandwiches. John had always been secretly pleased when her writing carried her away to the point that she forgot about dinner. Left to his own devices, he would have eaten soup and sandwiches as a steady diet. She wondered if Ransom was like that.

Ransom. Suddenly the afternoon washed over her, and she leaned against the counter, gripping the edge of it tightly and closing her eyes. They'd done it again, she thought. Once again they'd reached out to each other and crossed emotional barriers. They were a couple of people who knew better, yet couldn't seem to resist the temptation.

He'd wanted her body. He hadn't been able to conceal that. Even the memory of his desire stirred a coiling, warm heaviness in her. And she wanted him, too. But out there beneath the cottonwood, they had both wanted something more: the comfort of another person's caring. And that was an even greater danger than the yearnings to feel his skin, his weight, his hunger.

She would have felt a whole lot better if he'd tried to seduce her. That she could handle. Long ago she had realized that for men, sexual need and emotional need were entirely separate. In younger days her cool unapproachability had made her enough of a challenge that men overlooked her ordinary physical attributes. Ages ago she'd learned to handle those advances gently but firmly. Ransom's emotional needs were something else altogether. The last thing on earth she wanted to do was add to his pain.

But worse, far worse, than the reluctance to hurt him was her own growing sense of panic. She recognized the feeling; it came over her any time she sensed that her emotions were becoming involved. It closed in on her like a thick, suffocating blanket, darkening the corners of her mind and making the air too thick to breathe. The first tendrils of caring had put down roots in her heart, and she felt exactly as she would have if she had found her foot caught in the train tracks and, while trying to free herself, had looked up to see the train was almost upon her.

"I see you found the telescope," Ransom said as he stepped into the kitchen. He had seen it on the porch.

She whirled around, startled by his voice, but there was something in her face that went beyond surprise. Fear. He knew it as intimately as he knew pain. He recognized the look, scented the faint metallic odor of it on her. She was terrified.

"Mandy? What happened?" His first thought was that someone or something had threatened her. Immediately his posture altered; she saw him crouch ever so slightly, ready to spring. His eyes scanned the kitchen swiftly, missing nothing. "Mandy?"

"Nothing," she croaked. "Honestly. Nothing." She stared, seeing in his reaction the harsh reality of the life he had lived. He lived on a knife's edge. My God, how could she have let him come so close? He was a walking, talking promise of pain!

Ransom straightened slowly, not entirely reassured, and his blue eyes searched her face. Evil wizards. Suddenly he understood. The wise thing would have been to let the moment pass, let things fall slowly back into unthreatening casualness. He couldn't do that. He couldn't even pretend to ignore the fright in her eyes.

"Mandy," he said again, and before she could react, he gathered her close, tangling his fingers in her hair, drawing her head to his shoulder.

"Please," she said faintly, her voice muffled against his shoulder. "Please. Don't."

"Shh." He rocked her soothingly, as if she were a small, frightened child. One hand rubbed her back gently; the other brushed her cheek, her temple, her hair. "Don't be so afraid," he murmured. "Even when a princess is under an evil curse she's allowed to have a champion."

"You'll go away," she said almost inaudibly. "Everyone goes away. I don't want to depend on anybody. I don't want to care about anybody."

"I can't promise, Mandy. Nobody can make the kind of promise you need."

"I know." She sounded so lost and forlorn that he ached. "That's why I don't want to care!"

He scooped her up, startling her, and she instinctively wrapped her arms around his neck, afraid of falling. In silence he carried her from the kitchen into her study, where he settled down on the easy chair, taking her onto his lap. His arms were tight around her, denying her escape.

"My wife," he said presently, his voice sounding strained, "was in my line of work. We, uh, worked on a couple of projects together and became friends, I thought. In our business, friends weren't easy to come by."

Her own fears receded as she listened. His heartbeat was steady beneath her ear, but she could feel tension coiling in him. The ache in her now was for him, she realized. Dear God, it was already too late. Closing her eyes, she waited for him to continue.

"I, uh, didn't have any relationships with women over the years, because it didn't seem fair. I admit I had casual encounters, but I never went any further, because my job was dangerous, and I seldom knew from one minute to the next if I might be called away for an indefinite period."

When he was silent for a long time, she spoke softly, keeping her eyes closed. "Your wife was different." She knew he was remembering terrible things. The memory of pain was growing almost physically in the room around them. Instead of shying away from it, she felt driven to share it.

"I thought so." His voice had become mechanical, toneless. "She lived the same life. She understood. I didn't have to explain. She didn't have to explain. Between projects, we often got together for dinner or a show. Anyhow, eventually we became lovers. I guess I needed to know that somebody was waiting at home when the mission was done. Life didn't seem quite so empty."

She nodded her head against his shoulder, telling him she understood. Oh, indeed she understood. Loneliness was a devouring beast with harsh claws, and people would do insane things to evade it.

"Karen got pregnant," he continued flatly. "We got married. It was—I was—Mandy, I don't know if I can explain it. A child. *My* child. Suddenly I wanted out of the business. I wanted a home. I wanted to watch my child grow. Karen talked about abortion. She didn't want to give up her career. She was a lot younger than I was, a lot less worn out by all of it, I thought. For her it was still exciting. Anyway, I talked her out of it. I told her I'd raise the baby, she could keep working. It would cost her nothing but a temporary leave of absence. Our bosses were perfectly willing to go along with that, so we went ahead."

He drew a long, deep breath. "There was a mission I couldn't pull out of. Everything had been planned. If I didn't go it would have meant—" He caught himself. "Sorry, that's classified."

"It's okay," she said quietly. She didn't want to hear this, but somehow she *had* to. "I get the picture."

"So I went. I was supposed to be gone a month. I was gone four years. Karen aborted the baby and continued working. She was—" He cleared his throat once, then again, squashing down the jagged pain that always came when he thought of his lost child. "She was a double agent."

"Oh my God!" She sat up, staring at him, at the cold mask his face had become. She knew what was coming, knew it was going to be one of those things so vile that every feeling, every thought, would rebel against believing it. "She—"

"Yes." The word was clipped, short.

"Oh, Ransom." Casting aside all caution and fear in her pain for him, she threw her arms around his neck and hugged him as tightly as she could. This man knew betrayal in its deepest sense. He had mentioned that he'd been imprisoned for four years, but to think that he had been betrayed into that horror by his own wife! It was impossible to grasp the enormity of it. It made her own fears seem laughable by comparison.

"I, uh . . ." He was having trouble forcing the words out. "When I escaped and made it back, it became obvious. She'd been suspected, but there was no proof. What I had to say about what happened, well, the picture was clear to everyone after that. She was—she was—" He choked, unable to say it.

"Ransom?" Her hands cradled his face gently. "What?"

"Sanctioned," he blurted at last and buried his face in the curve between her neck and shoulder as shudders racked him repeatedly.

Sanctioned. Officially murdered. The word hung in the air for a long time as Mandy held him, staring blindly over his head into the dark. It was too much to comprehend. Like most people, she knew in a vague way that such things happened, but the reality of such a world was confined to movies and books. Ransom had lived in it. Good Lord, the scars, the wounds, he must carry on his soul! Her chest was so tight that she could scarcely breathe.

Gradually he stopped shuddering. She could almost feel the massive amount of self-control he exercised in calming himself. And he hadn't said one word about his feelings. Not one.

"I'm sorry," he said, sounding breathless. He raised his head from her shoulder, and she released him. He let his head fall back against the chair, closing his eyes.

"Don't be sorry," she said. With her fingertips, she touched his face, tracing the line of his brow, his nose, his chin. His beard was soft, silky, short, and through it she could feel other scars. His face had been ruined, too, she realized. Overwhelmed by it all, she sought out each scar with her fingers and then pressed a kiss on it, as if it would help. As if anything could help.

"Ransom?"

"Hmm?"

"How old are you?"

Once again he brought his arms around her. "Forty-one."

"It's been a long haul."

"Mmm."

"Why did you get into the business?"

He sighed. "After Nam, I couldn't seem to quite settle into real life. And I suffered from a dangerous combination of youth, idealism and a desire to make a difference."

"Did you? Make a difference?"

"Nobody makes a difference on that level, Mandy. If we're lucky, we make a difference on a one-to-one basis."

Her fingertips found another scar just behind his ear and paused there. "I'm finding this difficult to comprehend."

"I'm not sure I comprehend it, either, and I lived it."

"I can't bear to think what each of these scars means." Things inside her shriveled and clenched at the merest thought of how he must have suffered.

"That's over with. Don't worry about it."

"But I do." She bit her lower lip. "I'm mother-henning again. Tell me to shut up. But I have an almost uncontrollable urge to check you over from head to foot and assess the damage. Just like a hen checking over a chick who got into trouble."

At that a muffled chuckle escaped him. "I'd be glad to oblige you, except I couldn't answer for the consequences. I'm not damaged that way."

Color burned in her cheeks, and she had to battle an impulse to hide her face. Right now, though, other things were far more important than a little sexual reference. "I've noticed. How bad are your legs? You said they were nearly as bad as your back.''

He hesitated. "You've seen enough. You've heard enough. I don't want you to remember any more. I shouldn't have dumped this on you.''

"People need to dump. I'm willing. Tell me about your legs or I'm going to have to look for myself. I can't stand this.''

"Pandora," he cautioned quietly.

"Ransom . . ." Her tone was warning.

"The backs of my legs look like my back. I had to have them broken and reset with steel rods so I can walk. Enough?''

Her throat ached as if it were caught in a noose. "Finish," she said tightly. "All of it.''

"I had to have my left arm reset, too. And my face is a miracle of plastic surgery. Mandy—"

"What else? All of it, damn it.''

"Nothing major. A few assorted scars from cuts and burns.''

With a swiftness that astonished him, she slipped from his lap and hurried out of the room. Several minutes later, she still hadn't returned. He searched the house for her and failed to find her, so he looked outside. He found her in her garden, on her knees in the dark, digging up her marigold plants.

"What are you doing?" he asked, though he had a pretty good idea.

"Working out a boundless rage," she said tonelessly. "I was raised not to throw things.''

"Those plants—"

"Will die in a few days anyway." Shoving viciously with the trowel, she dug up another.

"Mandy." Bending, he yanked the trowel from her hand and pulled her to her feet. "You'll be mad at yourself tomorrow. Don't do this.''

She struggled against his grip. "I'm mad at the whole world right now. Being mad at myself sounds like a breeze by comparison. Let me go!''

"No. I shouldn't have told you. I shouldn't have upset you. My God, I'm so sorry."

"Stop it!" she shrieked. "Stop it."

"Mandy—"

"Shut up! I've been scared and hurt my whole damn life, and none of it's been under my control. I *want* to be mad. I want to be furious!" She tried to break free of his hold. "I want to shout and scream and smash things! I've had it. Had it! Do you hear me? I'm through! Finished! I'm not going to creep around anymore. I'm not going to be afraid anymore! If I could get my hands on those bastards who hurt you, I'd kill them. Kill them!"

"Mandy. Oh, Mandy." His voice sounded broken, and his arms were like steel around her as she struggled and pounded wildly on his chest. "Oh, my God, what have I done to you?"

Exhaustion ended her rage, leeching it from her until she hung limp in his arms, an occasional sniffle her only sound.

"All done?" he asked grimly, scooping her up for the second time that evening. She didn't answer. Her head lolled as he carried her back into the house and up the stairs to the bedrooms.

"Which one is yours?" he asked. A slight motion of her hand answered him. Carefully he set her down on the wedding ring quilt that covered the narrow bed. Its narrowness made it obvious that she no longer slept in the bed she had shared with John.

"I'll be back in five minutes," he said. "I expect to find you under the covers. If you're not, I'll undress you myself and put you there. Your choice, Mandy."

She managed it. When he returned with hot chocolate in two steaming mugs, she was under the covers, quilt drawn to her chin. Sitting on the edge of the bed, he slipped an arm around her shoulders and raised her.

"Drink," he commanded, and she sipped the warm, sweet liquid, too tired to argue, even when she realized the chocolate was laced with brandy. He must have found the bottle left over from Christmas four years ago.

"I'll be right here all night," he said as he eased her back onto the pillow.

"Go home," she whispered. "It's over now." Indeed, everything inside her felt as if it had shriveled, died and crumbled into dust.

"I'm not leaving you alone." He brushed her long, dark hair gently back from her face. "From time to time, a warrior keeps a vigil. It's good for the soul. Sleep, Mandy."

Chapter 4

He stayed with her all night. She slept restlessly, troubled by vague nightmares, and each time she opened her eyes he was there, sitting in the chair by the bed, watching her.

"Ransom," she mumbled the last time. "Go get some sleep."

"I'm okay," he answered quietly. "Sleep, Mandy."

When she woke again it was nearly dawn. Through the lace curtains at her window she could see the faint brightening of the eastern sky. Ransom's head had settled onto his chest and he was dozing. A fist squeezed her heart, and tears sprang to her eyes.

Suddenly his eyes snapped open, meeting hers. "Mandy?" he said softly, a question.

"I'm okay. For heaven's sake, get some sleep." Her voice was choked with unshed tears.

He shook his head slowly.

"Ransom, please." A tear spilled over.

A look of anguish passed over his face. He bent suddenly, yanking his boots off, and then he stood, unbuckling his belt and flinging it aside. Mandy watched, wondering, but not at all nervous.

He lay beside her on top of the quilt and drew her into the circle of his arms, bringing her head to rest on his shoulder. "There," he said quietly. "We'll both sleep."

It was late morning when she opened her eyes again. Ransom was sleeping deeply, his arms wrapped securely around her, hers wrapped around his waist. Her head was pillowed on his chest, the sound of his heartbeat strong in her ear.

She didn't dare move for fear of disturbing him, so she lay still, watching the sunlight move across the room as noon approached.

He was courageous, Mandy decided, as she thought over the painful things he had revealed last night. At first she had heard his tale filtered through her own fears, but now, in the bright morning light, she understood why he had told her. He was showing her that in spite of betrayal he was prepared to face the risks again. In comparison she felt like an abject coward.

Or maybe, she thought with a catch in her breath that she felt in her heart, maybe he had been telling her that he was just as scared, just as reluctant, as she was. And certainly with more cause.

"Morning." His voice was husky with sleep as his arms tightened.

She turned her head and met his blue gaze, saw the concern there. Searching rapidly through the dusty corners of her battered soul, she found a smile and offered it to him.

A pent-up breath escaped him as his eyes wandered over her face, measuring, gauging, until at last his attention settled on her mouth. "Amanda," he whispered. "Amanda Lynn."

The last person to call her that had been an angry second grade teacher. This was different. This was a recognition. Suddenly she was filled with courage.

As if he sensed it, he tugged her gently upward and brought her lips to his. His mouth opened beneath hers, asking her to explore its smoky, hot depths. How good he tasted, she thought, her kiss swiftly growing bolder. He let her lead, pressing for nothing, not even moving his hands against her back, though she could feel his growing tension.

"Ransom," she whispered. "Ransom what?"

"Ransom Richard," he answered huskily, tugging her mouth back to his.

"Ransom Richard Laird," she murmured, tasting his lips, his tongue, in short, sweet kisses. "A warrior's name. Ransom means son of the shield."

"Mandy." His control was shattering. She could feel it and didn't care. Explosions of need hammered her. Desire shot through her in electric ribbons. Never had she imagined such wild feelings really existed. It appalled her to think her fears might have prevented her from ever knowing this. It was nearly too much. He tasted so right, smelled so right, felt so right. This was her script, the one she had dreamed of since youth.

"Mandy." Her name was a groan, and he took command, kissing her deeply, tugging at the quilt until it vanished. He pulled her over him so their bodies met from head to toe, and he caught her face between his hands, taking her mouth hungrily, pillaging the warm sweet cavern as if he wanted to slip wholly into her.

She moaned softly against his lips and began to tremble with a need so great it threatened to rip her apart. Against her she felt his readiness, and it increased her excitement. Involuntarily she moved against him, pressing, and this time it was Ransom who groaned deeply. His hands flew from her head to her hips, pressing her closer yet, grinding himself into her softness.

"Yes, yes, yes," she chanted in a whisper. "Ransom..."

His hands suddenly swept down, then up, dragging the flannel nightgown upward with them, exposing her skin to his touch. Fire. His touch was like fire. She burned for him, flamed for him, resented the denim that lay between them.

A shiver racked him, and then, abruptly, he grew still and rigid. For an instant he didn't move, and she lay confused, dazed.

"Mandy." Swiftly he tugged at her gown, yanking it down, turning her with him so they lay side by side. He cradled her gently, the only sound their ragged breathing as the world gradually righted itself.

A long, long time later she raised confused eyes to his. "Sweetness," he said softly. "You are sweetness and purity. Amanda Lynn Tierney, I'd kill myself if I ever saw regret in your eyes because of anything I did."

"But..." He had awakened in her a sweet, savage wanting, and she wanted to tell him that she wouldn't regret, couldn't regret—yet some wise corner of her mind knew she would do precisely that.

He saw the flicker of understanding in her eyes and laid a gentle finger across her lips. "Now hush."

He finished the roofing that afternoon, and Mandy wrote like a demon. As page after page filled her computer screen, she knew she was writing this one for Ransom. This was his book, the story she would give him.

Her fears haunted her, too, dark shadows looming in the corners of her mind, but she bravely ignored them. Difficult though it might be, she had at last found something worth all the risks and terrors. She told herself she would deal with those demons one at a time and vanquish them. She would become whole for Ransom.

It was, of course, much easier said than done. Her momentary courage felt like a small, uncertain candle flame in the dead of the darkest night. Superstitiously, she could almost feel threat thickening the air around her. Somewhere along the way she had definitely developed the conviction that Amanda Lynn Tierney had no right to be happy.

When he stepped into the kitchen at dinnertime, they stood staring at one another for a long moment, recognizing the changes between them, the fears, the uncertainties, the needs. And then he held out his arms to her and she went into his embrace eagerly, turning her face up without hesitation.

"Sweet Mandy," he murmured, kissing her once, twice, three times. He hugged her tenderly until she stirred, muttering that dinner would burn.

* * *

"Ransom?"

His fork halted halfway to his mouth. "Hmm?"

"Are you going back to your old job?"

He searched her face closely and was amazed to see not fear, but a kind of sad courage. It was as if she wanted to measure the dimensions of an inevitable pain, accepting that there could be no escape from it. Slowly he set the fork down and pushed back his chair. Coming round the table, he pulled out the chair beside her and sat, claiming both her hands.

"I'm on six months' convalescent leave," he said slowly. "I don't have to decide until it's up."

"You haven't decided yet, then." Her brown eyes were huge, her lips compressed to still their quivering.

"I'm not sure," he said truthfully, hating himself for each word as he spoke it, knowing they struck her like blows. "I don't want to go back, Mandy. But I can't lead a purposeless existence."

"Nate said you were a driven man." She looked so brave that something inside him seemed to be breaking.

"That's not it. Not really. I just have to feel I'm accomplishing something worthwhile. It doesn't have to be my old job. In fact, I'd much rather it wasn't."

"What kind of purpose do you need?"

He shrugged. "I'm trying to figure that out."

"You were planning to quit before," she said quietly. "Nate told me. You told me."

"To raise a child." He nodded. "I think about that a lot. That might be purpose enough for me." He looked down at her hands and saw that they were trembling. Then he lifted his gaze to hers and considered asking the question that had been tumbling around in his head like an obsession since dawn when he had lain down beside her and taken her into his arms. In his entire life there hadn't been very many people he trusted enough that he could actually sleep in their presence. Mandy had enlarged that very small, very select group. "Will you go to the Harvest Dance with me?"

Tom Preston's men had mentioned the dance when they had helped with the barn roof. It was an annual event, they'd said, that gave the local ladies a rare chance to get duded up and spend the evening with men who for once didn't smell of horses, cattle and manure. Ransom had laughed along with them, but since dawn this morning it had become important to him to see Mandy "duded up." To see her smile and laugh. To see her carefree for just an evening.

Her eyes widened, and color drained from her cheeks. For an eternity she said nothing at all.

He understood, or thought he did. She felt they were tempting fate already, but this must seem like a step into the jaws of disaster. It was a superstitious attitude that he didn't completely understand.

He understood conditioning, understood how a person could become distrustful or afraid to take risks. A person's mind and soul could react exactly the same way to a bad emotional experience as they did to touching a hot stove. What he couldn't wholly understand was Mandy's apparent conviction that it was some kind of personal karma to lose everything she loved. Ransom was a firm believer that men were the captains of their fates, and that everything in a person's life could be traced directly to decisions made or not made. The universe wasn't out to get Mandy Grant. She had simply experienced the inevitable losses of life in a way that made her feel cursed. The random chances of life, for her, had come to seem like fate or destiny, an Evil Wizard. Personal. Directed. Deliberate. Somehow he had to change her mind about that.

But now, right now, he could see the flare of fright around her delicate little nose, see the dilation of her pupils, see the rapid rise and fall of her breasts. She was scared, but she wasn't running. She was, he saw, fighting for courage. Fighting to triumph over herself.

The sight of that struggle had an unexpected effect on him. Protective instincts that had been buried so long he had forgotten he had them suddenly rose in an almost painful rush. "Forget I asked, Princess," he said gruffly. "I forgot about the Evil Wizard."

Her eyes were huge, wounded, hungry for understanding and warmth, and yet terrified of what the consequences might be. "It's silly," she whispered. "This is all so silly...." She wriggled free from his hold and fled the room, leaving him in solitude to ponder just how silly it all was.

After a while Ransom stirred himself to clean up the dinner dishes. Silly? he asked himself. Maybe, maybe not. He'd been having the strangest fancies ever since he met Mandy Grant. Fancies of knowing her from elsewhere, of destiny and plans and eternal schemes. He'd never for one moment felt she was a stranger to him, and somehow neither had she after the first hesitancy. He could tell. They reacted to one another with an intensity that spoke of old acquaintance.

Pausing, he leaned his hip against the counter and stared out at the night. When had he first met Mandy Grant? Not when he walked up the drive to her house. When he read her first book? No, even then there had been a familiarity. He had the oddest sensation that he'd been seeing her face in dreams since childhood. He felt a sense of recognition that extended far beyond the past two weeks. Never in his life had he responded to another person on so many instinctive levels.

So what did it mean? Finishing the dishes, he turned his feelings around in his mind but could make no sense of them. A psychiatrist would tell him it was the result of his experiences of the past several years. He wasn't emotionally stable. Hah! He tossed the dish towel across the kitchen to land on top of the washer. He even knew exactly where he would find her this very minute.

Closing his eyes, he recalled the dreams and fantasies he'd had during his imprisonment. The woman hadn't had a face. He'd never seen her clearly. But he'd felt her and heard her, had known her need for him. Mandy.

Suddenly he was galvanized. Striding across the kitchen, he headed not for her office but for the living room. Somehow, he knew she'd fled there.

Mandy was trying to read a book when he appeared in the room. She sucked in a sharp breath as she looked up. He looked like an ancient warrior, she thought as the lamplight gleamed on his golden hair, battered and bloody, but not beaten.

"Amanda Lynn Tierney," he said firmly, "you and I have centuries of uncompleted business to take care of."

She held her breath now, staring wide-eyed, something rising wildly in her, acknowledging him and his words.

"I may have slipped my trolley," he continued, "but by God, we're going to finish it this time, this lifetime. You and I are going to the Harvest Dance next week. And that's final."

The funniest smile curved her lips. "You're as crazy as I am, Ransom."

Suddenly he felt like laughing. A real laugh. The first real laugh in a long, long time. "I know. Isn't it great?"

She laughed with him, because the sound was so wonderful, so infectious, because it did her heart so much good to see this man laugh. But behind her smile, behind her laugh, foreboding took root. It was dangerous to care. Tragedy took everyone she cared about. It was dangerous, but she cared anyway. It was too damn late.

Tom Preston stopped by a few days later to see if Mandy was pleased with the horses, and with a great show of reluctance accepted her check. Standing out in the yard, he watched Ransom scraping industriously at the barn as he prepared to paint.

"Looks like you got yourself a hard worker, Mandy."

"Seems so."

"I don't mind telling you I asked Tate about this guy when I heard about him. Said only good things."

"There are only good things to say."

Tom's gaze grew speculative, and he looked from her to Ransom. "Are you coming to the dance this year?"

"It appears so."

"With Ransom?" He hardly needed to see her nod, and his smile deepened. "We all loved John, Mandy, but it's

troubled us to see you alone and sad for so long. Guess I
ought to go over and meet the boy.''

"He's not a boy, Tom," she said as she walked with him
over to the barn. "Far from it."

Ransom saw them coming from a distance and hastily
pulled on his shirt, buttoning it rapidly. He didn't want
Mandy to have to face the looks he knew would result if
word got around about his scars, especially since he was
willing to bet gossip was already rife.

He shook Preston's hand cordially and endured the older
man's measuring look without any discomfort.

"Mandy tells me you're bringing her to the Harvest
Dance," Preston remarked.

"I plan to."

"Well, you'd better be prepared to undergo an inquisi-
tion. Everyone's been curious since they heard Mandy hired
a hand, but you come to the dance and you'll have to endure the prying of every biddy in Conard County."

Ransom laughed. "I've survived worse."

"Reckon you have. That's a hell of a big job you're fix-
ing to do." He indicated the barn.

"I've got plenty of time."

"You need to be looking at the fence, too, if Mandy
means to start a herd. Sheep, she said."

"That's right," Mandy affirmed.

"Good idea." Preston's look became mildly speculative.
"What do you know about ranching, Ransom?"

"I was raised on the Rocking L in eastern Montana. My
dad went bust one winter."

Preston shook his head sympathetically. "Seen too much
of that in my day. A couple bad winters in succession just
about puts anybody under. Ever raise any sheep?"

"Some. Our neighbors did. They survived the winters."

Preston's face relaxed into a grin. "You're gonna need
help."

Ransom glanced at Mandy, wondering if this conversation disturbed her. Preston was acting as if they were married and Ransom was running Mandy's ranch. It made him
uneasy. It didn't bother Mandy, though. She looked as if she

were used to it. Seeing his concern, she smiled almost impishly at him. He grinned back.

"I'll cross that bridge when I come to it, Tom," she said smoothly. "I'm not committed to anything yet, so I've got all the time I need to work things out."

The hint was subtle, but Preston picked up on it. He laughed good-naturedly, commented on the lateness of the first frost and headed back to his truck. When he was gone, Ransom put down the scraper and came to Mandy's side.

She tilted her head, smiling up at him. "How's a beer sound?" she asked.

"Like heaven." He followed her into the kitchen. "Are your neighbors always so nosy and chauvinistic?"

She laughed. "Sure. Come on, you claim to be ranch-bred."

"It's been more than twenty years. Guess I forgot. Doesn't it rub you wrong?"

"Why should it? This was John's spread. I'm a city girl in the minds of the folks around here—Casper being the city to them. They know I don't know much about it, and I'm not dumb enough to pretend I know what I don't. You're the rancher in their minds, not me. They're going to want to know how much you know so they can decide if I'm going down the trail to disaster or possible success."

"What if they decide it's failure?"

"Then I'll hear enough dire warnings to make Cassandra sound like an optimist."

He laughed at that, accepting the icy beer she handed him.

"I need to go into town this afternoon," she said presently. "I'm down to my last disk and my last twenty sheets of computer paper, and Dan Riley phoned to say my new keyboard is in."

"Great," he said, leaning against the counter and tilting his head back as he swallowed beer. "Can I invite myself along? I'm in desperate need of a barber."

"Sure."

But he caught a moment's hesitation and was troubled. He didn't know how to bring it up, however, so he held his peace. Finishing the beer, he crushed the can absently and started to go back to work.

"Ransom?"

He looked back.

"What's wrong?"

Turning, he leaned back against the counter, splaying his legs and pulled her up against him for a long, deep kiss. He was sweaty from his labors, but the smell was fresh and good. She leaned into him and gave herself up to the wonder of Ransom Richard Laird. For now her warning, frightened voices were silent, as if the magic of this tenderly budding relationship had smothered them. The past few days had seemed to exist out of time, in a land of perpetual sunshine.

His hands moved gently over her back, and his tongue brushed fiery patterns over the warm sweet interior of her mouth, drawing her into him, deeper and deeper.

"Ransom," she sighed, and his hands slipped downward, cupping her soft bottom. Slowly, oh, so slowly, he lifted her against him, showing her what she did to him. And just as slowly he raised his head and looked into her eyes.

"Amanda Lynn," he said softly, "you've got me in the palm of your clever little hand. So, before I make a complete ass of myself, maybe you'd better tell me why you weren't at all sure you wanted me to come with you this afternoon."

She flushed a cherry red and hid her face in his shoulder. In spite of himself, he smiled. "Come on, Mandy. My secrets are obvious right this minute. Share yours."

She shook her head.

Bending, he brushed a kiss on her ear. His breath sent a shiver coursing through her. "I'll torment you," he warned gently.

"You do already," she sighed, too far gone in the pleasure of his touch to care that he knew it.

"Mandy."

She tilted her head back but couldn't quite meet his eyes. "I have a doctor's appointment."

His hands tightened on her bottom. "What's wrong?" he asked sharply.

"Nothing." Her head ducked. "I was just going to get . . . you know."

"What?" And suddenly he understood. He caught his breath and held her so tightly that she finally complained she couldn't breathe. He gentled his grip and pressed his cheek against hers.

"No," he said. It might have been twenty years since he'd left, but he remembered all too clearly what a small community was like.

"No what?"

"You can't go into that gossipy little town for that. I won't hear of it. The whole damn county will be discussing your morals and we haven't even—I won't hear of it."

"I don't care." She stuck her lower lip out mutinously.

"I do. Damn it, Mandy, I won't have you discussed like that. I won't."

"But what if—" She could hardly believe they were discussing this, however circumspectly. She certainly couldn't bring herself to say it right out loud.

"Then I'll take care of it." He would borrow the truck and drive into the next county to buy condoms, but he would not, absolutely not, allow Mandy to become the subject of gossip.

An aching tenderness filled her, and she at last dared to meet his eyes. No longer empty, they shone with gentleness. They blazed with it. She reached up to clasp his face.

"Ransom?"

He almost smiled. "I'm listening, Mandy. Parts of me may be preoccupied, but my ears are wide open."

"John never liked—" Again color flooded her face and her eyes dropped. No amount of effort could bring her to say out loud that John had hated to use condoms.

But he understood what John had probably disliked. "As a temporary measure, it's not bad. Don't worry about that. Not that of all things, princess. In a minute, when I'm sure I can stand without my knees giving way, I'm going to let you go. And you're going to call and cancel your appointment. I'll stand right here until you do."

"Here." Mandy tossed Ransom the keys as she joined him at the truck.

He smiled, the creases by his eyes deepening. "Are you sure you're ready for this? I haven't driven in years."

"It's like riding a horse, Ransom. You never forget. Besides, these country roads are a great place to get back in shape."

Also, she was feeling a little too edgy to drive. She couldn't believe she and Ransom had discussed what they had earlier, especially when they weren't even lovers. Closing her eyes, Mandy remembered a discussion on the same subject with John. Three months after their marriage, he'd brought it up with a great deal of foot-shuffling and hemming and hawing. She'd never forgotten his embarrassment and had intended to handle matters this time so that it never needed to be discussed.

She stole a glance at Ransom. He drove as he did everything else, with easy confidence. As if he felt her attention, he turned and gave her a slow, lazy wink.

"How short are you going to cut your hair?" she asked. He was dressed in a fresh chambray shirt and almost-new jeans. No longer did he look out of place, as he had when he first arrived. As naturally as breathing, he'd assumed the local coloration. A chameleon. The thought jarred her.

"Why?" he asked. "Are you attached to my long, shaggy locks?"

"Sort of," she admitted.

He reached out and patted her leg. "I'll leave enough for you to get your fingers into," he teased. "If you want to."

She did want to. She very much wanted to plunge her fingers into his impossibly soft golden hair. Her gaze dropped to his forearms. His sleeves were rolled back, and fine golden hairs glinted against his tanning skin. And there, just under his left sleeve, she glimpsed a long, thin scar, still faintly red. From when they repaired his arm, she guessed. Inevitably, her eyes dropped lower to his lean, hard thighs.

"I'm blond there, too," he said.

Her eyes leapt to his, and she watched him smile as a hot blush flooded her cheeks.

"You're so lovely when you blush, Mandy. I just can't seem to resist teasing you."

Suddenly he braked the truck right in the middle of the dirt road. Twisting in the seat, he caught her shoulders gently and drew her closer, until they almost touched.

"Do you like what you see, Amanda Lynn?" he asked huskily.

Mesmerized by his blue eyes, she nodded mutely, embarrassment forgotten. Her heart had begun to beat with a steady throb, a pagan drumbeat of anticipation and hunger. So fast. He made her feel everything so fast and so intensely.

"I'm glad," he whispered, brushing his warm lips lightly against hers. "I like what I see, too. Very much." Impossibly, his eyes were smiling. "I steal looks at you all the time, and I wonder, too. And I'm enjoying every single moment of anticipation. If anybody had ever told me that someday I'd wallow in going crazy from temptation, I wouldn't have believed it. But here I am, tempted beyond belief, and I'm in absolutely no rush to put an end to my misery."

Not even John had made her feel as desirable as Ransom did right then. A small sound escaped her, and she slipped her fingers into his beautiful golden hair as he pulled her into him for a yearning kiss.

He tasted her hunger and returned it, but it still wasn't time. She cared for him, he knew, but most of her heart was still securely sealed behind fortress walls. With Mandy he wanted no half measures. If they ever made love, she was going to give herself wholly, without hesitation. She was going to know that the princess had been claimed by her knight.

"I love your hair," she said a short while later as they sat cheek-to-cheek. Her fingers played at the nape of his neck. "Don't you dare cut it all off."

"Just enough so I don't look like a middle-aged hippie."

A little gurgle escaped her. "Sorry, your expression isn't vague enough. You look too dangerous. Like a Viking. Are your ancestors Nordic?"

"My father was of Danish and Scottish extraction, and my mother was a Russian émigré."

"Really? She came from Russia? Do you speak Russian?"

"Fluently." And it had sure caused him enough trouble. It was on the tip of his tongue to ask about her family, but he caught himself. Poor little princess. She would never know those simple but important things about herself. He tightened his embrace.

"Do you speak any other languages?" she asked.

"A few, some so unusual that I can't tell you without revealing classified information."

Her eyes darkened, and he wanted to kick himself for reminding her of the many things she had to be frightened of. Gently, she pulled away.

"We'd better get going or you'll never get your hair cut and I'll never get my supplies."

While Mandy took care of her purchases, Ransom hit the barbershop across the street. A real, old-fashioned, genuine barbershop. He hesitated a moment, wondering if he might get his head shaved after all. Back east, you couldn't find a barber of any kind anymore, and certainly not one as old as this geezer. He would wind up with a military cut for sure.

"Howdy," he said to the barber.

"Howdy," came the answer, the measuring look. "What can I do for you?"

Ransom smiled. "You can save my life. I'm in desperate need of a little barbering, but my girl's threatening to kill me if I cut too much off. Do you think we can find a compromise somewhere between broken heart and effeminate?"

The barber's laugh was wheezy but genuine. "Step up, young fella. I ain't never ruined a romance yet."

The barber was naturally nosy, but Ransom had years of experience in answering such questions satisfactorily while revealing nothing. The old man got sidetracked on to something else finally, and Ransom relaxed.

Thirty minutes later he stepped out onto the street with the haircut he wanted and his beard neatly trimmed. Shoving his thumbs into his pockets, he strolled up the street to the Conard County Sheriff's Office. Mandy had said she would meet him there. He hoped Nate was around.

Halfway there, the back of his neck prickled and a warning heat settled between his shoulder blades. It was a preternatural instinct, honed by years on the edge. He hesitated midstep, convinced that somebody was watching him. Staring at him. Paying attention to him.

But that was ridiculous. He was believed to be dead by almost everybody in the world. Only his family and a handful of people at the agency had any notion that Ransom Laird had returned from the dead. None of them would advertise his whereabouts. And folks here didn't know who he was or who he had been, at least not enough to pass the information on to anyone who might actually care. After almost five years he should be forgotten, anyway.

Probably just some curious person wondering who the stranger in town was, he told himself. He was no longer an active agent. He didn't need to get paranoid every time someone looked at him. Forcing himself to ignore the sensation, he continued down the street.

The instant he entered the sheriff's office, he spied Nate and Mandy in Nate's office.

"Hey, Tater!" he called, and watched several deputies go from shock to laughter. Even Mandy smiled.

"Ransom, I'll kill you, you son of a gun," Tate growled. "I managed to keep that under wraps for twenty years." But he grinned and slapped Ransom's back while dragging him into his office.

"Tater," Mandy said, eyes twinkling. "I like it, Nate."

"It'll be all over town by tomorrow," the sheriff said ruefully. "Ransom was lucky. We used to call him King."

"King? Why?"

"King's Ransom," Nate explained with a smile.

She glanced quickly up at Ransom, and he caught her faint, secret smile. He knew exactly what she was thinking: *Lost kings return to rule.* He winked at her.

Nate spoke. "I was just inviting you and Mandy to have dinner with Marge and me before the dance next week."

Mandy and Ransom exchanged looks. Ransom nodded slightly.

"We'd love to, Nate," Mandy answered.

"We?" Nate brightened. "You mean all this matchmaking's for nothing?"

Ransom chuckled. "I already asked Mandy to go to the dance with me."

"Well, son of a gun. Wait 'til I tell Marge!"

The sun was low in the sky by the time they headed home.

"Is my hair okay?" Ransom asked as he turned off the highway onto the county road.

Smiling, Mandy slid closer and ran her fingers into the hair on the back of his head. "Well . . ." she said, drawing the word out.

"Damn, I told that barber my girl would kill me if he took too much off."

She laughed softly and blushed wildly, feeling younger and more alive than she had in years. "You didn't!"

"I did. And he told me he'd never yet ruined a romance."

A romance! His choice of words made something inside her turn all warm and weak. And for once all her fears failed to rear up and castigate her folly. "Well, he hasn't ruined this one."

He pretended to sigh with relief. "So it's okay?"

"It looks nice. You had your beard trimmed, too. Now you look like a yuppie."

"A yuppie!"

Suddenly, with an explosive sound, the windshield shattered into a web-work of cracks. Before Mandy really registered it, she was lying facedown on the bench seat. Ransom's weight was pinning her, his belt buckle cutting into her ear as he sheltered her body with his. Simultaneously he hit the brake, bringing the truck to a screeching, choking halt.

"Don't move," he said sharply, his voice low.

"I wouldn't dream of it," she said breathlessly. "Not when you consider where my head is." What the devil was going on?

For an instant she felt him stiffen. Then she gasped as he gently nipped her bottom. "There are possibilities in this position," he whispered back. "I knew you had guts."

"Guts?"

"Shh."

Guts? His meaning trickled through her slowly, stiffening her, accelerating her heart. The shattered windshield, his protective posture, his insistence on quiet. She knew exactly what he was thinking. The hair on the back of her neck prickled.

A very long time later he whispered her name. "Mandy?"

"Mmm?"

"I'm going to get up very slowly. Stay where you are, no matter what."

Galvanized, she reached behind her and managed to grab a handful of his shirt. "No."

"Shh. I know what I'm doing."

She supposed he did, but it didn't make her feel any better. "Please be careful."

His arm slipped under her, squeezing her waist, and then, to her utter amazement, she felt him kiss her bottom. The feeling that trickled through her had nothing to do with fear.

"Absolutely," he whispered. "I want to explore these possibilities a whole lot further."

Slowly he levered himself off her, keeping low. "Slide off the seat and get as far under the dash as you can. Quietly."

She obeyed, crouching into the small space. She could hardly bear to watch as Ransom sat up and peered out the side windows. Then, moving cautiously, he opened the door and slid out.

Nerve-stretching minutes passed in utter silence. Sunset passed into dusk, and finally she had to bite down on her knuckle to keep from calling out for Ransom. She should have known. What kind of fool was she? The minute she started to care, the minute she became involved, disaster struck. She fought to swallow a wild laugh as it occurred to her that maybe she ought to wear a garlic necklace to ward off evil.

"Mandy?"

Suddenly he was there, a shadow against the darkening sky. A muffled sound escaped her. In her relief, she forgot everything else, including her sense of self-preservation. Battling her cramped muscles, she struggled up on the seat and crawled across it to throw her arms around him. He caught her close.

"It's okay, princess," he murmured, stroking her mussed hair gently. "It's okay." But he didn't sound as if he believed it.

The windshield was shattered so badly that they couldn't see through it. While Ransom searched the toolbox in the back of the pickup for a crowbar, Mandy held the flashlight for him.

"What is it, Ransom?" she asked finally. "What caused it?" All the time she had been hunched on the floor of the truck, wild speculations had filled her mind. None of them seemed real, however, not even in the face of the shattered windshield. Nothing, that is, except evil wizards and good old-fashioned karma. She should have known better than to let herself care.

Moments ticked by in silence before Ransom answered shortly, "Buckshot."

Mandy drew a sharp breath, and he looked up at her. "Just some kids fooling around, Mandy. They're probably even more scared than we are." He turned back to the toolbox.

"Sure." She didn't believe it. The beam from the flashlight quivered, then steadied. "Ransom, kids around here don't play with guns. There's no need. Most kids are shooting by the time they're eight, and they own their own guns before they're twelve. It's not like the city, where Dad's gun is a big temptation." She bit her lip, recalling that he'd grown up in similar circumstances.

"I'm sure it was an accident," he said firmly. He found the crowbar and stood up in the bed of the truck. "Mandy, I found the spent shell. Just kids, probably looking for birds, and one of them tripped. I'm willing to bet they don't get a wink of sleep tonight." Bending, he grabbed the side of the truck and jumped down. When he hit the dirt, he staggered to one side and cursed.

"Damn it," he said shortly. "Somebody tell me how the hell steel legs can hurt."

Mandy bit her lip harder and followed him around to the front of the truck. "Ransom—"

He rounded on her. "Mandy, just think! In real life assassins don't use buckshot and shoot through windshields! They stalk their quarry and use high-powered rifles with sniper scopes or something equally effective. The worst—the absolute worst—that could have happened if that shot had penetrated the window is that one of us might have lost an eye."

"Okay." Her voice was thin, the word clipped.

Muttering an oath, Ransom threw back his head a moment, closed his eyes and drew a deep, steadying breath. Then, without another word, he moved her away and bashed out the windshield. When he finished, Mandy dug out the whisk broom she kept in the glove box and swept pebbles of glass from the seat and hood of the truck. She would not, she told herself, cry. Ransom had been short with her because he hurt, and besides, she knew better than to care, didn't she? No, she would *not* cry.

"Mandy."

Suddenly she was caught up in a huge bear hug.

"I'm sorry I snapped at you," he said.

All her hurt seeped away. "Do your legs hurt a lot?"

He sighed and kissed her cheek. "Count on you to be more concerned about my legs than the fact I snapped at you."

"You snapped because you hurt. I've been known to do that myself." She rubbed her cheek against his, savoring the softness of his beard. "Just forget it."

He lifted her into the truck and climbed up beside her, reaching for the ignition key. He hesitated for a moment, then leaned back, sighing.

"Mandy, can you humor an old warrior?"

"Sure." She turned to look at him, wishing the starlight was brighter.

"I really do think it was accidental, but I'm sitting here trying to battle twenty years of highly developed instincts. Will you please put your head on my lap and keep down while I drive?"

Her heart raced, whether from a sudden return of fear or the thought of resting her head on Ransom's lap she didn't know. Scooting over, she lay on her side and put her cheek on his thigh. As soon as he had the truck rolling, his right hand came to rest on her shoulder.

"This position has possibilities, too," he remarked, giving her a gentle squeeze. "Tell me the reasons why I shouldn't explore them."

She knew he was trying to distract her, but she was already distracted enough by her own awareness of his proximity.

"Mandy? Come on, give me all the reasons."

"Shut up. I'm too distracted to think."

A brief laugh escaped him. "Me too. I don't suppose you could move a little closer?"

In the dark, she blushed. "What happened to your instincts?"

"They're being superseded by an even older set."

Mandy knew exactly what he meant.

Chapter 5

Back at the house, Ransom pulled up right by the kitchen porch and turned off the ignition. His right hand clamped Mandy's shoulder, holding her where she was.

"Mandy. Humor me further."

"Okay." Wickedly, she nuzzled his thigh with her cheek. She heard him draw a quick breath, even as she drew one herself. What had gotten into her? Reaction to her fright? Or simply the warm, drizzly sexual feelings he awakened in her with such ease?

"Not that way," he said softly. "It's killing me to say that. Damn. Mandy, stay here while I check things out. My other instincts are still driving me crazy. Along with you."

She wiggled onto her back and tried to make out his face. "What's going on? You said it was an accident."

"It was. I'm sure of it. But I'm a trained—never mind. Just let me act out my craziness for a few more minutes."

"Which craziness?" Some devil was driving her into provocation, and even as she spoke she was a little shocked by her own boldness.

"The warrior craziness," he said firmly, but his hand strayed toward the swell of her breast, not really touching, but hinting. "Mandy?"

"Yes, Ransom," she said, suddenly breathless and past caring. "Act out your craziness. Either one. Both. Whatever."

A choked sound escaped him, and his hand touched her cheek briefly. "Stay here. Don't move. Don't make a sound. I'll be back in a little bit."

She lay there for at least ten minutes, unable to believe she had said the things she had. They were both crazy, she decided. Stark raving mad. It was easier, however, to consider her own mad behavior than to speculate about what it was that worried Ransom enough to make him act so cautiously. She had the uneasy feeling that his arrival had brought her into contact with an alien world. She couldn't imagine the darkness he must have known, and she didn't want to imagine that darkness invading her sanctuary.

"Mandy? Come on. Let's get you inside."

"But my stuff's in the back."

"I'll get it. You just get your rump inside."

While he carted in the boxes of paper and disks and the keyboard, Mandy started throwing together a quick meal. They were going to have to talk about these instincts of his, she decided. The warrior ones. She didn't miss the fact that he bolted the back door when he brought the last box in, or that he had already drawn all the curtains.

"Well," he said, returning to the kitchen after carrying the keyboard into her study, "I guess you can't decide whether to be scared to death or not."

"I was just going to mention that. Your behavior isn't exactly consistent." In fact, his behavior was giving her butterflies of dread in her stomach. She didn't want any more violence in her life. None. Never again.

He dug a beer out of the fridge. "I really believe it was an accident, Mandy. I'm not kidding about that. But I've been trained for years to check everything out thoroughly, not to make any hasty assumptions. My life has depended on that training more than once. Old habits die hard. Anyhow, everything seems to be kosher, so I was overreacting. Okay?"

It was hardly okay. Watching him take his precautions had reminded her of things she had been close to forgetting, little things, like the cost of caring.

She put a bowl of tuna salad and a loaf of bread on the table. "Would you mind making your own? I'm tired tonight, for some reason."

"No problem."

"I'll heat some soup."

"Forget it." He caught her hand gently and pulled her to the table. "Sit down. Let me take care of dinner."

"Ransom—"

"Cut it out," he said, pressing her down into the chair. "What's the matter? Cycles of the moon? Or are you just furious with me?"

Her eyes flew to his face. "I'm not mad at you!"

"Good. So what's on your mind?"

He stood over her, hands on his hips, waiting.

She gestured helplessly. "I don't know. I'm confused. I'm tired. I feel kind of sad. I'm scared but I'm not. I don't know."

"Frustrated."

She held her breath, looking down at her hands. "Oh hell, why not? That, too."

"Look at me, Mandy."

Slowly she looked up at him. He was magnificent, she found herself thinking. He looked like a well-barbered Viking warrior.

"Would things be easier for you if I packed my duffel and took off in the morning?"

The question hung in the air between them. Ransom stood as silent and still as a statue, awaiting her answer.

"Probably," she said finally. "But I don't want them to be easier. Sooner or later I'm going to have to deal with all this anyway." That much was obvious to her now. Her sanctuary had been invaded, and whether the warrior left now or later, his presence would leave its mark.

He gave a slow nod and pulled out a chair near hers. "How do you like your sandwich?" he asked, reaching for the bread. "Lots of tuna?"

"I can make it."

He turned, giving her an expressionless look. "Look, Mandy. My patience is wearing pretty thin right now. Don't argue, just answer."

"Just a spoonful of tuna, please."

She watched him make the sandwich and suddenly realized a couple of things. He looked tired, very tired. Beneath his deepening tan, he was pale, and there were lines of strain in his face. His mouth was compressed. She'd never seen Ransom's mouth compressed before.

"Ransom? Are you still hurting?"

He finished making her sandwich before he answered. "I shouldn't have jumped out of the truck, I guess."

"Did you hurt something?"

He shook his head. "Don't think so."

"Can you take anything for the pain?"

"Old blue jeans," he said suddenly.

Mandy blinked, then recalled the discussion they'd had last week about old jeans. "Cluck-cluck," she answered.

He flashed her a small smile. "I have codeine if I need it. I don't need it, though. It'll pass off."

"Cycles of the moon," she said slowly.

He turned, studying her face, then laughed. "Okay. Pax."

"Pax," she agreed.

Much later, it was obvious to Mandy that he had no intention of returning to his cabin that night. He joined her in the study while she wrote, and from time to time he would get up and walk through the house with a slow, measured tread. The last time he returned from prowling, she swiveled her chair and faced him.

"Ransom," she said.

"Yes, ma'am?"

"Are you trying to figure out how to tell me that your instincts, the warrior ones, are telling you to sleep here tonight?"

"Actually," he said with a small smile, "both sets of instincts are telling me to sleep here."

"There's a sofa bed in the living room and two guest bedrooms. Take your pick."

"Ouch."

She couldn't help but smile. "That's my best offer."

"I'll take it. Are you through writing?"

"For now."

"I made some hot chocolate. Can I interest you?"

"Just let me exit the program."

He returned with two cups just as she was switching off her computer. He set them down on the table by the easy chair and without a word drew Mandy firmly onto his lap.

She was surprised to realize there wasn't an ounce of resistance left in her. She was scared, but this was one moving freight train she couldn't step away from. It would end one way or another, but she couldn't bring herself to end it unborn. That was as scary as anything else, this lack of the will necessary to protect herself from certain pain.

So what? asked a little voice in her mind. She was thirty years old, too old to believe that another Ransom Laird would ever show up in her life, too old to believe that she would ever have another opportunity like this. The man touched her in so many ways that she was afraid to analyze it. He offered her glimpses of something beyond the ordinary, glimpses of light and life and color. Maybe, maybe, if she accepted his offering just once she could savor the gift without paying too highly.

"That's better," he said, when she was settled. He handed her a cup. "Careful, it's hot."

His free hand rubbed her arm gently. "You know, it's amazing, but just a couple of weeks ago I felt like I had hardly a friend in the world."

"You had Nate," she remarked.

"Nate and a few others, but that's not what I mean."

"I know," she said after a moment. "I know. Friends but not friends. Different levels of intimacy and understanding."

"Exactly. I don't feel friendless now, Mandy."

His blue eyes caught and reflected the lamplight. He was so close, Mandy thought. Hard beneath her, strong against her. If she moved two inches their mouths would meet. "I don't either," she answered softly. And that was absolutely the scariest thing of all.

His stroking hand paused, squeezed her upper arm, resumed its gentle caress.

"Tell me," she said, "what you were doing in the sixth century."

"Invading England with the Danes?" he suggested.

"Wasn't that the eighth century?"

He shrugged. "What were you doing in the sixth century?"

"Waiting for the twentieth. I spend all my time waiting. I'm beginning to think I'm the greatest time waster in eternity."

Leaning forward, she put her cup on the table. Everything inside her quailed at the realization that she was going to take this step for no better reason than that she would always regret it if she didn't. Surely, she told herself, the price of a single taste of heaven was something she could live with, for she certainly couldn't live with the price of passing it up. Gathering together every scrap of her courage, she said, "I'm through waiting."

Their eyes locked. For several heartbeats the universe stood still.

"Just tell me one thing, Ransom."

"Shoot."

"Is there somebody out there who wants to kill you?"

His face was suddenly inscrutable. "Not that I know of. I've been out of action for a long time, Mandy. Does it make a difference?"

She regarded him steadily. "No," she said finally. "Not now. In the long run, it might. I hate to think anybody might want to hurt you. But right now I wouldn't care if you were an inmate on death row." And that was downright terrifying.

He set his mug down. "Now *you* tell *me* something."

She nodded.

"Are you sure about this? Because, by God, if you're not, I'll understand. What I won't understand is if you regret this."

She drew a deep breath and expelled it slowly. "I think we've both got plenty of scars and wounds. I'm not looking to collect any more, and I'm not looking to inflict any."

"What were you doing yesterday, Amanda Lynn?" he asked softly.

"Waiting."

"And what will you be doing tomorrow?"

"Living." And hurting, too, probably, but she blocked that thought.

He smiled then, a gentle, warm smile. "I intend to see to it."

He kissed her tenderly, questingly. She responded without hesitation, welcoming the shaft of delight that plunged through her. She was committed now, and she threw restraint aside gladly. He made her feel so incredibly, wonderfully alive. He reminded her that for every pain, life offered a pleasure, if only you had the courage to reach for it.

His mouth was warm, tasting of chocolate, and it claimed hers with that beautiful rightness that only Ransom gave her, as if her mouth belonged to him, had been created for him, and his for her. The kiss deepened, and Mandy's head fell back against his cradling arm. His other hand stroked her gently, from her back to her hip and outer thigh, then up again. Slowly. His caress and kiss were deliciously slow, as if they had all the time in the world.

He smelled so good, she thought as her hand slid up his hard chest to his neck and then into his hair. Sun-kissed, musky and chocolaty. His beard was wonderfully soft against her cheeks and fresh smelling.

"Sweet, sweet Amanda," he whispered, raising his head a fraction. "You feel so good, taste so good. You fit so perfectly on my lap. I could almost spend eternity like this."

"Almost?" Her voice was a sigh.

"I'm only human after all," he said with a hint of laughter in his voice. "I'll succumb to temptation sooner or later."

"I'm all for succumbing," she answered, just as his mouth found hers again, this time in a sinuous, suggestive kiss that ignited the warm glow in her to an aching flame. "Oh, Ransom," she sighed. "Oh..."

Waves crashed in Ransom's head. Ocean surf pounded in his veins. He had thought he knew the dimensions of desire. Now he discovered he had only begun to explore them. Patience and gentleness escaped him. Panic lanced him. Abruptly he tore his mouth from Mandy's and hugged her tightly, stilling her. Her ragged breath was a warm torment against his neck.

"Mandy." Her name was an almost inaudible croak. He was trembling. God, how he was trembling! "Mandy." This time he found his voice. "We'd better not." Little in his life had been as difficult as saying those words.

Her hand made a convulsive movement against his chest, curling into a fist, pounding a single, painless protest against him. "What's wrong?" She sounded strained.

"Me." Closing his eyes, he battled for control. "It's been so long, and I want you so much. I don't want to frighten you. I'm like a bomb about to go off."

A minute passed, then another. His pulse slowed, and his panic became fear of another kind. And then Mandy raised her head.

"Ransom, if you don't want to frighten me, then you won't."

"You don't know—"

"You're right, I don't know. But I'm not afraid to find out."

"I want this to be perfect for you."

Mandy cupped his cheek and kissed his chin. "Perfection is an illusion. Why don't we shoot for it another time?"

She slipped from his lap and headed for the door. "Figure out what you really want. Me, or the illusion of self-control. I'm going up to bed."

The gauntlet was thrown, and he could almost see it lying on the floor.

Between them, he thought, they had enough devils and demons to do justice to one of her books. They needed to walk with care around each other in order to avoid treading in sore places. Ransom was exquisitely aware of the need for caution and delicacy in his relationship with Mandy, and right now he had the feeling he had transgressed.

She was right about the self-control, though. He was always in control of himself, if nothing else. It was why they had never been able to break him. He set very high standards for himself, standards he never sacrificed. Now he was close to losing that control, on the edge of sacrificing some of those standards, and she had challenged him to do it.

Could he go to her and take the one risk he had never taken? Could he take the risk of what he would see in her eyes later? Did he trust her that much? She had as good as told him that she trusted him implicitly. All he had to do was trust her in return.

Upstairs, Mandy had climbed into the king-size bed in one of the guest rooms. Tense, with a growing sense of disappointment, she waited. She understood, though. She had crossed enough hurdles of her own that she could sympathize with Ransom. This particular hurdle, she guessed, had taken him by surprise.

Ransom never came. Giving up finally, Mandy switched off the light and lay staring into the dark. Maybe he was right, she told herself, trying to ignore the slow, steady throbbing of her body. Maybe neither of them was prepared to be so vulnerable to another person. Ransom didn't want to lose control, didn't yet trust Mandy enough to come to her stripped of everything but his need. And if she was honest, she would admit that she'd had second thoughts almost from the instant she left the living room. She was coming to care deeply for Ransom, and in spite of her determination not to let her neurotic fears overwhelm her, she was nevertheless terrified. He would go away sooner or later, and she just didn't know if she would be strong enough to handle another loss. If she made love with him, her emotions would deepen. She didn't have a single doubt about that.

So let it ride, said the sane, sensible portion of her mind. Let it ride. It was too soon to know if she should risk this step.

But, oh, how empty her body felt, how she ached for his strength and weight. How alone and vulnerable she felt without him.

The feelings that Ransom had shelved for better than four years were shrieking to be let loose. He was up before dawn, and the pearly gray light found him splitting wood behind the barn. He had absolutely no intention of letting those feelings free. All his life, self-control had been the only thing that protected him. As long as he was in control of himself, no one else could control him. Once, just once, he'd relinquished some of that control for the sake of an unborn baby. That lapse had cost him dearly. Once he had trusted. It was suddenly apparent that he wasn't ready to do that again.

Sweat made a fine sheen on his skin as he split log after log. His breath rasped in the chilly morning air, drying out his throat. The demons were at the gate, and he didn't dare let them in. If once, just once, he allowed himself to feel any of the anger and anguish of the last four years, he might fall apart like Humpty Dumpty, never to be put back together again.

And then there was Mandy. Last night she'd offered herself without reservation, and he'd rejected her. It couldn't have made her feel too good, even though he'd told her that his reasons had nothing to do with her. He wasn't so much afraid of the strength of his desire for her as he was of breaching the dam. How could Mandy be expected to understand that? She couldn't, of course, so this morning she was probably feeling hurt and possibly humiliated.

So explain it to her, he told himself, swinging the axe once more in a savage stroke. Tell her you're sitting on a volcano of backlogged feelings. She'll understand.

Maybe, maybe not. At this point he wasn't even sure himself what he was afraid would happen if he let loose. He just knew it wouldn't be pretty.

"Ransom?"

Mandy's voice pierced his preoccupation. Altering his swing, he buried the axe head in the chopping block and then straightened slowly. Pulling a rag from his pocket, he wiped sweat from his face and neck.

She was behind him, and the knowledge made his back prickle. Shirtless, he was mercilessly exposed, and even though she'd seen his scars twice before, even though she'd made it plain they didn't repel her, he wasn't comfortable with it. He turned.

Mandy drew a deep breath as the full morning light bathed Ransom's face and chest, setting his hair on fire.

"You're so beautiful," she whispered.

Something in Ransom cracked, rupturing a fault so deep he knew he would never patch it. Instead of the furies he'd expected, however, there was a flood of warmth so healing that he caught his breath.

"I'm sorry," he said, surprising himself.

"What for?" Mandy asked. "We've both been racing headlong into something we're not ready for. I've been trying to convince myself I'm not frightened when I really am. And you—well, you're just not ready to trust enough to let go. I'm glad you pulled back, Ransom. I'm afraid we both would have regretted it if you hadn't." Turning, she headed back to the house, calling over her shoulder, "Breakfast is ready."

He admired her dignity. He didn't feel very dignified himself, standing there shirtless, covered with sweat, his muscles trembling from an attempt to smother the rage that sat like a cold lump of lead in his stomach. He didn't dare let it emerge. But didn't he have every right to be angry?

Muttering an obscenity, he turned toward his cabin. The least he could do was clean up a little and put on a shirt before he went to breakfast. He didn't want to think about any of it, but the fact was, he was beginning to wonder if he'd been crippled in ways that went far deeper than skin and bone.

A short while later, crossing the hard-packed earth to Mandy's kitchen door, he saw the missing windshield of her truck and was reminded of yesterday's events. Damn, he was slipping if his own inner turmoil could put something like that out of his mind. He'd clean forgotten about it.

"We'll have to do something about your windshield," he said to Mandy as he stepped into the kitchen. The screen door slapped shut behind him, and he closed the inner door against the morning chill. The kitchen was warm, quiet, inviting. Mandy sat at the table, a half eaten plate of scrambled eggs before her.

"Your eggs are cold," she said calmly. "I'll heat them in the microwave."

"Don't bother. It's my fault for dawdling." He pulled out his chair and sat across from her. At least she hadn't retreated to the far end of the table again. "About that windshield. Do you have insurance?"

"Against being shot at?"

He grimaced. "Against vandalism. Call it vandalism. It was an accident, damn it. I'll take it into town this morning and see about getting it fixed." It would give him an opportunity to make a phone call where she couldn't hear.

"There's no rush. I'll just call my insurance agent and tell him what happened. We can take care of it whenever it's convenient."

"It's also apt to turn into winter at any moment, and it'll be damn cold driving without a windshield, Mandy."

She shrugged. "Have it your way." What was eating him?

He ate the rest of his breakfast in silence. It was only as he pushing his chair back from the table that he looked at her. "I'm sorry," he said for the second time that morning. "I'm sorry about last night, and I'm sorry for being so angry this morning. Sometimes I just . . . get angry."

Her head tilted, and her expression gentled. "I guess I can see why you would. Forget about it. I will."

"Thanks. I'll take care of that truck now. Is there anything you want from town?"

Mandy shook her head. "I've got everything I need. I'll call ahead to my agent and tell him you're coming."

He moved around the table and bent over her, tilting her head up for a kiss. "It'll pass," he murmured. "I promise to come home in a better mood."

That was probably why he wanted to go to town, Mandy thought as she watched him turn the truck and head down the driveway. To get away until he got a grip on his anger. Well, if anyone had a right to be angry, surely Ransom did.

The drive to town cleared Ransom's head more than chopping wood had. Maybe it was the wind blowing in his face, or maybe it was just the silence and sunshine; whatever, he felt almost human by the time he pulled up in front of the sheriff's offices.

Nate was buried in his office, burrowing his way through the mounds of paper that came with his job. He always put it off until the last possible minute, preferring to be a lawman rather than a clerk, but at least once a month he paid the piper. Ransom's arrival was a welcome distraction.

"If I didn't know better," Nate drawled as he leaned back and peered up at Ransom, "I'd say you look like a man with weighty things on his mind. Where's Mandy?"

"At home."

"Pull up a chair, son," Nate invited. "Do we need the whole posse, or will I do?"

Ransom half smiled and folded himself into a chair. "You'll do, Nate. You always did."

"So what's up?"

"I came into town to get the windshield on Mandy's truck replaced. Somebody shot it out last night when we were driving home. Buckshot."

Nate let out a low whistle and leaned forward. "Did you see 'em?"

"Nope. I told Mandy it was just some kids, that one of them had probably tripped and the gun went off by accident."

"But you don't believe it."

Ransom shrugged. "Hard to believe it was anything else. But it's also hard to believe it was a couple of kids when I didn't see any kids. Unless kids in these parts lie low and deliberately shoot at passing vehicles.''

"Never had anything like that in all the years I've been sheriff.'' Nate rubbed his chin. "If it was an accident, you would have seen the kids fooling around by the road.''

"That's how I figure it. I would have seen *something*.''

"But nobody who seriously wants to hurt somebody tries buckshot through a windshield.''

"That also occurred to me.''

Nate regarded Ransom steadily. "You think it was a warning.''

"That's the only thing that makes sense. The question is, what kind of warning, and who sent it? People in my business don't play that way.''

"You think somebody's trying to scare Mandy?'' Nate sounded disbelieving. "Look, man, John Grant engendered a lot of goodwill in Conard County. Everybody who knew him had a lot of liking and respect for him, and most of that feeling applies to Mandy, as well. Folks around here would do just about anything for her if she'd let them.''

"I wasn't seeing it quite that way,'' Ransom said, with a quick shake of his head. "No, I think I'm the one being warned. The question is, why? Would somebody have reason to want me to move on? Maybe somebody with a personal interest in Mandy?''

"Mandy's gone out of her way not to encourage that kind of interest since John died. It kind of surprises me that she's interested in you, if you want to know the truth. Even if that weren't the case, you're talking about a sick mind. I'd like to think I'd have at least some suspicion if one of the folks around here was unhinged.''

"You feel you know everyone that well?'' Ransom asked.

"I've lived here all my life,'' Nate answered steadily. "Except for three years in Nam, at any rate. A sheriff's a politician as well as a lawman, Ransom, and there's not so many people in this county that I haven't gotten to know them all one way or the other over forty-odd years. I can't say for a fact that none of these folks would do such a thing, but I feel I'd have some notion of it if one of 'em was weird like this."

Ransom folded his arms across his chest. "So you tell me what you think is going on. I admit that twenty years in my line of work can make a man paranoid, but so can buck-shot through a windshield."

Nate laid his hands flat on the desk. "Are you sure you didn't bring one of your own problems with you?"

"I told you, people in my business don't work this way. A high-powered rifle would be more their speed, and they'd aim to kill, not frighten."

"So maybe somebody wants to play a little cat and mouse with you, make you sweat. I admit that calls for a weird kind of mind, but I can see someone from your business thinking that way a hell of a lot easier than I can see one of my neighbors pulling a stunt like this."

Ransom shook his head. "I don't like it, Nate. That's too easy. In the first place, I've been out of action for the last four-and-a-half years. Only a handful of people know I'm still alive, and the official word among the handful who do is that I'm taking a medical retirement. Anyway, I've been gone so long that I'm not a threat to anyone."

"Somebody thinks you're a threat," Nate said gruffly. "What're you going to do about it?"

Ransom yielded a heavy sigh. "Not a whole hell of a lot, Nate. Not a whole hell of a lot."

"Why not?"

"Just what am I supposed to do? Without any idea of what's going on, anything I do might be exactly the wrong thing."

Nate scowled. "You damn well better be careful. And you better look out for Mandy, too, or I'll be nailing your hide to the barn wall."

"Nothing's going to happen to Mandy," Ransom said grimly. "I can promise you that much. I won't let it."

After he left Nate's office, he hunted up a pay phone and placed a long distance call. The person who answered listened without interruption as Ransom spoke. When he fell silent, the voice on the other end said, "You're officially on leave." In other words, since he wasn't on a mission, he couldn't expect any help. The next sound was that of a phone being disconnected.

Ransom was in the act of slamming the receiver into the cradle when he realized he was being watched. That tingle on the back of his neck was unmistakable. Instantly, he spun around to catch the watcher.

There wasn't a soul in sight.

Not yet ready to believe his eyes over his instincts, he scanned the windows of the surrounding buildings for a sign, any sign, that someone was staring down at him. That was when he noticed the five-year-old child in the window of the convenience store. Relieved, he released his breath.

Damn, he was too much on edge. That was dangerous. He had to stay calm enough to act, not just react. Calm enough to think, weigh and plan. Calm enough to deal with the fact that he was utterly and completely on his own. Usually he was on his own only during a mission, when he always knew who and what he was up against. This time was different. This time he was looking into the dark, and he didn't have an idea in hell who was out there waiting for him.

Hell!

Well, if he didn't accomplish anything else today, he could go into the next county and get some condoms. If things got out of hand again, at least he would be able to protect Mandy from that much.

It was after four when Mandy heard the truck pull up outside. She caught herself just as she was rising from her computer and sat back down again. Considering the odd mood Ransom had been in that morning, she decided it would be better to let him look for her in his own good time. A few minutes later, when it was evident he wasn't coming into the house, she forced her attention back to her writing. Whatever had been bothering him that morning was clearly still working on him.

At five she started dinner, wondering if she were wasting her time. Maybe he was as unnerved as she was by their precipitate rush toward intimacy. Good grief, it had taken her nearly three years to get this close to John.

The thought set her back on her heels. Her hands started to shake, and her mouth went dry. What was she thinking of, to let her feelings grow so swiftly, and for a man about whom she knew so little? He was just a drifter, pausing briefly in her life while he healed. In no time at all he would go back to his job and his other life and leave her once again in solitude. How could she risk her hard-won peace this way?

"The truck is fixed, Mandy," Ransom said from behind her. The slap of the screen door punctuated the sentence.

"Thank you." The words were muffled, difficult to say with parched lips and tongue. To still their trembling, she clasped her hands on the counter in front of her.

"Something wrong?" His booted feet halted right behind her.

"No. Nothing."

He didn't believe her. Strong, hard arms closed around her from behind, folding across her stomach just below her breasts. His warm lips found the vulnerable side of her neck, right below her ear, and a helpless shiver passed through her in response.

"Are you mad at me?" he asked, his warm breath caressing her ear.

"Of course not," she managed to say. Mad? There was no room for anything else with all her panic. Why was it that every time he touched her, her common sense flew out the window? Her hands were shaking now for a different reason, and all she wanted to do was turn around and melt into his embrace.

"Then look at me," he demanded quietly.

She turned within the circle of his arms because she was helpless to do anything else. She was starved for the sight of him, the look of him, the Viking warrior harshness of his bearded face.

"What scared you?" he asked gently, tracing her cheek with a gentle fingertip.

"How do you know I'm scared?" The words were little more than a rush of breath.

"I can smell it on you," he said bluntly. "I can feel it in the way your heart is racing. Are you afraid of me?"

Not even in a desperate need for self-preservation could she tell that lie. "No."

"Then what?"

"Me," she admitted, her head dropping.

He understood. His hand left her cheek, and both arms tightened around her in a comforting embrace. With her face pressed to his hard chest, with his masculine scent rich in her nose, Mandy knew a sense of security that was as utterly irrational as it was undeniable.

"I'm scared, too," he admitted, closing his eyes and pressing his lips to the top of her head. God, yes, he was scared. He was forty-one years old, and for the first time in all those years he felt ties forming, strings that were binding him, tugging on him. He was being pulled to Mandy in a way that was steadily limiting his options. All day, ever since he'd left Nate's office, he'd been telling himself that it was time to move on. Something was wrong, somebody was after him, and he didn't want to risk any harm coming to Mandy. Yet here he was, holding her once again, knowing damn well that not all the furies of hell could take him from her side. Not yet. Not yet.

She was, he was sure, feeling the same way. It was as if neither of them could survive the wound of ending their relationship, even though they both were convinced that the damage would only be worse if they waited. What a hell of a situation.

"Dinner's going to burn," she said faintly against his chest.

He let her go reluctantly.

That night, Ransom didn't sleep worth a damn. He let Mandy think he had returned to his own cabin, but instead he chose to maintain his vigilance over her. She never locked her doors, once a pardonable omission considering where she lived, but pardonable no longer. He made a mental note to tell her first thing in the morning that she had better start locking her doors. He had avoided such discussions because he didn't want to alarm her, but now he acknowledged that had been a dangerous decision.

Until he saw her bedroom light go out, he waited outside, listening and watching. When he was certain she must be asleep, he let himself into her house, leaving the chilly, empty night behind. He could have stationed himself in the living room, but it had been a long time since he had stood night guard-duty, and he wasn't sure he could count on his battered body and mind to stay awake. Instead he sat at the kitchen table, on one of the uncomfortable oak chairs. He made coffee and sat in the dark waiting. Watching. Listening.

And remembering. That was the damnable thing about the long, empty hours. His mind filled the void with images, and those visions were too often unwelcome memories. In the dead of night he discovered just how many appalling memories he had. Surely that said something about him. Well, hell, he already knew it was time to re-evaluate himself.

He also found himself reviewing rusty skills in his mind and considering how he might best secure Mandy's castle against intrusion. Nate could do little except keep an eye out for strangers in the county and tell his deputies to stop by the ranch a couple of times a day. For full-time guard-duty there was only himself, and after so many years he doubted his abilities.

There had been a time when he had been confident that if he slept, he would wake at the first sign of anything untoward, no matter how subtle. During his days as a captive, however, he had learned to sleep deeply and let nothing disturb him. It had been a survival skill, and, like most of his survival skills, he had learned it well. So well that he wasn't at all sure anything short of a nuclear attack could wake him.

How long could he keep this up? He asked himself the question and had no answer. He was being foolish, he guessed. A man had to sleep sometime. Nevertheless, he couldn't stand the thought of sleeping while Mandy was sleeping, because she would be defenseless. Someone had to watch over her.

That meant he was going to have to devise a means of safeguarding her while he slept. In the long, lonely hours of the night, he forced himself to consider Mandy's protection and shied away from other thoughts.

Somewhere deep inside, he knew he had become a hunted man. Who was after him, or why, he couldn't begin to fathom, but with gut certainty he knew that someone was hunting him, toying with him like a cat just before the kill.

And with equal certainty he knew he had to protect Mandy. He had led them to her, and they wouldn't forget her if he vanished. No, they would try to use her, and he couldn't expose her to that.

So he sat in the chilly hours before dawn and wondered what the hell he was going to do. The warrior had led the damn evil wizard right to the princess's walls.

Chapter 6

An unusual fog bathed the dawn in pearl gray mists. From the window of her bedroom Mandy looked out to discover that she couldn't even see as far as the barn. In fact, she could hardly see the ground below.

It was as if they had been plucked from the planet and set in some alien world, she thought whimsically. Whimsical or not, the sensation created by the thick fog was eerie and unnerving. Evil. She turned from the window suddenly, feeling the back of her neck prickle with fear. Ridiculous, she scolded herself. Your imagination has always been too vivid.

The morning's damp chill had penetrated the entire house. She washed up swiftly and climbed hurriedly into a thick, warm jogging suit, a baggy navy blue number that she loved for its comfort and warmth and which did absolutely nothing else for her. She'd had it for years, and John had teased her about it being a security blanket. Maybe it was. It certainly felt like armor against some of the malevolence she sensed in the morning.

She found Ransom in the kitchen making coffee and frying bacon. One look at him and she knew he hadn't slept a wink. Not a wink. Did he really think he could fool her?

As she stood in the doorway of the kitchen, a storm whipped through her, sweeping away a mountain of illusions to which she had been stubbornly clinging. She couldn't escape life. Not really. She had buried herself as far out and as far away as she could get, and life had simply walked right up to her door and dragged her back into the game. A truly dangerous game, to judge by Ransom's attempts to dissemble for her.

Her knees turned to water and her mouth became as dry as cotton while she contemplated the reality that lurked beyond her fortress walls. Fortress walls that she had apparently built from the diaphanous stuff of fantasy rather than substantial brick and mortar.

Almost stunned, feeling as if she were standing brutally exposed on a high, windy precipice while cold winds threatened to topple her over the edge, she turned away and headed for the shelter of her study. She had thought she didn't ask much of life. How much, after all, was it to want to simply be free of hurt and terror? Too much, evidently.

Perhaps, she found herself thinking almost numbly, if she couldn't escape the hurt and fear, then maybe she was an utter fool to pass up the joy and pleasure. But her every instinct for self-preservation recoiled from that concept. Caring made the pain even worse.

She might conceivably have spent the entire morning staring numbly at her computer while she tried to cope with her shattered illusions of safety, except that once again life refused to let her hide. The unexpected sound of a car coming up the driveway dragged her out of her preoccupation.

Must be Nate, she thought, or one of his deputies. They were the only people who stopped by without calling first. Glad of the distraction, she hurried out to the kitchen in time to find Ransom setting breakfast on the table and Micah Parish, one of Nate's deputies, climbing out of his dusty Blazer parked near the kitchen door.

Opening the inner door in greeting, Mandy watched the deputy come across the dusty, hard-packed dirt to the porch steps. Other deputies had come to check on her before, but never Micah. She guessed he *had* thought she resented him, and she was suddenly very glad she had spoken to him the other morning.

Micah had come to town four years ago, just after John died. Mandy still remembered him getting out of a battered old pickup and crossing the sun-drenched main street toward Nate's office. She had been there to pick up a box of John's personal effects, and she had watched Micah Parish's approach with a fascination that had briefly pierced her grief. He had been wearing desert camouflage, and Nate, who had served with him in Vietnam, hired Parish, newly retired from the army, on the spot.

"Morning, Micah," she said as he reached the lower step. "Do you have time for some breakfast?"

He mounted the three steps and gave her one of his small, rare smiles. "I've got plenty of time, Mandy. Thanks. Is Ransom around?"

"Ransom's doing the cooking," Ransom said from right behind Mandy. She felt him, felt his heat. Just knowing he was there, right behind her, and that all she had to do to be in his arms was take a step backward, nearly erased her awareness of everything else. Ransom broke the spell by reaching around her to unlatch the screen door. "Come on in, Micah."

That was when Mandy realized that these two men knew each other. There was something in the way their eyes met— Ransom's so blue, Micah's so black—that spoke of understanding.

"How long have you two been acquainted?" she asked.

Ransom looked down at her with a faint smile. "Since Nam."

No further explanation seemed to be required. Even if it had been, she didn't think she would get it. Sensing that if she pushed she was going to run up against a couple of stone walls, she held her peace for the time being and helped Ransom finish putting breakfast on the table.

Men could be the most frustrating creatures, she found herself thinking a few minutes later. Two women friends who hadn't seen each other in years would be talking up a storm. These two men didn't say a word. Instead they ate in a silence that somehow seemed more companionable than any conversation she had ever shared.

Not until he had finished the last bite did Micah speak. "Nate figured you'd be getting pretty sleepy around about now."

A smile nudged one corner of Ransom's mouth. "Nate figured right. More coffee?"

"Thanks."

Ransom refilled all three mugs. As he did so, he looked at Mandy, looked her right in the eye. It was a look that seemed to see all her uneasy and contradictory thoughts and feelings.

Disturbed, she looked away. "Why did Nate think Ransom would be getting tired?" As if she didn't know. It was suddenly, painfully apparent that Ransom had spoken to Nate and shared concerns that he had refused to share with her. *Kids fooling around in the grass, my foot!*

Micah looked at Ransom as if for permission to answer her, and Mandy suddenly resented it. This was her home, her life, and these men had barreled into it without so much as a by-your-leave, bringing all their violence and ugly games with them. She set her mug down with a sharp crack and rose, drawing their eyes to her.

"If I'm not old enough to hear it, intelligent enough to understand it and trustworthy enough to be told, then I guess I'm too young, too dumb and too unsteady to be involved. This is my home, gentlemen. Take your problems elsewhere!"

Ransom caught her in the hallway outside the kitchen. Grim-lipped, he wrapped an arm around her waist and hauled her into her study. There, he leaned back against the closed door and tugged her into the V between his legs, pressing every inch of her torso intimately to his. And then he kissed her. Violently. Savagely. Like a Viking warrior claiming an unwilling captive.

And just as suddenly, before she could do more than register an explosion of internal heat, he lifted his head and glared down at her. His voice was little more than an angry whisper.

"If I thought my leaving would keep you clear of this," he growled at her, "I would have been gone two nights ago. Unfortunately, princess, any chance of keeping you out of it was gone the minute they found me."

Her wits seemed to have scattered to the four winds before the fury of his kiss, and it was a moment before she collected herself enough to whisper, "Who? Who are they? What do they want?"

He shook his head, every line of his face bleak. "I wish I knew. I wish I had even a foggy idea. I made a call yesterday and couldn't find out a damn thing. The simple fact is that this shouldn't be happening, because only a handful of people have any idea I'm alive, or that I'm here. I've been out of action so damn long, there shouldn't be anyone who wants me, anyway. I've spent the last day and a half racking my brains trying to figure out who could possibly have a score that big to settle with me. Anyone else would have long since forgotten me."

Helpless to stop herself, telling herself she ought to still be angry, ought to feel somehow betrayed, she reached up and touched his face. At the moment all she seemed capable of knowing was that this man was pursued by demons he couldn't seem to shake. The injustice of it was bitter bile on her tongue, and she felt helpless to console him. Unable to tell him these things, she simply said, "What now?"

"I guess Nate asked Micah to spell me so I could sleep. Other than that, I don't know. I just plain don't know, Mandy."

He looked so tired, so... defeated, somehow, as if this were the last straw. Maybe for him it was, after everything he'd been through. He was, after all, just beginning to recover from his last battle, just beginning to find his feet and his direction and his purpose. Aching for him, Mandy leaned into him and wrapped her arms around his waist. With her cheek on his chest, she listened to his heartbeat.

"It's okay," she said pointlessly, the soothing, meaningless incantation of a person with nothing else to offer in the way of comfort except caring. "It's okay." A hard little kernel of resolve began to grow in her. She had no idea how she was going to find the courage to do it, but somehow, some way, she would stand beside Ransom through this. He'd been alone long enough, she thought.

When they returned to the kitchen a few minutes later, Micah was waiting for them as patiently as the earth and trees. He looked up impassively, not even by the minutest flicker of a muscle betraying what he might think.

"You get some sleep," he said to Ransom. "I'll spell you. And then between us maybe we can come up with something."

The fog clung throughout the day. Every time Mandy looked up from her work, gray ghosts swirled slowly beyond the windows, pressing inward. The gloom invaded her writing until finally she had taken an entirely different turn in the tale than she had planned to. Uncertain whether the turn was right or wrong for the story, she gave up in disgust.

Micah made it clear he wasn't a guest and didn't want to be treated like one. He wandered in and out of the kitchen, accepting nothing but a mug of coffee from time to time. He spent most of his time outside, prowling. Patrolling. Guarding. Evidently it was good enough for Ransom, because he slept a solid eight hours.

Mandy was cooking dinner and had persuaded Micah to take a seat at the table when Ransom finally made his appearance. His hair was wet from a shower, his shirttails hung out, and he was yawning hugely as he stepped through the door.

Micah grinned faintly. "You sure needed that, man."

"Yeah." Smothering another yawn, Ransom headed for the coffeepot. "I went out like a light."

Without the least bit of self-consciousness, he startled Mandy by bending to kiss her cheek as he reached for the coffeepot.

In that moment, as color flooded her face and her heart skipped a beat or two, Mandy envied Ransom. He saw what he wanted and he went for it. He didn't analyze every little thing to death the way she did. No. He wanted to kiss her, so he kissed her, and to hell with Micah and the rest of the world. Why couldn't she be a little like that?

Ransom joined Micah at the table, turning his chair so that he could sit sideways to the table and stretch out his long legs. He looked so damn relaxed, Mandy thought, watching from the corner of her eye as he crossed his booted legs at the ankle and smothered another yawn. As if everything were perfectly normal. As if he weren't being hunted.

His first words dispelled that illusion. "Did you get wind of anything today?" he asked Micah.

Mandy's hands froze in the process of stirring the browning meat and onions. A moment later she started stirring again, not wanting either of the men to know how intently she was listening.

"Mebbe," was Micah's laconic answer.

Maybe? *Maybe?* When Micah said nothing to elaborate, Mandy had to restrain an urge to turn on him and demand an explanation. She didn't know Micah well, but she knew him well enough to know he wouldn't say a word he didn't choose to.

After an endless pause, Micah spoke again, dropping his rare words like pebbles into the pool of silence. "Show you after supper."

In the silence that Micah seemed to carry with him like a cloak, Mandy realized just how accustomed she had become to Ransom's companionship at the table. The two of them always talked, always discussed the day's events, and often discussed more momentous things, things like memories and past events, things like hopes and feelings.

Micah short-circuited all that. Anyone would have had some effect on the direction of Ransom's and Mandy's conversation, of course, but she doubted anyone else would have cast a pall of complete silence over them. Micah clearly felt no need for casual speech and appeared utterly unperturbed by the silence. If Ransom was disturbed, he showed no evidence of it, seeming to find the lack of talk completely normal.

It was a mark of the changes in her that Mandy did *not* find it either unremarkable or normal. In fact, it seemed downright unsociable. The only alternative, however, was to make conversation simply for the sake of filling the silence, and that she refused to do. After all, the only safe, neutral topic would be weather, and, like most writers, she had a horror of the trite, even if she *did* occasionally have to resort to it.

After dinner Micah complimented her cooking and then pushed his chair back from the table. "Come on, I'll show you what I found. Then I gotta get back and take care of my livestock."

He led them outside and toward the front of the house. Just before they reached the corner of the porch, he stopped beneath the living room window and hunkered down. Ransom hunkered down beside him, and Mandy peered over Ransom's shoulder.

Micah reached out and pushed aside a marigold plant. There, in the softer topsoil of her garden, she saw a footprint. A small, fresh footprint.

"Too big for Mandy's foot," Micah remarked. "Might almost be a man's size eight or nine. Figure it was someone weighing maybe 130, 140 pounds."

Mandy's heart had begun to beat rapidly, a nervous, unhappy tattoo. "And just what do you think someone was doing in my marigold patch, Micah?" There was, of course, only one thing they could have been doing, but it was so outlandish and outrageous, she wanted someone else to say it.

Micah looked at Ransom as if for permission, then said, "Reckon they were looking in your window, Mandy. Ground's too dry away from the flower beds to tell if they looked in any other windows. Or where they might have come from."

She was suddenly cold in a way that had little to do with the evening's chill. Straightening, she rubbed her arms vigorously, torn between a desire to walk away from this into the house and a need to hear whatever might be said between these men. The fog was creepy, she thought, as icy fingers of fear danced along her spine. It would be dark soon. She had never been terrified of night in her entire life, but now, suddenly, she dreaded the approach of darkness.

"Let's get you inside."

Ransom's voice startled her, and she looked toward him to discover that he had risen and was studying her closely. "I'm fine," she lied.

"Like hell." One corner of his mouth lifted in a humorless smile. "You look like someone just walked over your grave." He slipped an arm around her shoulders and drew her close to his side as he turned to face Micah. "Thanks, Micah. I'll call you later."

Micah nodded, touched the brim of his Stetson hat to Mandy and strode off toward his Blazer.

"Come on, princess," Ransom said gruffly, and guided her toward the kitchen porch. When she stumbled over something, he simply swept her up in his arms and carried her.

"Put me down, damn it," she protested, somehow managing to sound as if she didn't mean it.

"Just as soon as we get inside. You know, I always wanted to be a knight in shining armor and rescue some damsel in distress. I can get used to this."

She scowled. "Don't. I'm not interested in being anybody's damsel, in distress or otherwise."

"I know." The teasing note vanished from his voice as they stepped into the kitchen. Gently, he lowered her feet to the floor. When he was sure she was balanced, he slackened his hold and with one finger tilted her face up to him.

"Day by day," he said quietly, "I get stronger. Little by little, I mend. And more and more, I feel like a man. Especially around you, Amanda Lynn. Especially around you." Bending, he covered her mouth with his.

It was a kiss that was astonishingly gentle, that made unnamed, unknown places in her heart and soul ache with a keen longing. A sound escaped her, a soft sorrowful sound like the mournful note of a dove, a sound that spoke of unfulfilled hopes and dreams, of losses and disappointments. Her hands rose and dove into the golden silk of his hair as pain and yearning warred within her. Why? she wondered dazedly. Why was everything that mattered always denied to her?

Ransom pulled away suddenly, but before she could protest, his purpose became clear. He closed and locked the door, switched out the kitchen light, then scooped her up again. He carried her into her study, and once again she found herself on his lap. And once again he tilted her face to his so that his mouth could seek the softness of hers.

As night gathered around the house, something else gathered around the two of them. Not quite passion, not quite hunger, not quite... Not quite. It was a promise more than a fulfillment, an intent more than a deed.

"Ah, princess," he sighed raggedly against her mouth just before his tongue made a provocative foray into her silken heat.

He knew how to kiss. Nobody, Mandy thought dazedly, nobody ought to be able to cast such a stirring spell with a simple kiss. His tongue stroked hers in a supple, evocative rhythm. Slowly. Deeply. Tenderly. There was nothing demanding, nothing harsh or hungry or cruel; there was only a gentle invitation. And he kissed as if the kiss were itself the consummation. There was no hurry, no sense that he wanted to move on, or that this was merely a step in a journey. No, his kiss was the beginning and end, a pleasure he savored with undisguised enjoyment.

From time to time he paused, lifting his head so they could catch their breath, and then he scattered small, soft, warm, loving kisses on her cheeks, her chin, the tip of her nose.

"Amanda Lynn," he whispered once, achingly, and then bent to steal her breath yet again.

A wizard's spell, she thought dazedly. A mage's enchantment filling her with a burning ache that made her insides throb in a slow, deep demand for more. She felt, but could not prevent, the rise of her hips, the instinctive undulation that signalled her need. Lifting, she sought relief and found only temporary surcease as her thighs clamped together.

He felt the slight movement of her bottom against his lap as she responded to her woman's nature. Awe struck him, causing him to tear his mouth from hers to look, to see that she was indeed so needy for him. He was a good lover, he had always satisfied his partners, but he had never brought one to this kind of response with only a few kisses. Touched, humbled, he was also frightened. Too much. Too soon. He wanted her willing compliance, not her seduction. Her seduction would wound them both.

Bending his head, he kissed her once more, but differently, with a gentler, more comforting quality. He wrapped his arms around her more snugly, tucked her into the sheltering curve of his torso and soothed her tenderly.

He wanted this woman with a terrifying ache that went deeper than the hot throbbing of his loins. He wanted her, but he had no right to take her. Not so long as he was hunted.

Mandy might have been embarrassed, except that Ransom held her so tenderly, as if she were incredibly precious to him. He trailed soft kisses along her jaw until at last she let go of her body's tension and relaxed against him. When she gathered courage to open her eyes, she found him smiling down at her, his blue eyes warm like summer skies.

But neither of them said anything. They trembled on the verge of discovery, but neither of them dared look over the edge.

"I'm afraid."

She said the words aloud at last. Standing with her hands submerged in soapy dishwater, acutely aware that Ransom was prowling the house like a guard again, even as he made occasional stabs at helping with the dishes, she admitted her fear. Saying it, facing it, helped a little. But only a little.

Ransom's arms closed around her waist from behind, and he pressed his face warmly against the side of her neck. "I swear," he whispered huskily, "I won't let anything happen to you, Mandy."

"That might not be entirely under your control," she replied a little unsteadily. Nor was it her biggest fear.

"They'll have to kill me first." There was no huskiness in that statement. It was a simple, flat declaration of fact.

She believed him. *That* was her biggest fear. And that was the yawning gulf between them. In that instant she became sharply aware of who and what he was. Stepping aside, she reached for a towel to dry her hands, then turned to face him.

A warrior. A man whose life was shadowed by violence and blood. A man who had lived by the sword. A man who might now die by it.

Closing her eyes against the sudden grip of pain, she found John's memory waiting for her. John had been a warm, loving, gentle man. Vividly she could recall the tenderness of his nature, the way children had instinctively trusted him. Gentleness and kindness notwithstanding, he had been torn from her by the sword of violence and hatred and fear, by the sword of the world men had created with their savage natures.

Now she opened her eyes and faced Ransom, who watched her narrowly with both concern and an elemental distrust. Elemental because she was sure it was a deeply ingrained part of his nature. When had he last been able to trust anyone? Certainly he couldn't even now.

Every line of him spoke of hardness and harshness. He made no allowances for himself, she sensed, but always demanded he live up to some high ideal. An ideal of being tougher, harder, faster, smarter. An ideal that encompassed honor and duty. An ideal that would make him step between her and any kind of danger. An ideal that would make him die in the place of others.

John, too, had shared that ideal in his own gentler way. *A greater gift hath no man....*

And heaven help the women who loved these noble, honorable protectors. These warriors on the side of right. These guardians of civilization. These men who were prepared to sacrifice everything to protect the flame of decency. God help them.

Once again she turned, away from Ransom this time. She understood these men because her tales were full of them. She recognized some part of them inside herself, comprehended their devotion to what they saw as their duty. She respected them, she honored them, but dear God, she didn't want to care about one of them ever again.

"Mandy?"

"Forget it," she said. "Just forget it." The dishes could wait. Everything could wait. Turning on her heel, she tossed the towel aside and headed for her study. There, at least, it was all fantasy. The pain wasn't real.

The fog was unnatural, Ransom thought. It was nearly midnight, and he left the house to prowl around outside, to look for anything untoward. He wasn't a man who believed in ghosts or magic or other supernatural things, but this fog, natural as he knew it must be, still *felt* unnatural.

Well, he thought, as he moved with a silent stealth he had feared he might have lost, this weather would sure make a great background for one of Mandy's stories. It would be easy, too easy, to believe that some evil wizard had created this fog to dull his senses and block his vision, to conceal the approach of sinister things in the dark.

He grinned into the teeth of the night, amused by his own fancifulness. The amusement didn't last long, however. He had read Mandy's expression earlier in the kitchen, and he had a good idea of where her thoughts had strayed. She was scared again, emotionally scared. Strange, but he didn't think she feared for her physical safety nearly as much as she feared emotional pain.

Nor did he have any right to cause her *any* kind of pain, physical or emotional. That was what his presence here had done, though. Damn!

And his conversation on the telephone with Micah a couple of hours ago hadn't helped any. Nate had warned all his deputies to keep an eye out for any strangers in Conard County, but other than the usual snowbirds headed south, no strangers had been sighted. That didn't mean there weren't any, of course, but without a hint about where to begin, there was little any of them could do.

All the combined skills and experience of Nate, Micah and Ransom had yielded no better plan than to be vigilant. Hell!

Nor were his contacts in the agency any more helpful. In theory, beyond a small handful of highly trusted, highly placed persons, no one knew that Ransom was back from the dead. Even in the hospital he had been shielded behind a false identity.

Still, like a green fool, he had come to a place where he had ties in the form of Nate Tate, a public figure. But it had never entered his head that anyone in the world might be trying to find him, never entered his mind that he might need to exercise discretion. That made him a complete and total fool, he guessed, albeit a forgivable one.

The unforgivable part was that he had jeopardized Mandy.

He would have muttered a string of obscenities, but long practice kept him quiet. If someone was watching or listening in this fog, they mustn't be able to detect his passing. Like a gray wraith, he slipped through the swirling mists in total silence.

Mandy heard Ransom come in a short while later. She couldn't sleep, and when she had heard him go outside, any desire to try had vanished. The relief she felt upon hearing his return absolutely staggered her, and without another thought she pulled on her bathrobe and hurried barefoot down the stairs.

She found him in the kitchen making yet another pot of coffee. He stood in the dark at the stove, the blue of the propane flame the only illumination. It was eerie, she thought as she paused on the threshold. The blue glow reminded her of the magic she often described in her books, and it shrouded Ransom in unearthly light.

"Can't sleep, princess?" His query was soft as he turned his head to look at her.

There was a stillness in him that blended with the night, a quiet that was more than superficial. She sensed, as surely as if she could read his mind, how acute his senses were right then, how preternaturally alert he was at that moment. She would have had no trouble believing he could hear the swish of her flannel nightgown against her thighs.

"I . . . heard you go out," she said, because she couldn't speak her real thoughts. Thoughts about his magnificence, his virility, his sheer masculine impact at this moment. Thoughts about how much his safety had come to mean to her.

"Just checking things out." His voice remained little more than a whisper, as if he didn't wish to dull his senses with sound. "Everything's okay."

She took a hesitant step into the kitchen, wondering if he wanted her to go, or if perhaps he wanted her to stay, wishing she had the simple courage to reach out for what she wanted the way he did.

Instead, he reached out for her. In a straightforward gesture of invitation that made her throat tighten, he held out one arm, asking her to step up against his side and into his embrace. And when she did, his arm settled around her shoulders, making her feel both safe and welcome.

While the coffee perked, they stood together in the silence and said not a word. He smelled of the night air, and of man. The combination was enticing, and she rubbed her cheek against the side of his chest like a contented cat. His hand tightened a little on her shoulder, a gentle gesture of pleasure and encouragement.

"So we just wait?" she asked finally. "Just wait for somebody to take another potshot at you?"

He sighed and rubbed her shoulder. "Damned if I can think of anything else at the moment." He squeezed her, then released her so he could turn off the flame and poured a couple of mugs of coffee.

Mandy accepted the coffee and waited, missing the comfort of his arm, but unable to ask him to hold her. For a moment he was both silent and motionless, and then he said, "I guess we could sit in the living room."

Why the living room? she wondered as she led the way through the darkened house. The curtains there were drawn, shielding them from any prying eyes, but she understood when he took her mug and set it on the coffee table.

"Come here," he said as he sat beside her, and the next thing she knew she was lying full length on the couch with her head cradled on his lap. He lifted his booted feet to the coffee table and settled back, sipping coffee and stroking her arm and shoulder.

"You don't really want that coffee," he murmured. "It'll keep you up."

Keep her up? What the hell did he think *he* was doing by putting her head on his lap and stroking her? Every nerve ending in her body had suddenly decided to wake up and join the party.

Just as she was trying to decide if it would be wiser for her to return to bed or give in to her hammering impulses, Ransom reached for the clip that bound her hair and released it.

"I don't know how you can sleep with your hair caught up that way," he said quietly.

She didn't know how she could possibly sleep now that it wasn't. His fingers had slipped in among the long silky strands and were gently massaging her scalp, easing tensions she hadn't been aware of and replacing them with new tensions. Sensual tensions.

"Just close your eyes, Amanda Lynn," he murmured. "Just close your eyes."

How long, he wondered, was he going to able to endure this? Time and again she turned to him with a trust that stole his breath, then turned away again in fright. She wanted him, there was no doubt of that in his mind, but that wasn't enough, not for either of them.

With a self-control that astonished him even as he exercised it, he continued to stroke her hair and scalp soothingly, to caress her shoulders reassuringly. With the strength that had carried him through his captivity, he ignored his own needs and the ache of his body for satisfaction.

And gradually the tension seeped from him and something reminiscent of contentment replaced it. He had been alone in the dark with his demons for a long, long time. As one small, frightened woman slowly sank into sleep against him, he at last found some surcease.

Chapter 7

"Don't move."

The growled command followed hard on the heels of a disorienting sense that she had heard something in her sleep. An instant passed as she struggled to place herself and then remembered that she was lying on the couch with her head on Ransom's lap. But Ransom's lap was sliding away.

"Wha—"

"Shh," he whispered sharply. "Stay where you are, Mandy. Just stay. You're safe here, and I don't want you in the way." Safe because nobody in a million years would look for her on the couch at this time of night when the house had been completely dark for hours.

"But what—" She pushed herself up on one elbow and fell silent as she realized an orange glow was coloring the tall curtains on the barn side of the house, and that a deeper orange light seeped around the edges of the curtains. "Fire." The word slid out on a sharply expelled breath. Fire was a deadly threat, and it could leap to her house in no time at all. They needed the hoses, the...

"Mandy, stay put. Just pick up the phone and call Nate and tell him we've had an explosion."

Against the fiery glow, she saw Ransom move toward the hall and the kitchen.

"Ransom—"

He whirled then and came back to her, seizing her shoulders to gently shake her. "Listen," he commanded, low-voiced. "It was an explosion. That means it may have been deliberate. I'll do what I can to control it, but you stay here and call Nate. Promise me, Mandy, or so help me I'll stay here with you and we'll both watch it burn to the ground."

He meant it. He meant every blessed word, she realized. "I promise." How she loathed saying those words. It was *her* ranch that was in danger. Her property, her life.

She called Nate at home, rousing him from slumber, but he came instantly alert.

"I'll get help out there," he said swiftly. "You stay in the house, Mandy. I mean it. You do exactly what Ransom says."

Why, she wondered numbly, did the whole world seem to think she was utterly helpless? She wasn't.

Her promise to Ransom fulfilled, at least technically, by her phone call to Nate, she was suddenly galvanized. In the dark, with the familiarity of long years, she ran upstairs and dressed in heavy overalls, boots and a denim jacket. From her bedroom window she could see that it wasn't the barn after all, but Ransom's cabin that was burning.

The meaning of that penetrated her like an icy cold dart from hell. Refusing to give in to sudden tremors and fear, she clattered back down the stairs and headed out the kitchen door to help fight the fire.

She had taken only one step onto the kitchen porch when strong arms seized her in an iron grip. She gasped, ready to fight for her life, and then sagged with relief as Ransom's familiar scent filled her nostrils.

"Damn it!" His growl was barely audible over the roaring crackle of the cabin's destruction. "I told you to stay put!"

"The fire—"

"The cabin's a dead loss. All I can do is make sure the fire doesn't spread. Damn it, Mandy, the person who set the fire might still be hanging around!"

The person who set the fire? Disbelief exploded in her mind like a nuclear blast, and for an instant she was empty of all thought, empty of everything except the blinding white flash of shock.

"Mandy?" Ransom felt her stiffen against him and in consternation tried to read her expression. He could understand that she might be horrified, shaken, scared, furious—there were a dozen things she could feel that wouldn't concern him at all. Her silence, her unresponsiveness—that was something to worry about.

Finally she started to breathe again. "They might still be here?" she repeated quietly, lifting her gaze to his.

Grimly he nodded. "That's right. And they might be looking to make more mischief." He didn't say what kind of mischief, because he figured her imagination was good enough to fill in the blanks—and if it wasn't, then he didn't see any point in alarming her further.

She drew a deep breath. "Well, then," she managed to say steadily, "you sure as hell shouldn't be out here. Come inside."

"The fire—"

She shrugged. "You're worth more than a damn barn." Then she hesitated, remembering the livestock in the barn. "The horses?"

"I let them out into the corral." He had felt a lot of things for this woman. He had felt awed by her talent, touched by her concern, impassioned by her kisses—so many things. Right now, however, he felt admiration. He wouldn't have guessed that she would prove to be so cool under fire.

And right now, with all the dignity of royalty, she took his hand and tugged him back into the kitchen with her.

"We can watch the fire just as well from here," she said calmly. "Or even better from upstairs. Which is the better defensive position?"

"Well, I'll be damned," he said, giving voice to his admiration. "Upstairs would be better."

* * *

By the time Nate arrived with the volunteer fire fighters, the cabin had collapsed inward on itself and burned like an immense bonfire. They began hosing hundreds of gallons of water onto it from the pump truck, but only to keep the flames from spreading to the surrounding buildings or the tall, dry grasses beyond the packed earth of the yard. There was little hope of putting it out before it burned to embers, and little reason to, since everything that mattered was gone.

Needing to be useful in some way, Mandy dug out the huge coffee urn she and John had used when they threw a barbecue, and made coffee. Then she started making sandwiches, mountains of sandwiches. Those volunteers were apt to be at this for hours.

Feeling hollow inside, she watched as Nate, Micah and Ransom drew apart to hold a low-voiced discussion. They were excluding her, and she tried to muster some resentment. After all, she *was* involved. Ransom had made that clear when he said it wouldn't make any difference if he left now. He meant, of course, that they might try to use her against him, and she knew with deep certainty that Ransom was honorable enough and decent enough to make it possible for them to get to him that way. Of course, they— whoever *they* were—could also use Nate or Micah against him.

She didn't doubt for a moment that Ransom was acutely aware of those possibilities, and she was sure he damned himself for coming to this place and endangering his friends. He was that kind of man.

Her throat tightened, and she forced her attention back to the burning cabin, a visible orange and yellow inferno. The thought she had been avoiding since she awoke to the fire suddenly shouldered its way past all her defenses.

What if Ransom had been sleeping in the cabin?

Maybe, just maybe, he might not have had time to get out. The explosion must have been the propane tank blowing. It might have been the trigger for the entire fire, or it might have blown after the fire had been burning for some time. Either way, Ransom might never have known. He might have died.

Closing her eyes tightly against a sudden shaft of angry pain, she leaned against the counter and battled for calm in the middle of the hurricane.

The world would be a poorer place if Ransom was lost. She believed that as surely as she knew that her own life would be poorer without him. He had brought a touch of magic into her life. He had brought the sound of laughter to her. He had moved her and awakened her. He had made her care.

He was also a man whose every step was apparently dogged by a curse of violence and destruction. Whatever she might feel for him, however much she might care for him, she could never endure the violence of which he was a part. The violence that was so much a part of him.

It was nearly noon by the time the last volunteer fire fighters staggered out of the yard. After she had personally thanked the last of them, Mandy dragged herself into the kitchen and collapsed wearily at the table. Nate had long since gone to work. Micah, however, stood guard over the smoking rubble while Ransom went to the corral to look after the horses. With a sigh, she put her head down on her arms.

Ransom's voice roused her. "Nate is asking the arson investigator to come out here."

Mandy raised her head, and she saw him standing just beyond the screen door. "He told me. Let me get you some coffee."

"Stay put." He pulled the door open and stepped inside. There he halted and stared at her.

He was covered from head to foot in soot, and he smelled like smoke and sweat, but she had never in her life seen anything or anyone she wanted as much as she wanted Ransom in that instant. Her desire pierced her like daggers of glass, and yearning clawed at her, but fear was ice in her veins.

He saw the fear. He smelled it. And he figured he couldn't put up with any more of this crap. He *wouldn't* put up with any more of it. Until the lady made up her mind where she stood, he was out of the game. He had, quite simply, reached the last straw with a lot of things, not the least of them Mandy's flip-flopping feelings toward him.

There was another survival skill he had learned and learned well, and as simply as flipping a switch, he closed off his feelings for Mandy. Eventually, he found himself thinking with all the detachment of a third party, he was going to pay a price for walling off parts of himself. And as soon as he thought it, he gave an indifferent mental shrug. He had survived things that would have driven other men mad simply because he could cut off his feelings. The piper hadn't caught up with him yet, and considering recent events, he might well be dead before the payment came due.

Without so much as a sigh, his face grew shuttered, his expression bland. Mandy saw it but was too tired, too saddened, too frightened, to wonder at it.

"Let me get you coffee," she said again, struggling for the energy to rise.

"Forget it." He turned toward the hallway. "I need to use your shower, and then I have to go to town."

"Ransom, you need rest. Micah and I will watch over things. You get some sleep." Even in her fright at what this man might mean to her, she couldn't ignore his needs.

"I need something to wear," he said flatly. "Every damn stitch of clothing I had with me is now nothing but soggy ash." He looked at her. Reluctantly, it seemed to her. "The book you autographed for me is gone, too."

He said that last almost thoughtfully, as if he were testing some idea for validity. What was wrong with him? she wondered groggily. Why did he seem so distant?

He saw the confused questions begin to form in her expression, so he turned and left her before she could get started. Damned if he was going to sit still for the third degree from her—or from anyone else, for that matter. He'd had it. He had absolutely, positively *had it!*

His clothes were filthy, stinking and sooty, but he didn't have a change, and anyway, he'd been filthier in his day. He needed the shower, though. *Damn!* God bless America and the hot shower. If he'd had to make a list of what he missed

most in captivity, a hot shower would have been near the
top, right after freedom and a warm, soft woman. Mom and
Apple Pie was a myth. The truth was more like Michelle
Pfeiffer and Hot Water.

Except, he thought as he turned his face into the hammering spray, it wasn't really Michelle Pfeiffer he wanted.
Not then. Not now. Karen had had that kind of delicate
beauty. The stuff of men's dreams. She had also been the
coldest bitch it had been his misfortune to encounter. No,
what he wanted was the kind of beauty that reached the
soul. The kind of beauty a man could warm his heart on for
fifty or sixty years.

Scrubbing his head savagely, he thought about the blatant fear he had seen earlier in Mandy's eyes. She'd looked
as if he had brought the dragon to her palace gate. And he
guessed maybe he had. But, damn it, did she have to look
at him as if he *were* the dragon?

That was when he realized he was furious. Enraged.
Wrathful. Hell, there wasn't a word to encompass it. He
could have chewed nails, punched holes in steel. He felt as
if he were verging on a core meltdown.

Dusk had fallen by the time Ransom returned to the
ranch.

"Everything's okay," Micah told him as soon as Ransom climbed out of the truck. "You want me to hang
around while you take a nap?"

"Naw. Thanks, Micah, but I'm not sleepy. I'll probably
crash tomorrow."

Micah searched his face, then nodded. "Yeah," he said.
"Yeah." They both knew about anger, real anger. "See you
in the morning, man."

"Thanks, Micah. I mean it."

"No problem."

The kitchen door was open in defiance of the evening's
chill, and golden light spilled forth, beckoning with a
promise of warmth and welcome. Just an illusion, Ransom
thought as he paused at the foot of the porch steps. There
was no real warmth or welcome in there.

Mandy was frightened, and during the course of the afternoon he had wrestled with himself enough to acknowledge that she was entitled to be afraid.

After all, she had lost every damn thing she had ever loved. And solitude, genuine emotional solitude, was the best fortress in the world. He ought to know. He'd lived like that for nearly twenty years, locked away from everything human and hurtful. And on his one foray into the light, he had found it an illusion.

So why the devil was he trying to step into the light again, and why the hell was he condemning Mandy because she was afraid to?

Because he was stark, raving mad, of course. Because everything inside him had been one great big jumble of confusion ever since he had learned he wasn't going to die after all. For four years he had believed himself to be a dead man. Surely he couldn't be expected to play Lazarus and then act as if nothing had ever changed?

"Ransom?" Mandy stood in the door, silhouetted in the golden, inviting light. "Ransom, are you all right?"

Damned if she didn't sound as if she really cared. "I'm fine." His tone was flat.

"Dinner's ready."

With feet that seemed to be encased in lead, he climbed the steps and entered the kitchen. Distrustful of the deepening night behind him, he closed the inner door and locked it.

"I made your favorite," Mandy said. With a swift glance, she took in his spanking new jeans and shirt, and the two General Store bags he carried that appeared to be full of clothes.

She sounded as if it were a perfectly ordinary evening. That surprised him, jarred him. He dropped his bags in the corner and stepped over to the table. Watching her place the hot beef sandwiches on the table, he wondered why everything seemed wrong.

"Ransom?"

She was frowning at him now, worry evident in her brown eyes, in the set of her mouth.

"Ransom, are you all right?"

"I . . . don't think so." He was surprised to hear himself say it, surprised to realize it was true.

She flew to him instantly, as if she weren't afraid of him at all, and touched his forehead and cheeks. "You feel warm."

"I'll be okay. I'm just tired." Somehow he didn't want her concern.

"Would you rather go lie down?" She looked worriedly up at him. "I'll save your dinner for later. I put fresh sheets on your bed. Go on. Lie down."

Fresh sheets on *his* bed? Until that instant he hadn't realized just how much of a trespasser he had felt in her house during the last couple of days. So she thought of it as *his* bed, did she?

She followed him, fluttering like a nervous butterfly. He wanted to tell her not to flutter, not to worry, to just go away because he would be okay as soon as he slept, but the words didn't want to come out.

And then he remembered he was supposed to be watching over her, that if he slept she would be unprotected. He hesitated halfway up the stairs, then felt her hand in the small of his back, pushing him on.

"Bed, Ransom. Now."

"Mandy . . ."

"Upstairs. Go on. Damn it, you're too big to carry."

He took another upward step, noting that his legs felt heavy, too heavy. "Promise me," he said around a disobedient tongue, and halted, refusing to move another step.

"Anything, if you'll just get to bed."

"Promise . . . Call Nate. Tell him I'm sick."

Because he was. He knew it suddenly and certainly as the first shiver ripped through him. Time was running out fast. Now he knew what he was in for. More by strength of will than of body, he climbed the last stairs and headed to the bedroom.

"Nate," he said again as he slumped onto the bed.

"I promise. Ransom, what is it?"

He forced out one last word just as another shiver gripped him and rattled his joints. Between clenched teeth, he said, "Malaria."

Poor Nate, she thought as she dialed his number. The man was probably wishing her and Ransom into the next county. Last night he had lost his sleep; tonight she was going to disturb his dinner.

"Sheriff Tate."

"Nate, it's Mandy. I'm really sorry to interrupt your dinner...."

"Hush, sweet face. Dinner's over, and you're never any trouble. Is something wrong?"

Nate had such a wonderful voice, she thought irrelevantly. So soothing and reassuring. "Ransom wanted me to call you and tell you he's sick. Malaria, he said."

Nate muttered an unprintable word; at least, it was a word *her* publisher considered unprintable. "Okay, doll. First it's chills, really bad chills. You'll probably need every blanket you've got to warm him. Then he's going to have a really high fever. He might get delirious from it."

Mandy bit her lip. She didn't know a darn thing about real illness. She was never ill, and John had been healthier than a horse. "Do I need to try to keep the fever down?"

"Yeah, I guess. You might try to get some aspirin into him. And find out what kind of medicine he's been taking for it so I can tell Doc Randall when I round him up."

"You're getting the doctor?" That was such a relief.

"Absolutely. Now run and ask him what medicine he takes. I'll wait."

She dropped the phone on the bed and hurried into the next room. Ransom was shaking from head to foot like a man possessed. One hand pulled futilely at the bedspread, trying to drag it over him. At once Mandy grabbed it and tugged it around him.

"I'll get some more blankets," she told him. His blue eyes looked glazed. "Ransom?"

"Yo." He squeezed the syllable out between his teeth.

"Nate wants to know what kind of medicine you take."

"Chloroquine." A huge, racking shudder shook him.

"Okay. I'll be right back."

It wasn't easy, but he forced himself to keep his attention focused outward. He couldn't leave Mandy unprotected. The worry plagued him, kept him alert long past the point where he would ordinarily have turned inward in his misery. He swallowed three aspirin, no mean feat when he was shaking like San Francisco in 1906. He was conscious of Mandy fussing over him, aware that she felt helpless and frustrated, but hell, there wasn't anything anyone could do.

He heard Nate finally, heard the doctor who wanted to take him to the hospital. "No," he managed to say through chattering teeth. "No. Be ok-k-kay by m-morning."

"I imagine he's been through this often enough to know," said the disembodied voice of the doctor.

"Reckon so," Nate replied, his familiar voice soothing Ransom, who had relied on it often in circumstances that were far more dangerous. "Ransom? Ransom, I'm stationing a deputy here overnight, so don't worry about Mandy. She'll be looked after."

Shaking so hard that he had to keep his teeth clenched, Ransom managed to mutter a slurred, "Thanks."

Secure in the knowledge that Nate would look after Mandy, Ransom let go. The Beast had caught him fully in its grip, and there was nothing for him to do except get through it. Nothing he *could* do except get through it. Closing his eyes, he gave himself up to it.

He had long thought of his malaria as the Beast. It had a tendency to spring on him out of nowhere, almost always when he could least afford it. It snatched him up in its cruel jaws and shook him until he ached miserably from head to toe. Then it took malevolent delight in singeing him with its hot breath, until he felt as if his skin would shrivel up and blacken from the heat.

But worst were the dreams the Beast inflicted. Beyond the rational edges of the mind, incomprehensible horrors lurked. There, lying in wait and ready to spring, were nightmare visions compounded of the jeweled jungles of three continents and the unspeakable realities of international intrigue.

Maybe, he hoped, as another shudder racked him, maybe this time he wouldn't get delirious. Maybe this time the fever wouldn't rise so high that he half lost his mind. It was a vain hope, but he clung to it anyway.

Nate stayed with Ransom while Mandy went downstairs with the doctor. He'd been here himself a time or ten, and he looked down on Ransom with sympathy. "Let's get you out of your boots, old son," he said gently, bending over his friend. "When did you catch this bug, buddy? I thought you got out of Nam clean."

Ransom stiffened and jerked with another shudder, then abruptly relaxed. For a minute he just tried to catch his breath.

"You couldn't have had this all along," Nate remarked, filling the silence the way he often had in the old days, when he and Ransom had faced bad moments. Talk was distracting. "Uncle sure wouldn't have let you go undercover with this little parasite roaming your system." With a powerful tug, he pulled off Ransom's boot.

"In the camp," Ransom said. "I caught it in the camp." Another shivering bout was building. He could feel it deep inside, a kernel of growing tension as his brain decided it needed to bring up his temperature to fight the invasion.

Nate straightened. "Hell, man, did you get any medical attention at all?"

"You're kidding, right?"

Nate swore savagely. "You always were a mule's butt, son! Why didn't you just come home from Nam and stay put like the rest of us?"

"Like the rest of you?" Ransom gave a ragged laugh. "Right. Like which rest of you? The ones who hide in the mountains and wait for attackers who never come? The ones who sit lost on street corners because nobody wants them?"

A sound caught Nate's attention, and he turned to find Mandy standing in the door, a bottle of pills in one hand, the other hand clapped over her mouth. She stared at Ransom in apparent distress.

"Oh, I don't know," Nate said casually, returning his attention to Ransom. "Like me, I guess. It's possible to fight the good fight just about anywhere. You don't have to hang around in jungles and slave labor camps to find a devil to wrestle with. Hell, buddy, we grow plenty of 'em at home!"

Ransom's grin was little more than bared teeth as another round of tearing shudders grabbed him.

"Get all the blankets you have," Nate told Mandy. Then he returned his attention to Ransom. "Come on, let's get you out of these clothes."

"D-damn you, I d-don't want a nursemaid!"

"Maybe not," Nate said calmly. "I know I never wanted one, either. Tough patooti, pal. When your fever starts rising, we're going to need to cool you down, and it'll be a hell of a lot easier if you're stripped."

"Go home, Tater. Drive your k-kids crazy."

"Fat chance. I've been wanting to get even with you for years. And I'm never one to pass up an opportunity." He looked up with a reassuring smile for Mandy as she entered the room with her arms full of comforters and blankets. Then, with utter disregard for her modesty or Ransom's objections, he stripped Ransom with swift efficiency, leaving him nothing but his black briefs.

Mandy stood on one side of the bed, Nate on the other, as they piled on the blankets. Their eyes met once, sharing mutual horror at Ransom's scars, but neither of them let him know how they reacted to the sight. For an instant, just an instant, their eyes locked and Mandy saw her own outrage mirrored in Nate's usually calm gaze. Normally the gentlest of people, she felt capable of murder just then. Nobody, *nobody,* should ever be treated the way Ransom apparently had been.

"Go home, Nate," Ransom sighed as the warmth of the blankets began to relax him. "Go home."

"Yeah, I will. Later." He looked across the bed at Mandy and smiled reassuringly. "Sure could use a little coffee. Mind if I make some?"

"I'll make it, Nate." If that was the only useful thing she could do, then by gosh she would make coffee until it came out his ears.

Twenty minutes later, just as Mandy was filling a couple of mugs with coffee, Nate joined her in the kitchen.

"He's being his usual uncooperative self," he remarked with a half smile as he accepted a mug from her. "Shivering like hell and telling me to drop dead."

Mandy gave him a half smile back but recognized the male bluster for what it was. "*Should* he be in the hospital, Nate?"

He leaned back against the counter and shook his head. "I used to get this regular as clockwork myself, and I always preferred to ride it out in my own bed. It's miserable as all get-out, but he'll live. The main thing is to keep the fever down." He looked down at the mug in his hand, hesitating visibly. Then, reluctantly, he added, "He's safer here than he would be at the hospital. In other ways."

She caught her breath as fear returned. The hairs on the back of her neck prickled. "Who is it? Do you have any idea?"

He shook his head. "If I had any idea at all, I'd be combing this county for lice. That man upstairs saved my life more than once, and that's only part of it. I intend to make damn sure no harm comes to him, but I don't have a clue where to even start looking." He sighed. "Maybe the arson investigator can come up with something. At this point, though, there's nothing to be done except keep a sharp eye out."

Shivering against a draft, Mandy rubbed her arms and noticed with shock that it was nearly ten. "Nate! Look at the time! You ought to be home."

"Sorry, doll, you're stuck with me. I told Marge I'd see her when I see her. You can't cope with this alone."

"Of course I can," she said stoutly, although inwardly she wasn't all that confident. What if she couldn't get his fever down? What if he became delirious and she couldn't prevent him from hurting himself? "Besides, you need your sleep. You have a job to do tomorrow, and you can't do it properly if you haven't slept.''

"Don't see why not. I have before."

"That doesn't mean you did it properly."

He laughed, his face creasing with genuine humor. "How about a compromise? We'll split it into shifts. I'll promise to call you if I need help with him, if you'll promise to call me."

That was how she came to be lying in her bed across the hall, listening to the deep rumble of Nate's voice as he talked quietly to a restless Ransom. She'd missed a lot of sleep last night and ought to be dead on her feet, but tension infused her with wakefulness. So much had happened in the last few days. Too much to absorb, really. She needed to think about it all, evaluate it, analyze....

Sleep pounced and caught her mid-thought.

"Come on, Bertie. We'll make it."

The sound of Ransom's voice jerked her out of deep, dreamless sleep. She sat up immediately, but needed a couple of moments to remember what was going on. Ransom. Malaria. And Nate was looking after him.

Rubbing her eyes, she glanced at her clock and was astonished to see it was nearly three a.m. Damn Nate, she thought, instantly awake. Shifts, my foot!

She grabbed her robe, jammed her feet into her slippers and hurried across the hall, tying her sash as she went.

In the dim light from a single low-wattage lamp on the dresser, Nate bent over Ransom. The covers had all been cast aside, and Ransom thrashed restlessly, muttering as Nate sponged him with a cloth. Mandy hurried to Nate's side. He glanced at her.

"Honey," he said softly, "he wouldn't want you to see him like this."

"Tough. How high is his fever?"

"Pushing 105, near as I can tell. And this isn't doing much good." He sighed. "Go fill the tub, Mandy. Skin temperature. I've done this a time or two with my kids, and it hasn't failed yet."

"You're going to put him in the tub?"

"That's the idea."

Ransom flung out an arm. "Come on, Bertie, don't quit! Damn it, man..." His words trailed off into a mumble.

"Bertie was one of our medics," Nate said. "Got hit in a firefight. Ransom carried him out."

Mandy bit her lip until she tasted blood. "Did... did he make it?"

"Bertie? No. He died right after Ransom put him on the Dustoff—the medevac chopper."

Mandy fled. There was no other word to describe her rush down the hall into the bathroom. Filling the tub busied her hands, but it couldn't empty her mind.

She was torn between wanting to comfort, yearning to heal and soothe, and an overwhelming desire to flee before caring cost her any more than it already had. Damn, he looked so vulnerable lying there on the twisted sheets, his scarred body thrashing in the delirium of high fever. So vulnerable and yet so damn strong and powerful that her throat tightened and her breath caught with something she couldn't even name. A felled giant. A fallen warrior. A hawk with a broken wing.

All kinds of crazy similes filled her mind, but they were easier to handle than the idea that Ransom was still so deeply troubled by something that had happened so long ago. Wounds. All kinds of wounds. So many kinds of wounds.

"Mandy?"

She turned swiftly, blinking back tears she only now realized she was weeping. Nate and Ransom were easing through the door, Ransom's arm slung around Nate's neck, his eyes half open as he tried to maintain his grip on consciousness.

"It's ready," she said, bending to turn off the taps.

"Come on, old son," Nate said. "It'll feel like ice. Sound good?"

Ransom was so incredibly beautiful, Mandy thought, as she watched Nate steady him while he stepped into the tub, still wearing his briefs. He might be flushed with fever and barely conscious, but he was still beautiful with a golden sleekness that made her ache.

The sigh that escaped him as he sank into the water was one of pure relief, and the expression on his face was suddenly one of sheer bliss. The tub wasn't really big enough. His knees were bent and rose above the water, which, even when he leaned back, didn't come much above his waist. Scarcely giving it a thought, Mandy reached for the cup she used to rinse her hair. Kneeling, she ladled the lukewarm water over his chest and shoulders.

"I'll get his robe," Nate said. "He'll probably cool down fast now."

She nodded, then remembered. "Nate?"

"Yeah?"

"I don't know if he has a robe. All his clothes are in the two bags down in the kitchen."

"The fire. I forgot."

"John's robe is in the closet at the end of the hall. It'll be a little short, but it'll sure go around." Some part of her was surprised to realize that the thought of Ransom wearing John's robe didn't bother her. Yet just a few short months ago she had gone on a crying jag over that same robe when she had come across it by accident.

"I'll just get a blanket," Nate suggested.

She turned her head and looked up at him, meeting his gaze head on. "It's all right, Nate. Really."

Turning back to Ransom, she resumed her ladling.

"Mandy."

Surprised, she lifted her eyes from his chest and found Ransom staring straight at her. His blue eyes looked a little glazed and sunken, but he saw her. Really saw her.

"How do you feel?" she asked swiftly, touching his cheek with damp fingertips. Still warm, but not burning.

"Like hell." A corner of his mouth hitched upward just a hair. "This is humiliating."

"Screw humiliating," she snapped, not caring if she sounded vulgar. She was too tired to have any patience with macho male hang-ups. "Even Superman has to deal with Kryptonite."

"I probably wouldn't feel so bad if it were Kryptonite that got me. I shouldn't be putting you through this. I should have gone to the hospital."

"Right," she said sourly, dumping more water on the broad chest that she really wanted to nuzzle, wet or not. "Then Nate could have gone crazy trying to protect you from all the people wandering up and down the corridors and pushing into your room demanding blood samples and urine samples and—"

"Okay, okay." He let his eyes close, and his head dropped back against the edge of the tub. "Mandy?" His voice had grown so soft that she had to lean toward him to hear.

"Yes?"

"Mandy, don't be afraid of me. Please don't."

"I'm not afraid of you, Ransom." Her throat tightened around his name, nearly cutting it off. "Not of *you*." Leaning closer, she kissed him lightly on the corner of his mouth.

Behind her, Nate cleared his throat. "Don't mind me," he said, laying his hand heavily on Mandy's shoulder. "Well, old son, have you cooled off enough to let me take your temperature?"

Ransom's eyes fluttered open again, skimming Mandy's face swiftly before they rose to Nate. "I never saw you in the role of nursemaid, Tater."

"That's only because you ain't seen me playing daddy to my girls. Now hold this under your tongue."

Something very like humor glimmered deep in Ransom's eyes as he obediently took the thermometer into his mouth.

Mandy went down to make more coffee while Nate put Ransom into dry underwear and back into bed. From the sounds that trailed down the stairway to her, she thought Ransom sounded almost like himself. When she went back up with her coffee, she managed to persuade Nate to catch some shut-eye on her bed while she kept vigil over Ransom.

"You'll wake me if he gets worse?"

Mandy shoved him across the hall. "Why do you always treat me like I'm some kind of fragile crystal, Nate?"

"Because that's how John always thought of you, sweetie. As something fine and precious and fragile."

A couple of months ago, she probably would have burst into tears. Tonight she simply shook her head. "I'm about as fragile as a horse, Nate. That ought to be obvious by now. Get some sleep."

Back in Ransom's room, she hesitated beside the bed, and then, driven by needs she was too tired to even question, she lay down beside him and closed her eyes. If he got restless, she would know instantly, she assured herself.

Rolling onto her side, she pressed up against his back and burrowed her nose right into the sheet that covered him. In some way, in deep, seldom-noticed places, she felt her world right itself. It was okay, she thought hazily. He was here, and he would be all right.

No one could touch him or harm him with both her and Nate watching over him. No one.

And for the moment, nothing else mattered.

Chapter 8

She hadn't even closed the curtains last night. That was her first thought when her eyes fluttered open and she discovered that the night's black velvet sky had lightened just enough that she could detect the change despite the dim yellow glow of the lamp on the dresser.

The next thing she realized was that Ransom's arms were wrapped around her and that her back was tucked up against his chest and bent thighs. It was a warmly intimate embrace, and in the unguarded state of just waking, she snuggled back into those arms, moved deeper into his embrace.

He made a soft sound near her ear, a sound that resembled a pleased mumble, and then his hand slid sleepily up from her waist to cup her breast with unmistakable possessiveness.

He had never touched her like that before, and the sharp stab of yearning that pierced her brought her fully awake. This is ridiculous, some part of her mind scolded. The man's out of his mind with fever! Just move his hand away....

But oh, how right it felt! With Ransom it always felt so right, as if she had been created for his mouth, his hands. A tremulous sigh escaped her, and she squeezed her eyes shut, holding herself rigid against a tempest of unfulfilled longings.

She could, with a backward look, measure the barrenness of her life. In retrospect, she guessed she had been as much to blame as her series of foster parents for her sense of alienation. None of them had been bad people, and none of them had intentionally made her feel like an outsider. In fact, considering that she'd felt like an outsider from earliest memory, it was likely that the feeling was something she had been born with—or that had been created with the loss of her birth mother.

Ransom made a soft sound and drew her even more snugly against him, curving his body to a tighter fit against hers. The hand that cupped her breast so possessively tightened a little and stroked softly for a moment before it relaxed.

He was probably having a delightful dream, she thought, holding her breath as awakening desires shimmered throughout her like wisps of magic. How easy it would be to sink into one of her own.

With a sigh, she forced her body to relax and squeezed her eyes shut. For the first time in her life, she felt compelled to stand back and look at herself. Even John hadn't made her take stock the way she so clearly needed to.

No, John had come into her life like a balmy breeze, fitting into almost every nook and cranny so gently and warmly that he was there almost before she knew it. He had made her feel secure and loved, and yet he had never managed to banish her sense of apartness. She had felt as if she were Amanda Tierney playing at being Mrs. John Grant. He'd been a man to grow old with, and yet she had never believed she would grow old with him. She had never felt permanent.

Ransom, on the other hand, made her feel as if she had spent eternity waiting for him. It was odd—disturbing—the way she felt no alienation around him. She knew many people and felt friendly toward some, but no one had ever before made her feel as if she had come home at last.

And that was why she was fighting so hard and feeling so frightened. He would go away. Whether he got killed or not, his life was elsewhere. He was destined to leave her behind, because she would not leave with him. Here, on this ranch, isolated from everyone but a few select friends, she was safe. She had found the castle where she could live out her days and write her books. So what if she refused to face reality? She made her living by creating fantasies for other people to escape into. Beyond her basic requirements, she had no need of reality.

And Ransom was reality. He was a terrifying reality, because he made her every emotion awaken, her every nerve sing. Around him, she could not remain only half alive.

Instinctively, she began to ease away from him, but his hold tightened at once.

"No," he mumbled. "Stay."

She hesitated. He probably didn't even know who she was. Any warm body would do. Again she attempted to ease away.

"Amanda," he muttered. "Don't go. Stay." His arm tightened, and his hand stroked her breast persuasively through her cotton gown. "Please," he mumbled.

So she stayed, her heart swelling painfully with unnamed emotions, her body aching with unfulfilled needs. Eventually, she even dozed.

The next time she awoke, the sky had lightened to lavender and Ransom's fever had broken in a bath of sweat that had soaked both of them and the sheets that were wrapped around him. Instantly concerned that he might take a chill, she started to get up.

"Don't go."

Turning her head, she looked over her shoulder to find Ransom's eyes wide open and very definitely aware.

"You're soaked," she said, ignoring the way her heart started to beat with a heavy rhythm. "I've got to get you some dry sheets before you get chilled."

For a moment his blue gaze searched her face as if seeking something, and then his hold on her relaxed. He let his eyes close, and his head fall back on the pillows. "I've probably ruined your mattress."

Mandy sat up, battling an urge to simply turn and hug him in her relief. "Don't worry about it."

For the briefest moment his eyes opened again and met hers.

"Are you hungry?"

"I'm just tired. I'll be fine, Mandy. Really."

Nate heard her moving around and came to help her change the sheets while Ransom watched listlessly from the rocker in the corner. As soon as they got him back in bed and under the blankets, he fell into a deep sleep.

"He'll be back to normal in a few hours," Nate assured her as they went downstairs together. "He'll wake up as hungry as a hibernating bear, though."

"Are you sure I can't make you breakfast, Nate?"

He dropped a quick kiss on her forehead before he stepped out the back door. "Marge and I always eat breakfast together, sweet face. It's a sacred time. No matter how many things disrupt the rest of the day, we *always* have breakfast together."

Halfway across the yard to his Blazer, he looked back. "You need sleep even worse than I do. Go to bed, Mandy. Charlie Huskins is here, and Micah will take over in an hour or so."

First, however, she took a long, hot shower and slipped into a fresh cotton gown. Before climbing into her own bed, she crossed the hall to check on Ransom and make sure he didn't need anything. Maybe she should have expected it, maybe she was just fooling herself, but she was astonished when he reached out and caught her wrist.

"Lie down with me," he said, and his eyes were both clear and alert. "Lie down with me, Amanda Lynn."

"You need to sleep," she argued, but her limbs went as soft as hot syrup, and she was obeying his demand before the words completely left her mouth. Melting, she climbed under the covers beside him, turning into his arms as he drew her closer. Her head rested on his shoulder, and somehow, as naturally as if it had always been this way, her legs tangled with his.

"Now I can sleep," he said, as if her presence had been all that was lacking before. "Now we can both sleep."

And they both did.

Much later, Ransom looked down at the woman who slept soundly beside him. He could have her, he knew. If he reached out and touched her now, she would turn into him and open like the rose she really was beneath that grim exterior. It would be so simple, he thought as he traced the delicate lines of her face with his eyes. It would be so easy.

And it would ruin everything. She wanted him, she even cared about him, but she had to come to him freely, and he was beginning to despair that she ever would. Poor Amanda Lynn, to be so frightened of what was so right.

Sighing, he lowered his head to the pillow again and closed his eyes. He was still weary from last night's fever, but his strength was returning rapidly.

And maybe it was time he did some thinking of his own. After all, Mandy wasn't the only problem here. She wasn't the one with a murderer on her tail. She had every right to be scared, and he was acting like a numskull, pretending that her fears were phantoms she needed to overcome. No phantom had shot out her windshield or burned down his cabin. No phantom was toying with him, like a cat with a mouse.

And what about the rest of it? What about the past five years? What about his failure to deal with the absolute waste of all he had suffered? Hell, it wasn't as if he had suffered in some great, noble cause. Not one damn thing had been accomplished by his imprisonment except to satisfy a vindictive streak in a woman whose heart evidently had a temperature of absolute zero.

That, he admitted, drawing a deep breath to steady himself against a sudden surge of futile anger, was what really bothered him. If he could have believed that even one little thing had been bettered by his captivity, just one little thing, he could live with the cost. But to pay that price for nothing at all...!

When he came right down to it, he thought grimly as he rode a tide of barely leashed anguish, he could say that about his entire life. All the things that had seemed so important at the time became trivial in retrospect. He had wasted his life, it seemed, risking everything on trivialities.

Well, maybe some of it hadn't been trivial. There had been that terrorist thing in Libya. He'd made an important difference there, had probably saved a life or two. A couple of other times, even in hindsight, his achievements had mattered. But it wasn't a hell of a lot to say for a lifetime.

And it didn't make up for four useless, wasted years in that camp, when nothing at all had been gained.

So who the hell did he think he was, trying to wear down Mandy's defenses and get behind her walls? What did he have to offer her, anyway? A battered, scarred body, a wasted past, and possibly no future at all.

So maybe he'd better get his act together. Maybe he'd better make sure he *had* a future, and then figure out what kind. Only then would it be fair to ask anything at all of Mandy.

Firm in his intention to do the right thing by her, he allowed his fatigue to drag him back into sleep. He had to be rested up by tonight. He had to be ready to deal with this strangely amateurish assassin. With this cat that stalked him in a deadly game.

The best laid schemes... The words of the Scottish poet were rolling loosely around inside his head when he struggled awake late in the afternoon. Before he was fully awake, he knew why. Snuggled against him was an enticingly soft morsel of femininity, but he might have been able to resist that. Hell, he had resisted it before. What was harder to resist was the silky thigh that was caught between his legs, pressing intimately against him, making a mockery of the thin barrier of his briefs.

He should be able to move away. That was what he told himself. And told himself yet again. But there was something so exquisite about the warm pressure of her thigh against him, especially for a man who hadn't found release in a woman for nearly five years, that he was paralyzed.

His eyes weren't paralyzed, however, and opening them, he found himself looking straight down the gaping neck of Mandy's cotton nightgown. Deep within, he could see the soft, shadowy cleft between her breasts, and *that* made him aware that he could smell her. God, she smelled good. Warm. Feminine. Sexy.

Damn!

He definitely had to move away. Now. Before he did something dishonorable, such as take advantage of an innocently sleeping woman. Never in his entire life had he done such a thing, and it wasn't that he'd never had the opportunity. It seemed wrong, somehow, to look or touch while she slept, because they weren't lovers. So that made it wrong for him to lie here suspended between heaven and hell by the thigh pressed so intimately against him.

Right.

So move, damn it!

But he didn't move. Instead he lay as helpless as a newborn babe, the breath locked in his throat turning solid while all the air in the universe thickened.

Because *she* moved.

She moved into him, turning closer, snuggling closer, burying her leg even deeper between his, so that he knew with mind-stunning certainty that the soft mound at the juncture of her thighs was pressed snugly against him. Oh yeah!

This was what made it all worthwhile, this sweet, piercing, aching shaft of need that could only be assuaged by another person. By a particular, *special* person. This was no ordinary hunger, no itch to be scratched, no mere accident of hormones. This was the hunger of a warrior for his fairytale princess. This was what sent a man out to slay dragons.

But it wasn't his to take.

Mandy stirred again, rubbing drowsily against him like a cat. He had to stop this now, before he lost control and claimed her before she even opened her eyes.

"Mandy. Mandy, wake up." His voice was husky, catching on the breath that wanted to stay locked in his throat. The hammering surf of desire was pounding in his veins again like a force of nature, a force so primal there was no arguing or reasoning with it. He steeled himself to ignore it, steeled himself for her inevitable shock when she awoke enough to realize how intimately she was wrapped around him. Sleep had lowered all the barriers she had tried to erect against him, and she was going to be horrified when she realized it.

"Mandy."

She awoke slowly, stretching and making little noises deep in her throat, reminding him of a kitten. Only a kitten wouldn't have this effect on him. Kittenish or not, Mandy was all woman, and his body recognized it.

"Ransom?"

It was, he admitted reluctantly, priceless to watch her eyes flutter open and grow aware. Precious to watch the color rush into her cheeks like cherry juice when she realized the intimacy of their embrace. Exquisite beyond belief when she recognized his state of arousal and yet didn't yank herself away.

"Ransom?" she said again, this time very tentatively, as if she were afraid to shatter the tenuous moment.

What was she asking him? He didn't know, and suddenly he didn't care. Turning on his side, he pressed his hand against her lower back and pushed her even more intimately into the cradle of his thighs. A groan was torn from him, and his hips, with a will of their own, began a helpless, relentless rocking against her.

He took the time, just enough time, to look down into her startled gaze. As he stared, amazement vanished and her eyes closed. And then, to his stunned wonderment, her mouth curved into a soft smile and her hips rolled responsively against his.

Way back in his mind a warning bell sounded, reminding him to protect her. The condoms he had bought days ago had been moved into the bedside table here when he started watching over her. Not that it really mattered, because if he got this woman pregnant he would bust a gut with sheer happiness. But Mandy probably wouldn't feel so happy, so he forced himself to take a few seconds to dig out the foil package and put it within reach. And then he stripped off his briefs so she wouldn't mistake his intention. He was reaching his point of no return.

Mandy was watching him when he turned back to her. The sheets had been thrown back, and she lay with her nightdress provocatively tangled around her thighs. She was beautiful, he thought. Exquisite. His fairy-tale princess. He should, he thought, offer her a chance to say no, a chance to get up and walk away. But her eyes were soft and hazy, not at all reluctant looking, and his need was strong, so he propped himself on one elbow and said nothing at all.

Her nightgown was made of white cotton eyelet, demure, fresh and clean, yet it gave him tiny, enticing glimpses of the satiny skin beneath. It was, somehow, a perfect nightgown for her and for the moment. It appealed to him in a way that the most provocative satin and lace confections never had. It was...wholesome. Like Mandy. God, how he needed her wholesomeness. Her cleanliness. Her rightness.

Slow. He swore he would go slowly, giving her every bit of pleasure he was capable of. He would worship her and display his reverence for her so that she would never wonder if this was merely a moment of lust. He wanted her to know that it was more, so much more.

Gently, listening to the quickening of her breath, he reached out and swept the hem of her gown upward. Inch by inch he exposed her to his gaze and knew that he had never seen such a beautiful woman. He wished there was some way to tell her that so she would believe it. It wasn't that she was perfect. The pale lines of stretch marks on her tummy took care of that. No, she wasn't perfect, and she was so much more beautiful for being imperfect.

When he tugged the gown over her head, he saw the uncertainty in her gaze.

"Tell me," he said. "Talk to me, Mandy. What worries you? What frightens you?"

His sensitivity tightened her throat. Closing her eyes, she took her courage in her hands. "I want to please you," she whispered. "And I don't know how." A whole flood of insecurities had risen in her, swamping her desires. In her life she had made love with only one man, and one man's measure, so long ago, was hardly enough to reassure her. She was older. She was out of practice. What if...? A whole string of "what ifs" began to form like mocking faces.

The admission tore at him. A woman who had been married, he thought, shouldn't be so lacking in confidence about her skills or attractions as a lover. It was a man's place, most especially a husband's place, to make sure a woman knew her attractiveness and discovered her skills. He felt a spark of anger toward John Grant, but quickly smothered it. It had been four years, after all, and four years was enough to weaken anyone's self-confidence. Truth to tell, his own confidence level wasn't any too high at the moment.

"Princess," he murmured softly, finding first her eyelid and then the lobe of her ear with his kiss, "this old warrior is feeling pretty shaky himself right now. I want this to be so good, so perfect for you—"

Her eyes flew open, and she quickly silenced him by pressing her fingertips against his lips. "I told you, we can shoot for perfect another time."

Behind her fingers he smiled and felt his tensions let go. "That's a two-way street, Amanda Lynn."

Bending, he took her mouth in a kiss that offered no quarter and ran the palm of his hand up her side to her breast. Smooth. Silky. Soft. Warm. Woman. *His woman.*

Ahh.... The sigh was long, heartfelt, and he didn't know if he heard it only in his mind or if he'd really sighed like that, but her hands were touching him, drawing him closer until his hard chest pressed against her soft breasts, until his aching, throbbing manhood was pressed against her yielding heat. This woman's small, soft hands reached for him and drew him closer, and it felt so good, so damn good, to be wanted.

Maybe that was what undid him. With a roar that filled his ears, internal restraints crumbled and long-defended walls crashed. Every last shred of his self-control vaporized in the heat of his hunger.

He took her like the warrior he was. He took her like a soldier who'd been gone too long and had come home at last. All his good intentions blew away in the shock wave. He was man, she was woman, and not one other damn thing mattered.

Mandy felt his control shatter as surely as if shock waves had blasted through the air around her. The firestorm broke over her as he surged into her in a helpless, convulsive plunge, stretching sensitive tissues that hadn't been stretched in years. The pain was a small thing, brief, fleeting, inconsequential beside the need of the man who inflicted it.

She felt the fine tremors of his muscles as he bent over her, ripped by low groans that escaped him with each thrust of his hips. She had thought she knew desire. She had thought she had experienced hunger and need. Now she looked into the tortured face of relentless, driving need and knew that she had never understood what it could be. The thrill of his invasion, the swift, clenching response of her insides to the pleasure of being taken, melted away in a warm compassion, in an overwhelming desire to give what he needed.

This was no soft, sensual claiming. This was raw, vital, a challenge in the face of life, a tearing, throbbing, convulsive ripping of pleasure from the moment. This was as elemental as life and death.

Responding instinctively, she wrapped her legs around his hips to take him deeper, her arms around his shoulders to draw him closer and assure him of his welcome. Closing her eyes, she kissed his cheek and surrendered to his needs as women have always surrendered to their chosen warriors, with tenderness and softness, with welcome and love.

"Mandy, I can't. . . ." The words were little more than a muffled groan.

"Then don't," she said in sudden fierceness, then dug her nails into his shoulders, urging him on.

His back arched suddenly, drawing his head back so sharply that she could see nothing but his throat. His flesh plunged deeper, so deep that she was sure they would fuse permanently. And then, with a groan so low it sounded torn from him, he erupted into her.

Afterward he tried to roll away, but she wrapped her arms around him and held tight, refusing to release him. Her woman's instinct warned that if she let go now, he would never return.

"Mandy..." Again he tried to pull away.

"Hush." She wrapped her legs around him, pinning him to her as best she could. Little by little his body was withdrawing from hers, and she thought how sad it was that the greatest moments of honesty between man and woman had to be so fleeting. And she thought how sad it was that now he would be ashamed because he had lost control.

Lifting one hand from his back, she stroked his hair with all the womanly understanding she felt so full of at this moment. He thought he had become an animal. She thought he had merely responded like a human being. Like a man who had spent too much time in hell, who had been deprived of every bit of life's goodness and rightness and pleasure for too long. But he wouldn't see it that way, because he was a decent man who believed he had just behaved in an indecent, uncivilized manner.

"Nobody," she murmured softly in his ear, "nobody has ever made me feel as desirable, as beautiful and as wanted as you just did. Thank you."

She felt a tremor run through him. Suddenly his face, until this moment turned away from her, turned toward her, nuzzling the side of her neck.

He said, "Yeah?"

She laughed then, a clear, joyous sound, a sound that had been absent from her life for so long. "Yeah," she assured him. "Absolutely yeah."

He stirred again. "Princess, I'm too heavy for you."

She knew it was safe then, for the moment at least, so she let him go. As he rolled onto his side, he took her with him, and then it was he who cradled her.

"I'm sorry," he said gruffly.

"Don't be. I'm not." His arms tightened around her, and she became acutely aware of each and every place his body touched hers. Lifting a hand, she touched his tousled golden hair, his silky golden beard, and smiled when he turned his head to press a gentle kiss on her palm.

"You might be," he said, his voice still gruff. "I clean forgot to protect you."

"It's the wrong time," she assured him swiftly, though she wasn't sure of that at all. The last thing in the world she would be able to endure was having Ransom hang around only because she might be carrying his child. Better that he think there was no possibility. And if she *was* pregnant— well, she would deal with that if it happened. Underneath, though, in the warm soft places of her soul, she knew she wouldn't mind it at all if she had a child. If she had *his* child.

She pressed her face to his chest and inhaled deeply. "You must be starving." She wanted the subject changed *now*. Lying had never been easy for her.

He recognized the change of subject for what it was and wondered if she found the thought of having his child *that* repugnant. The idea pained him. "A little," he admitted, but tugged her even closer. "First, I want to pleasure you."

"No."

The word shocked him. Shocked her, too, she realized as he looked swiftly down at her. "No?"

Color flooded her face. "Uh, not right now, Ransom. Later. You're tired and hungry, and I don't want you to get sick again."

And that was a bold-faced lie, he thought as he let her go and watched her scramble away as if he had suddenly developed the plague. What the hell was wrong with her?

But he kept his mouth shut as she snatched up her nightgown and hurried from the room, promising to have dinner ready in an hour.

He might have thought his behavior had repelled her, had driven her away, except that she had already assured him it hadn't. Closing his eyes, he tested her words in his mind, listened again to her tone as she spoke them. His memory, trained by years of working under conditions where it would have been hazardous to write anything down, reran the conversation verbatim.

No, he hadn't disgusted her. Of that he was sure. Her assurance had been genuine. Then what? What the devil had gotten into her?

She shouldn't have let him get so close to her, Mandy thought as she entered the kitchen later, freshly showered and dressed. Last night's untouched beef sandwiches had congealed on the plates, and beyond the window she saw Micah standing with his head thrown back as he watched the afternoon wane.

Poor guy. She had completely forgotten he was standing guard today. He was probably ready to kill for a cup of coffee.

She called out an invitation to him, and he came readily into the kitchen, waving aside her apology.

"After some of the guard shifts I've pulled," he said, "this one's a vacation."

For Micah, that was a long statement. "I sure appreciate what you're doing."

He shrugged. "Forget it."

She couldn't talk him into staying in the kitchen, though. After the fire at the cabin, nobody was going to relax their guard. He took his coffee outside and resumed his watch, leaving Mandy to face Ransom alone.

Well, she was going to have to face him sometime, but she sure didn't know how she was going to explain her panic in a way that didn't reawaken his self-disgust. How could you possibly explain to someone that you didn't mind playing Lady Bountiful to his needs, but that you were scared to death to let him touch upon your own? Too late, she had discovered her terror of allowing herself to be so vulnerable. Too late, she had realized that with each touch he gave her, she came to depend on him even more.

How could she possibly tell him such things? How could he possibly understand? He was a man, and for men such things were clear cut. For men, sex didn't necessitate emotional involvement. Unhappily, Mandy had just realized that for *her* it did, and that she wasn't prepared to take that step. Might *never* be prepared to take that step. How could she possibly explain?

Ransom appeared for dinner damp from a shower, wearing jeans and a black T-shirt. He looked dangerous, powerful and very masculine. Any lingering frailty from his imprisonment or from last night's attack of malaria wasn't visible. He was beautiful.

In a flash her body betrayed her by reminding her that just a short while ago this man's body had claimed hers. Nerve endings, imprinted like photographic film, tingled with remembered sensations. Standing there, looking at him, she felt again his weight on her, felt again the smooth heat of his skin and the steel of his bunching muscles beneath her hands. Felt again the thrilling shock of his penetration. Shimmering heat engulfed her, turning her legs numb and making her hands shake.

She wanted him. Oh, Lord, she wanted him as she had never, ever wanted anyone or anything. The ache was so deep, so sharp, that it was going to kill her. With terrible certainty, she foresaw the coming anguish.

"Oh, God, Mandy," Ransom said harshly, crossing the kitchen toward her with swift strides. "Mandy, don't look like that!"

The haven of his arms closed around her. He held her, simply held her, while the storm ripped through her.

"It doesn't pay to want anything," she heard herself sob. "If you want things, then someone can take them away from you. If you want things, you can be hurt."

"It seems that way, princess," he murmured. "It sure seems that way sometimes."

"Somebody wants to kill you," she said, as if that were the incontestable proof of her argument.

"It does seem that way."

"Well then!"

"Well then, what?" he demanded, holding her even closer. "Damn it, Mandy, if that's how you feel, maybe you should kill yourself right now. I mean, what's the point of dragging through the next forty or fifty years if you never want anything, never enjoy anything, never *do* anything? I plain don't understand how anybody with your guts can be such a damn mouse!''

"Guts? What guts?" She was sounding more and more hysterical, but she didn't care. "A mouse has more guts than I do!"

"Come off it." His temper was rising. "You had the guts to write a book, didn't you? You had the guts to let somebody else read it, didn't you? In other words, lady, you had the guts to put yourself on the line for something you wanted. And you want to keep writing, don't you? You don't cash in your computer and quit because you're afraid that someday you might not be able to write, do you?"

He slackened his hold on her just a little and drew a deep, steadying breath. "You've got guts, Amanda Lynn. You've got enough guts to go for what you want, enough guts to succeed. You just won't see it. And that makes me so damn mad at you that I could shake you until your teeth rattle."

Abruptly, he let her go and stomped out the kitchen door. Sniffling and wiping at her eyes, Mandy saw him fall into conversation with Micah. *Guts enough to go for what she wanted and guts enough to succeed.* Hah.

Who the hell was he to get mad at her, anyway?

The defender of her castle gates, that was who. The man who had breached her emotional barriers, that was who. The man she wanted with every fiber of her being.

Nate showed up after dinner, while Mandy was washing dishes and Ransom drying, both of them pretending that nothing, absolutely nothing, had happened. Nate seemed to sense some of the tension between them, or so Mandy thought uncomfortably when she caught a curious twitch at the corners of his mouth, as if he were trying very hard not to laugh.

He settled at the table, accepting a cup of coffee but turning down an offer of dessert. "You're looking a hell of a lot better, old son," he told Ransom.

Ransom straddled a chair and faced him, smiling faintly. "You didn't come all the way out here to tell me that."

"Might've come to see with my own eyes," Nate suggested, but the teasing twinkle was gone from his gaze. Noticing its absence, Mandy sat slowly, clutching a dish towel like a lifeline.

Ransom spoke. "It was arson."

Nate nodded. "The investigator called me this afternoon. He found the remnants of a crude timer and some blasting caps, which were used to blow up the propane tank. I'd say they're definitely out for your hide—but you already figured that out."

Ransom didn't even bother to nod. Mandy watched his eyes turn flat, almost blank, and she shivered. There was a stillness to him, a watchful sort of waiting, that she could almost feel. Something in him had shifted.

She found herself thinking that it was as if he had moved to another reality, that although his body remained here, his mind was no longer functioning on the same plane with the rest of them. He had, in the blink of an eye, become a predator. A thrill of fear made her scalp prickle.

"Yeah," he said in a voice gone gritty. "I already figured that out, Nate."

"Well," said Nate, as calmly as if he were discussing the weather, "what the hell do you want to do about it?"

Ransom's blue eyes, hard as glass, fixed on him. "I don't want you to get involved. I don't want anybody else involved in this."

"I figure it's already too late for that." Nate lifted his mug, made a production out of taking a sip.

Mandy looked from one man to the other, sensing some kind of byplay between them that was far deeper than words.

"You've got kids, Nate."

"Sure. I've also got friends, and two of them are in deadly danger. If you think I'm going to stand by and let somebody try to hurt you or Mandy, you've got another think coming. And while we're on the subject, I reckon you should know that Micah feels the same way."

"Been discussing it, have you?" Ransom's eyes remained flat, distant.

Nate hesitated, and for an instant his gaze slipped to Mandy, as if seeking something from her. She stared steadily back.

"Well," said Nate after a moment, "I sent my wife and kids to visit her cousin Lou in Colorado. Marge and Lou hate each other, so I figure nobody in a million years will look for her there. So they're safely out of this. That leaves Mandy. If we can get her out of here—"

"I'm not going," Mandy interrupted, aware of her intention only as she spoke.

Nate and Ransom both ignored her, and Nate continued speaking. "I figure somebody might want you bad enough to use people to get to you."

"That crossed my mind," Ransom admitted.

"Yeah, which is why I sent Marge away. Getting Mandy away might be a little more difficult. Everyone in the county seems to think you two have something going, and everybody knows Mandy. Putting her on a bus won't work."

"I'm not going," Mandy said again. The certainty was like steel in her backbone. However timid and afraid she might be, however frightened of risk and loss, she would not abandon her home, the only home she had ever really known. In fact, she realized with absolute conviction, she would die rather than leave. She pushed her chair back from the table and went to the kitchen door, where she looked out over the twilit yard.

"Mandy," Nate began in the patient tone of one who intended to argue reasonably with someone who was irrational, "you really—"

"No, Nate." She cut him off without apology. "I will not budge. This is my home, and no assassin is going to drive me out of it."

"It's only temporary—"

She turned and faced him. "No, Nate," she said again, calmly. "I won't be driven away, not for a week, not for a minute, not for a second."

Ransom understood at a level so deep it was painful. It was a scar she refused to accept because she knew the wound would never heal. Mandy Grant had lost her last battle and accepted her last wound. She had narrowed her horizons to these thin walls and the roamings of her imagination in a defense against previous wounds that had never healed, and now she wasn't going to sacrifice another square inch of her tiny world.

He wanted to go to her, hold her close, offer her a knight's promises of protection and success, but he had no right to do that. After all, he was the one who had brought this threat to her world; it was because of him that she was at risk. Besides, she wanted nothing from him. She had made that abundantly clear. She had let him spill his seed into her, had opened her arms and legs and taken him into her, had borne his desperation and hunger, and then she had turned from him, unwilling to take even the smallest thing he might have given her.

"She stays." He spoke the words in a voice that was rough with feelings he couldn't express. Feelings she didn't want. Feelings he couldn't afford to have. For now, for this dangerous time, he could afford nothing but anger. Cold anger. The kind of anger that sat in the belly like an icy lump of lead. The kind that kept his head clear and his attention narrowed.

Mandy looked at him, and once again her scalp prickled. She had written of such things, but never before had she seen a man so furious that there was no room left in him for anything else. Never before had she seen such cold, icy rage.

The Ransom who had wooed her with such gentleness was gone.

Chapter 9

Ransom and Nate sat in the kitchen for a long time, discussing and discarding strategies. Mandy paid them little attention. If there was anything she could do, they would let her know. Until then, she had nothing to offer. Instead she retreated to her study and the world of the book she was working on. It was easy to hide in the cocoon of her imagination.

Eventually she heard them leave the house, the slap of the screen door loud in the stillness of the evening. Later she heard Ransom come back in. She would recognize the sound of his footsteps anywhere, she realized. There was something distinctive about the way he set his feet down, about the slight hesitation in his loose-jointed stride. She heard him prowl the house, heard him moving around in the kitchen, and finally she heard him come into the study behind her. Her shoulders tensed defensively.

He sat in the easy chair, and she could feel his gaze on her as she typed gibberish into her computer and filled the screen with glowing amber symbols that made no more sense than her pounding heart and tightening body.

She felt her awareness of him settle into her abdomen, down low between her legs. It was the first time she had ever felt that kind of awareness, and her fingers fumbled on the keys. All the other feelings in her body seemed to fade away in direct proportion to the awakening sensations down there. The light caress of her jeans when she shifted in her chair was suddenly a pleasurable torment.

"Do you want me to leave?" His question was a quiet growl in the stillness.

She drew a deep breath. "No." Her voice sounded level, but her aroused flesh had begun a slow, steady pulsing that was taking more and more of her attention.

"You could fool me."

She faced him then, intending to— Whatever she had intended, she forgot it when she looked into Ransom's face. The withdrawal to some cold plane that had frightened her earlier was no longer evident. Behind his stony face, in the window of his blue eyes, she saw his pain. Pain she had caused. The pain of rejection.

She drew a sharp breath and closed her eyes against the understanding of what she had done. In an act of unwarranted cruelty she had encouraged him to expose himself, encouraged him to display the ultimate vulnerability, and then she had turned her back on him. He might understand her fears, he might even forgive her for them, but that didn't prevent him from being wounded by what she had done. And she had made it worse, because, while she had run from him like a coward, she had refused to run from the real danger that threatened them all. Despite what she had said earlier, she had acted as if she *was* afraid of him—and only of him.

"Mandy, are you all right?"

The gentle concern she was used to hearing in his voice was conspicuously absent. His tone was matter-of-fact. He asked the question as he might ask it of any stranger.

And that hurt her. Which she deserved, she guessed. Oh, yes, she deserved it. How could she possibly make up for what she had done?

"Mandy?"

She shivered, a huge, ripping shiver that shook her from head to foot. What a fraud she was. She sat here in her carefully orchestrated universe telling herself and the whole world that she was happy with her life, happy with the way things were, that there was nothing she wanted except to be left alone to write her books. Not only did she lack the guts to step outside her ivory tower, she even lacked the guts to admit that she might want to.

"Mandy?"

The indifference had evaporated from his tone. Concern, just a small echo of it, was there now as he reached out and touched her hand.

"Mandy, what's wrong?"

It was that small, fragile hint that he might actually care about her that opened the floodgate and fractured the dam that contained her feelings. A huge sob escaped her, and she reached out blindly, needing his warmth and strength, needing his *reality,* and finally admitting it to herself.

Perhaps the most amazing thing of all was that he gave it to her without a moment's hesitation. He gathered her onto his lap and into his arms, and his hands rubbed her soothingly, gently, while he murmured reassuring nonsense. Incapable of a coherent word, never mind a coherent thought, she pressed her face to his neck and hid within the sanctuary of his arms.

He was, she thought much later, an incredibly generous man. She wasn't at all certain that in his place she could have displayed anything approaching his kindness. She lay quietly against him, her head throbbing, her eyes swollen, her throat raw, her tears dried up. Even then, even knowing the storm had passed, he didn't evict her from his embrace.

"Ransom?" Her voice was a tired croak.

"Hmm?"

"I'm sorry."

A breath escaped him, not quite a sigh. "There's nothing to apologize for, Mandy. It's been hard on you."

How could she explain? For a wordsmith, she was suddenly short of words. "I have plenty to apologize for, and you damn well know it." Scratchy but defiant, her voice grew firmer.

He astonished her then by laughing. It was a quiet, tired sort of laugh, but a laugh all the same. "So okay," he said on a warm chuckle. "Apology accepted."

"You don't even know what I'm apologizing for."

"For this crying jag, I presume."

She sat up straighter on his lap and grabbed his chin, forcing him to look at her. "That's only part of it."

His faint smile vanished completely. "What's the other part?" His gaze was now wary, watchful.

He had a right to be wary of her, she realized with a pang. "I'm sorry for running from you this afternoon."

"Mandy, I—"

She silenced him by placing her fingers over his mouth. "I know you understand. You're a wonderfully understanding man. But that doesn't make what I did right. And it doesn't mean you weren't hurt by it. So I'm sorry. I'm very, very sorry."

For a long moment he was silent and motionless, his eyes holding hers. She returned his measuring look bravely, wondering what it was he saw, and whether he was going to accept her apology. He surprised her by asking a question.

"Why are you telling me this, Mandy?"

"Because...because I want you to know...I realize that what I did was...hurtful. That fear doesn't excuse me."

Not a flicker of a muscle betrayed what he might be thinking. "Fear excuses a great deal."

She shook her head. "No. It doesn't excuse a damn thing, and it's time I faced it. Fear is an instinctive thing—any animal can act on it. A human being isn't supposed to respond to every instinct and impulse that way. We're supposed to think, to reason, to use our minds to see beyond such things. I haven't been. I've been...I've been..."

Before she could find an adequately demeaning description for her behavior, Ransom stole her words, her intent and her breath with a devouring, demanding kiss. "Say it, Mandy. Damn it, just this once tell me the truth. Quit thinking, quit analyzing, quit trying to explain things rationally. Just tell me what you *feel. Tell me.*''

She knew what he wanted. She knew because she needed so desperately to hear it from him. "I want you," she admitted hoarsely. "I want *you.*''

He cut her off with another kiss, this one deeper but gentler. "I want you, too, Amanda Lynn. God forgive me, I want you so much...."

Those words tore down the last of her barriers and made a joke of her fears, because, God help her, she needed him the way she needed air to breathe. If she had ever had a choice in this, it had long since been lost. The point of no return had passed unnoticed, fading into the mist.

For a moment, just a brief, almost undetectable moment, they both resisted fate and destiny, they both made one last hopeless and human attempt not to succumb. Caring meant hurting, a lesson they had learned so painfully that it was branded on their very cells. But being human, they were driven by hungers deeper than pain, needs greater than safety.

With a deep sigh, Ransom cupped her cheek in the palm of his hand. Her head was already resting on his shoulder, but at his gentle touch she managed to snuggle even closer. Bending, he pressed his face to her hair and remembered how he had dreamed of holding her just like this during the long, lonely, endless nights of his captivity. It didn't seem odd that he hadn't even met her then, because he had known her in his soul and in his dreams. Later, perhaps, he might be embarrassed by such fancifulness, but at this moment, wrapped in a filigree of feelings that could be described in no other way, he didn't feel foolish at all. He was just grateful he had the opportunity to really hold her, to actually wrap his arms around her and hold her tangible warmth against him. So few dreams ever took substance.

Her fear stood between them, though. Despite her capitulation, he knew she was still afraid. If he said anything to her about his feelings, she would feel he was tempting fate and become even more frightened, so he held his peace and cuddled her close.

There was, too, on his part, an awareness of his own self-ishness. He had no right to disturb her hard-won tranquility, to surmount her defenses, not while someone wanted to kill him. Not while he couldn't afford to soften the edge of his anger. Not while he couldn't offer her a future.

Despite feeling selfish, he was unable to draw back from her. It was as if, in some elemental way, he knew that they could have no future together unless she was able to face the present beside him.

To hell with it all, he thought in a sudden, savage burst of feeling. He'd had little enough in his life that had felt as right and as good as this woman's soft warmth curled up on his lap. In fact, there had been *nothing* as right and as good as this. If it made him a selfish bastard to be unable to relinquish these few precious moments, then he was a selfish bastard with no regrets.

As unselfconsciously as a kitten, encouraged by what he had said and the way he held her, Mandy nuzzled Ransom's silky beard and breathed his warm, wonderful scent deep into her lungs. With her head on his chest, the steady beat of his heart filled her ear as she rested against him and his hands roamed gently over her side, her shoulders, her hip. When one of those hands slipped between her legs and squeezed her gently, it seemed a natural extension of the embrace. She shifted, making herself available to him, letting him know that this time she truly welcomed him.

"Can we?" she asked breathlessly. "Is it safe?"

"Shh." He brushed feathery kisses on her eyelids, her cheeks, her lips. "Nate left us guarded tonight. Shh."

Every nagging, pulsing yearning she felt for him settled right between her thighs. For a fleeting moment his hand abandoned her, but only to turn out the light. In the dark, he returned to her, unsnapping a snap, tugging down a zipper, slipping his warm fingers beneath denim and cotton to hot, moist, eager flesh.

"Ransom..." His name was a sighing whisper.

"Shh...shh...just let me," he whispered back. "Let me give this to you, Amanda Lynn. Let me."

She undulated upward against his pleasure-giving hand and let reality slip away. In the dark, in the warm, welcome dark with Ransom so close, nothing else mattered. "Ransom...you..."

"Shh," he murmured soothingly. "Shh... We should have started this way earlier, princess. Slowly. Easily. One long, hot step at a time. I want your pleasure. Every single hot, wet, aching moment of it."

The thrills that ripped through her were generated as much by his huskily whispered words as by his touches. She had never imagined anyone talking this way, speaking so frankly, so passionately.

"Do you like that?" he asked as his fingers glided between her hot satin folds and slipped into her slick depths.

Like it? She had never experienced anything quite like it. She had the brief, hazy thought that John had been a very conservative lover, a tender but unimaginative partner. Until this very moment, she had no idea that she might have missed anything. She opened her mouth, wanting to tell Ransom something of what he made her feel, fearing he might take her silence as rejection.

But he read her silence correctly, and when she opened her mouth he took it with his in a deep, plunging kiss that mimicked the slow, sweet penetration of his fingers. Every blaze of pleasure and excitement he had hitherto ignited in her paled suddenly as his hand and tongue unleashed a conflagration.

She twisted against him, arching upward against his hand with a groan that communicated the intensity of her aching need. His own desires spiraled through him and knotted in his groin. This woman was tinder to his senses even as she was balm to his soul.

They had this little bit of time, just this little window of opportunity, when they could be a man and a woman together. In a couple of hours he was going to have to become an agent again. He was going to have to devote his every attention and effort toward devising a means of drawing the assassin out. But now, for just these few, brief hours while Charlie Huskins and another deputy stood guard, he could forget all that. For just this little bit of time he could claim the colors of his princess to carry into battle with him.

They both moaned when he shifted his hand and dipped even deeper into her receptive, hot depths. Her jeans were a definite hindrance now, and he found himself remembering the full, creamy, pink-tipped breasts that were hidden beneath her blouse. He wanted her naked. Completely naked. He wanted to love her from head to foot so that she would never forget him, would always know that she had belonged to him. So that her every nerve ending would be imprinted with his memory.

He groaned again, this time in a different timbre as he reacted to the most basic of masculine needs: territorialism. Taking his hand from her, ignoring her whimpering protests, he shoved his arm beneath her knees and stood. His strength was suddenly almost superhuman, but he hardly noticed it. He was driven to make this woman his, and the only place to do that completely and securely was in bed. Her bed. It was essential that it be *her* bed. Even as he acted on the imperative, some part of him realized the mystical significance of claiming the princess in her own bower. No other place would make the claiming as complete. No other place would signify her total surrender to him.

He mounted the stairs swiftly, holding Mandy as effortlessly as if she weighed nothing at all. In her room he laid her on the counterpane and stood over her, stripping off his clothes with swift efficiency. There was little light, but even so, he saw her eyes grow wide with knowledge.

And then, depriving him of breath and filling him with fierce triumph, she rose to her knees and began to discard her own clothing. At last. At long last. She was coming to him at last.

His boots delayed him for a few moments, but soon he was free of the final restriction. When he straightened, he found Mandy ahead of him, lying back against the pillows and waiting. He paused, savoring the moment, lingering just a little longer on the brink. And then she lifted her arms toward him.

"Ransom," she sighed yearningly.

His every cell throbbed with the same demand as his loins, but first he had another purpose to accomplish. Instead of sinking into her arms, he knelt beside the bed and touched a finger to her soft lips.

"Shh..." he murmured. "Shh..." Let me worship you, he thought. Let me adore you and cherish you with my mind, my mouth, my hands, my body. Earlier she had met his mindless need with selfless understanding. He needed to show her how much that meant to him. He needed to give her something of what she had given him. And he needed to do it now, because life might deprive him of another chance.

"Ransom?" Her breath caught on his name as his hand swept over her, lightly teasing a nipple, dipping tenderly into her navel, finding its goal at last in the downy thatch at the juncture of her thighs. "Oh..." It was a sigh and a soft whimper as he brought her again, instantly, to a fever pitch.

She should have been embarrassed. Some vestige of her mind was astonished by her wantonness as she lay beneath his hands and let him—no, encouraged him—to touch her in any and every way he cared to. Some part of her wanted to draw back from the totally consuming eroticism of his caresses. Some part of her was afraid to give him the complete capitulation he demanded. She had never, ever, lost herself in the way he was asking of her now, and she was terrified to do so.

He demanded that she drop her deepest, most closely guarded barriers. He demanded ... only what he had given her that afternoon in his bed. He demanded that she relinquish her self-control and trust him to carry her through this unscathed and safe. As he had earlier trusted her.

Remembering how he had lost himself in her and how she had intuitively understood how naked and vulnerable he felt, she suddenly understood the true meaning of intimacy. And it was intimacy that Ransom was demanding of her now. Not sex. Not a simple scratching of superficial itches. Not love, not caring, not passion or even need. No, he wanted intimacy, a far more terrible thing, because it ran so deeply and so closely to the most tender and easily damaged parts of a person. Intimacy meant shucking the spiritual skin and leaving every emotional nerve ending open and exposed.

She wondered wildly if she could do it, if she should do it, and then she *was* doing it. Seizing his head, she drew his mouth to hers, claiming him as fiercely as he had claimed her. Her legs parted, opening like a blossom to his deep touches, encouraging him to take more and yet more of her. Let him know, she thought crazily. Let him know how much I want, how much I need, how much he means. Let him know.

And then she gave him the gift of her pleasure. Rising up against his hand, she went to him as he wanted, with her ecstasy offered freely and honestly.

And then, before the pulsing aftershocks had even begun to subside, before she could think about what she was doing and grow embarrassed, she tugged at him, pulling him onto the bed beside her, drawing him over her.

"Now," she said fiercely. "Now!"

He grabbed the foil packet he had thrown on the night table when he discarded his jeans. As soon as Mandy saw it, she snatched it from him. "Let me," she said hoarsely, astonishing herself even as the thought of what she was about to do sent fresh lightning along her nerves. Oh, yes, she wanted to touch him like this, and more. And later, when they were calmer, when the needs had gentled and there was time, she was going to touch him and explore him and learn him.

Straddling her hips, Ransom clenched his jaw and let her do as she wished. No one had ever put a condom on him before, and he found himself suspended between heaven and hell, wondering if he would be able to survive her ministrations. His breath caught as she touched him, and his mind served up a list of all the ways he would *like* her to touch him, stiffening him even more.

"You should have let me go to the doctor," she mumbled thickly, breathlessly, as she rolled the barrier onto him. "You feel so much better naked. . . ."

He also wouldn't have missed this experience for the world. There were no words to describe the fresh flood of passion her gentle touch elicited; there were no words for how it made him feel to watch her touch him with trembling hands, to see her hesitations and her shy delight in what she was doing.

Then, in a single incandescent instant, he claimed her. Buried deep within her, he froze briefly, reluctant to let go of this absolutely perfect moment in time. Around him, he felt her rippling contractions as she responded to the bliss of their union.

Earlier he had taken her as a warrior who had been away too long. Now, with deep, slow thrusts, he took her as a warrior who had come home. He watched her convulse beneath him and around him, watched culmination draw her tight and fling her to the stars. And then he let her watch him, let her see the hunger twist his face, let her hear the groans of driving need that were torn from him.

She felt his climax in her womb. More, she felt it in a deep place that heard what hadn't been said. He had shown her what he could not tell her, what she wasn't willing to hear.

The knight had claimed his princess.

Ransom woke at dawn. Opening his eyes slowly, he saw that the curtains had been drawn back from the window to let in the pink and lavender light. Slowly, cell by cell, he remembered where he was. Facedown in Mandy's narrow bed, he was sprawled widely in a posture more relaxed than any his body had dared adopt since childhood. She had done that to him, he thought hazily. She had unwound him that far.

Almost as soon as he had the thought, he tensed. A movement told him that Mandy was awake, and more, that she was kneeling beside him, looking at him. Oh God! He knew she had seen it before, in bed yesterday and when he'd been so feverish with the malaria. He had the vaguest memory of sitting in her tub while she ladled cool water over him. So she had seen the scars all along his body in the light before. Certainly she had seen his back. She wasn't repulsed.

But every hair on his body stood up with fear. He felt so exposed. He couldn't bear to imagine what she must be thinking, couldn't bear the thought of her seeing his ugliness like this. Even while he knew it wasn't rational, he nonetheless felt ashamed. All the tangled feelings of a victim rose in him, a textbook web of shame and guilt and humiliation. He had to force himself to lie still beneath her eyes, and he did so only because he knew they had to get past this.

His hammering heart forced him to suck in a deep gulp of air, a ragged, tormented sound.

"Shh..." Mandy leaned over him, pressing her palms to his shoulders. She knew. She didn't know how, but she knew, and her heart ached for him, an ache so deep it threatened to destroy her. "Shh..." She leaned closer to kiss the nape of his neck just beneath his shaggy, molten gold hair.

"I was sitting here," she murmured softly. "Just sitting here and admiring you."

"Mandy..." Who the *hell* did she think she was kidding?

"Shush. Let me finish." Her tone sharpened with command, then softened again as her lips found the first scar that slashed across his shoulders. "You're so beautiful, Ransom. So beautiful. I thought so the first time I set eyes on you. Oh, you were too thin and pale, and you looked as if you'd been sick for a long, long time, but there was more than that. Something so beautiful it shines out of your eyes."

With each word she kissed yet another scar, working her way slowly down his back across the tortured map of four years of his life. He caught his breath and tried to swallow the lump that was clogging his throat, but his throat just got tighter and her kisses just kept coming, finding every hurt, every scar, every damaged part of him.

"The instant I saw you," she murmured huskily, "I knew you were a warrior. I knew you'd been in battles so terrible

there's no way I can imagine them. I knew..." Her voice
broke and then steadied. "I knew you'd been beaten and
bloodied." She drew a ragged breath and kissed the scars
that marred the backs of his strong, powerful legs. When she
spoke again, her voice was thick with tears. "But I knew you
were still strong. All I had to do was look at you to know
just how valiant and undefeated you are."

He couldn't handle any more of this. She was ripping him
open with tender words and soft caresses. He started to roll
over, unable to speak through his closed throat, but she
stopped him by covering him with her body. Where before
he had been so brutally exposed he could hardly stand it,
now her soft nakedness covered him from shoulder to
calves. Her cheek lay between his shoulder blades, her
stomach pressed softly against his rump, and her thighs lay
gently over his. Reaching up, she laced her fingers through
his.

She wanted to tell him that she would shelter him and
protect him, that she would place herself between him and
the cold harsh world, but she left the foolish words unspoken. At this moment, everything seemed possible, but she
knew that wouldn't last. When faced with hard, harsh reality herself, she was going to dive into the nearest hole and
hide. This was a moment out of time, a fantasy wrested
from the night, and it would evaporate in the light of day.

As the pink light of dawn brightened slowly into gold,
Ransom lay beneath Mandy's protective warmth. He didn't
want to move for fear of shattering the tenuous tenderness
between them. This woman, the woman who covered his
exposed pain with her nakedness, this woman was the
Amanda Lynn Tierney who wrote fantasies that moved him
and touched him. This was the woman who lived only in her
fantasies because she was afraid of being hurt.

And damn it, he didn't know how he could possibly prevent that. In her books, good always triumphed over evil,
but this wasn't a book. This was real life. When she remembered that, she would run from him again. Needing so
much more, he contented himself with tightening his fingers around hers.

"Princess?"

The husky murmur sent shivers of longing pouring through her. "There's a custom," she said, "that when a lady bestows her colors she also has promised her favors."

Her fingers felt so fragile between his that he dared not squeeze any harder. Instead he drew her hand to his mouth and kissed it. He felt another tremor pass through her, and his body responded in kind. Strength flowed through him.

"I thought," he said huskily, running his tongue over one small fingertip, "that a knight had to be victorious before he claimed those favors. It seems to me we got it backward, princess."

She shifted against him in a sinuous, sensuous movement that made him acutely aware of where each and every one of her delectable curves was located.

"Oh, no," she said, her voice suddenly breathy and deep. "We got the colors part backward."

"How so?" Gently, very gently, he bit her fingertip.

Mandy gasped and tried to press even closer. "You've won all your battles, all your victories, already. We can pretend I gave you my colors years ago. I should have."

And probably wouldn't have, he thought, even as he twisted beneath her and brought them, at last, face-to-face and chest-to-chest. Mandy's legs fell between his, and he smiled at the way her eyes darkened when she felt the proof of his arousal.

"Lift up," he said roughly, and positioned her so that she straddled his hips, her most intimate secrets utterly exposed to his marauding hands. He slipped a finger along her moist folds and found the slick nub of her desire. He watched as she arched and whimpered softly at his touch.

"You wouldn't have given me a second look, princess," he told her gruffly. "You would have found me hard and cruel and insensitive. You would have recognized me as a necessary evil, but you wouldn't have wanted me to touch you."

"I would—" Her breath and voice broke as he rubbed her gently.

"You wouldn't," he said flatly. "I was a warrior. I was everything a warrior needs to be. I did everything a warrior needs to do. You'd better understand that before you give me your colors, because I'll do it again if I need to."

He would. She didn't doubt it for a minute. And whatever he said, she had seen the truth in his eyes. A warrior did what he had to. It was *why* he did it that made a difference.

Suddenly, shocking her with his strength, he lifted her until she straddled his shoulders. Then he gave her a kiss so intimate she couldn't believe what her senses were telling her.

"Ransom, no..."

"Mandy, yes," he growled. "I mean to have every one of your favors, princess. Every one. Every way."

She writhed, pinned by his hands, pinned by pleasure so exquisite it was pain. "Ransom...Ransom..." She cried his name as her torment mounted, yet still he kissed her relentlessly, his tongue stripping her of her last inhibitions. Higher and higher he drove her, sending her so far beyond thought that she could only feel.

He felt her break apart. She shattered like crystal reaching its resonant note. He gave himself a moment to taste her pleasure, and then he rolled her over, gathering her close and rocking her until the storm passed.

She wept. Her tears might have frightened him, except that she was also clinging so hard to him that he knew he would have a new set of scars on his shoulders. The pain felt good. Pain was as much a proof of existence as pleasure. Without pain there could be no pleasure. It was the hills and valleys of the emotions that gave life its perspective and its contours. He understood that. She needed to understand it, too, but he didn't know how a lesson like that could be taught. She would have to find the knowledge somewhere within herself.

Before her tears fully ceased, she moved her hands over him, telling him that she was still receptive. He released a breath he hadn't even known he was holding and closed his eyes against the sheer delight of her hands on his flesh. She traced every contour of his hard, powerful chest. When she found the small, hard beads of his nipples, she stroked and licked and nipped until he thought he would go out of his ever-loving mind.

"Mandy..." His voice was a harsh groan of protest, but already she was moving on, sweeping lower in her hungry search, approaching and then skipping away from his manhood in a teasing dance that suspended him between laughter and despair.

And then, stunning him into utter stillness, she reciprocated with her own shy, intimate kiss. He felt her warm, satiny lips and her hot slick tongue on him, and if a squad of commandos had burst through the door right then, he couldn't have twitched a muscle in his own defense.

"Mmm..." she purred as she felt his helpless response. "Mmm."

All that had gone before between them had been shrouded in a dreamy haze, an aura of fantasy that had answered some deep need of their souls. Now, however, that mist was gone. Each sound, each movement, each sensation, took on the hard, distinct edge of reality.

He heard the whisper of his own skin against the sheets as she made him writhe. He had never, ever, let anyone do this to him before, had never, ever, permitted himself to be so vulnerable and defenseless. It didn't matter that he had just done the same thing to her. Adrenaline shot through him as part of him tried to flee, as part of him cried out to escape from this exposure. Hell, yes, he wanted to run. He couldn't bear the thought of a woman, any woman, knowing she had this kind of power over him. He couldn't stand the thought of anyone seeing him helpless like this. Reaching up, he grabbed the headboard, heard himself groan, a sound that rose from the very bottom of his soul. He jerked sharply, and his legs stiffened.

"Ransom...?" A hazy, husky question.

Their eyes met across the expanse of his torso, and what he saw in her soft brown gaze undid the last of him. Closing his eyes, he gave her what he had never given anyone else. "That...feels...so...damn...*good!*"

Good didn't even begin to cover it. Ecstasy didn't come close, either. There was something about what was happening that was reaching beyond the physical to the emotional, and it was exhilarating him. Tearing at him. Clawing at him.

And finally, good wasn't enough. Reaching for Mandy with hands that trembled, he tugged her up beside him and tucked her beneath him. "I need you," he muttered roughly. "*Now*, Amanda Lynn. Now!"

In the radiant early morning light, she saw him above her, a golden warrior with eyes the blazing blue of the Wyoming sky. Beautiful. Wild. Powerful.

Unconquered.

Chapter 10

He felt like one great big exposed nerve ending. Standing beneath the shower's heated spray, letting water pummel his face and shoulders, he gave serious thought to just rolling up into a tight ball and pretending he'd never been born.

Men weren't supposed to feel that way, but hell, he'd been on enough battlefields to know that men damn well *did* feel that way, and he was feeling that way right now. Too much, too soon, too fast. In one flaming night of passion, tenderness and soul-on-soul contact, he and Mandy had gotten closer than he'd ever been to another human being.

Well, no, that wasn't exactly true. Back in Nam he'd been that close to Nate and Micah. When you stood eyeball-to-eyeball with the Grim Reaper day after day, with nothing to rely on but your buddies, you damn well got close. You got so you knew another man's smell as well as you knew your own, you knew what he wanted, what he dreamed and what he feared.

But since Nam, Ransom hadn't had anyone to rely on but himself. He'd been a loner. Was still a loner. Even wolves ran in packs, but not Ransom. Last night he'd let Mandy cross the invisible stone wall he kept between himself and the rest of the world. Superficially, he'd seemed no different than anyone else. He let women into his bed, friends into his life, but no one, absolutely no one, got within that invisible wall of stone.

Now someone had, and he felt as if he had been flayed, as if every single inch of his skin had been peeled away. Worse, the only way he could think of to protect himself would hurt Mandy, and he suspected that she felt every bit as skinned this morning as he did. After all, she lived behind some very high walls of her own.

He needed some distance. He needed it savagely. If he didn't get it, he might take it brutally. The thought worried him. He knew himself. Some things were instincts so deep that he acted on them before his mind had a chance to intervene. That was half the point of this shower: to gain time and distance and the chance to think before he acted.

And he sure as hell couldn't spent the rest of the morning hiding in here. Raw as he was, he wasn't sure he even wanted to. The thought of her lying on those rumpled sheets in her narrow bed waiting for him was enough to make being skinned alive seem like a small inconvenience.

Nearly groaning, he turned his face into the spray once more. There was another inconvenience he had been forgetting but couldn't afford to forget any longer: the would-be assassin.

Swearing under his breath, he turned off the water, threw the curtain back and grabbed a towel. He had wasted enough time. In fact, when he thought about it, he couldn't believe how laid-back he'd been about it so far. Mandy had distracted him. Like a witch, she had cast some kind of spell on him, a spell he was so reluctant to break that he was hanging his butt in the breeze just asking somebody to take another shot at it.

Damn!

With the towel wrapped around his hips, he strode down the hall and stepped into her room, words of explanation and excuse already forming in his mind.

She was gone. He stared at the carefully made bed, and then slowly, reluctantly, a smile tugged up the corners of his mouth.

It seemed he wasn't the only one who was panicking.

Mandy heard Ransom's booted feet on the stairs, heard his familiar, faintly hesitant step behind her. She was afraid to face him, she realized. Embarrassment over her actions was only a small part of it. Intellectually she knew that they had done nothing that millions of couples all over the world didn't do nightly. Emotionally, it might take her a little longer to believe it, but that was the least of her problems.

She was afraid that he would expect continued intimacy. She was afraid that he wouldn't let her retreat from the feelings that had overwhelmed her. She needed time. She needed distance. She needed to find her hard-won equilibrium. She needed to reestablish her control over her life.

"Mandy?"

Slowly she turned, her wary gaze rising to his. They stared at one another like ancient antagonists who had met unexpectedly and weren't sure whether to continue an old battle.

"You know," Ransom said abruptly, "I've got the weirdest sensation I've been here before. That I've done this before. Do you suppose we've both been running scared for all eternity?"

Her jaw dropped, but before she could muster any kind of response, he shrugged and a mask dropped over his face. "You crawl into your foxhole, and I'll crawl into mine, princess. It's the safest place to be."

He stomped out of the kitchen, looking both disgruntled and relieved. She should have guessed Ransom was no happier about this than she was. He would be moving on just as soon as he was well again. Just as soon as his convalescent leave was up. Nothing he had said or done suggested that he would do anything else. Surely a man who had been a secret agent his entire adult life needed more excitement than he could find in Conard County.

He might call her princess and say nice things, but when you came right down to it, there was no reason on earth why a man like him should really want a dull brown mouse like her.

The thought hurt, but she refused to consider why. Instead she assured herself that she and Ransom were adults. They were perfectly capable of assuaging their physical needs without becoming tangled in skeins of unwanted feelings. They could, and would, keep a safe emotional distance.

After all, they had both learned their lesson the hard way. Neither one of them was likely to forget it.

The day had turned surprisingly warm, and the sun beat fiercely on Ransom's back as he scraped blistered paint off the side of the barn. He stayed on the side where he could see the house and keep a better eye on Mandy. From here the blackened heap of burnt wood and ash that had been the cabin was invisible. To his left was the corral, where the horses frolicked and grazed by turns. Since the fire, he was loath to keep them in the barn. If the "cat" decided to resume the game, he didn't want the animals to be caught helplessly in the way.

From time to time he dropped the scraper, scoured the sweat off his brow and went to prowl the area, watching for any sign that the person who was stalking him had again come close. When he passed beneath the open window of Mandy's study, he could hear the tap-tap of keys as she wrote, and he could just make out her shadow in the dim interior. She didn't say anything when he looked in on her, and he didn't expect her to.

By now, he figured, she probably despised him. It was a discomforting thought, but one he accepted stoically. If something happened to him, it would be better for her if she hated him.

In fact, in retrospect, he could see that he had been unpardonably arrogant in some respects. He'd had the utter gall to pity her, for one thing, when he was guilty of the same weaknesses. Human weaknesses. She was disinclined

to care and he was disinclined to trust, and they were both
afraid of the very same thing. It was all very well to philos-
ophize that pain gave life its shape and contrasts, but it was
something else entirely to volunteer for another fall down a
jagged slope into a spiritual abyss.

Ah, hell, he thought, and wished for a beer. He knew for
a fact that there was a cold six-pack in the fridge, but he
wasn't going to indulge himself. He couldn't afford to cloud
his senses or slow his reaction time, even by the effect of one
beer.

He was, he realized, awakening from some kind of daze
that had clouded his mind for months. Ever since he had
discovered he was safe and protected in the hospital, that he
no longer had to fend for himself because others were caring for and protecting him, something inside him had shut
down. It was almost as if, in believing that he was safe, he
was able to withdraw into some dark, warm internal cave
from which he could view everything from a distance. Even
the feelings that had been necessary to keep him alive, the
anger and the hate, had been shut off behind layers of cotton batting, muffled and nearly silenced.

The return of his anger had been a sign, he realized. The
healing hibernation was over. Last night had been part of
that awakening. Time and again, during his short stay with
Mandy, he had felt himself reaching out, moving out, feeling again. And time and again he had felt himself pull
sharply back into the numbness. Last night had stripped
away too many layers. There was no way he could crawl
back into his cocoon. There was no way he could be numb
again.

Instead, he was angry. Instead, his senses were sharpen-
ing and clearing as the cobwebs blew away. His foxhole had
been filled in behind him, and now there was no choice but
to stalk. To hunt. To patiently await the first sign of his
quarry.

He was in pain. He was suffering sheer, gut-wrenching,
soul-searing, sharp-edged emotional pain. Awareness of
what had been done to him twisted like a hot knife inside
him. He needed to forget and he couldn't. He needed to

forgive, but he wouldn't. The actual physical pain he had endured didn't come close to the psychic pain. And unlike physical pain, psychic pain didn't go away.

Events had driven all thought of the Harvest Dance from Mandy's mind. She was utterly floored several days later when Ransom reminded her it was that night and that she had promised to go with him.

"But..." A million objections rose to mind, but not one of them constituted any real excuse other than, "It won't be safe for you."

"I'll be perfectly safe, and so will you."

"But in a crowd—"

"Nate tells me this won't be just any crowd. He says a stranger will stick out like a sore thumb."

"That's true, I guess." The population of the entire county was around 5,500 souls and Nate and his deputies recognized every one of them on sight. Out of those 5,500, less than two hundred usually showed up for the dance. TV, satellite dishes and VCRs made it easier and a lot more pleasant for most folks to stay home.

None of which answered her most important question. "Why do you want to go, Ransom?"

They were eating a lunch of grilled cheese sandwiches and vegetable soup at the long table in the kitchen. He kept his gaze trained on his meal, a custom he had developed since their passion-filled night together. It was a custom that made her long to throw something in order to get his full attention. She refrained, knowing the distance he was keeping was safer for them both.

"I asked you," he answered.

"Well, you can just un-ask me." Her tone took on an uncharacteristic tartness. "I can't imagine why you want to spend an evening dancing with me, much less why you want to spend the evening in a crowd. You're not a crowd type."

"No, I'm not," he agreed. The complete opposite, in fact. "But I *do* want to dance with you." That, too, was a fact, and admitting it to himself was even harder than admitting it to her. He wanted an excuse to hold her again. That would be the safest way to do it, too, because you couldn't make love on a dance floor. You couldn't expose your soul and all your tattered nerve endings. You couldn't make yourself helpless before your own needs. You *could* drive yourself crazy with longing, but he would deal with it.

There was more to it than that, Mandy thought. After the way he had been avoiding intimacy with her—with her co-operation, admittedly—she found it a little difficult to accept that he wanted to go to the Harvest Dance simply to dance with her.

Sighing, she pushed her plate aside and propped her chin on her hand. "Ransom, we really need to talk."

He barely glanced at her. "About what?" He hoped she didn't want to discuss what had happened between them the other night. If he lived to be a hundred and fifty, he didn't think he would ever be able to discuss what had really taken place between them. Some things... some things just came too close to the bone, too close to the soul. Too close to private places that weren't meant to be shared.

There had been magic in the air that night, he thought now. Wild magic. Things had happened that could never be explained. Talking about it would simply debase it.

"About what's really going on here," she answered finally. "If somebody is trying to kill you, they're sure going about it in a funny way. Even *I* can see that. It's been days now since anything at all happened. If somebody really wants to hurt you..."

"Somebody really wants to hurt me," he said flatly. "You don't shoot out windshields and burn down buildings for a joke."

"Then... you're being toyed with." The feeling was like cold slime running down her back.

"Looks that way."

"That's... that's vicious!"

"So's murder." He looked up finally, and met her worried gaze head-on. "We'll keep you safe, Mandy. Nate and Micah and I will see to it that nothing happens to you."

"It's not *me* I'm worried about." And she wasn't. Throughout all of this, she couldn't recall feeling a twinge of concern for her own safety. "Somebody would have to hate you an awful lot to do something like that."

Ransom heard the question in the statement but didn't know exactly how to answer. "I imagine I've made a few people hate me that way, but it's been so long...." He shrugged. "Who knows? I'm still trying to figure out who it might be, especially when I've been gone so long."

"Have you contacted anyone at your agency? Wouldn't they be able to help?"

Ransom shoved his plate aside. "Let's just say they really don't have anything useful to contribute to this situation."

"Nothing? Nothing at all? What good are they if they can't do *something* to help you?"

Ransom's eyes were like twin shards of blue ice. "Have you heard the term 'out in the cold'?"

Mandy drew a sharp breath, and there was a strange prickling sensation in her scalp. "But you're on convalescent leave. You haven't quit."

He shrugged. "There's really nothing anyone can do, Mandy. Not a thing. No one has a clue. As far as the agency is concerned, this appears to be a personal problem of my own, and there's no evidence to the contrary. I've been inactive for so long, even *I* find it hard to believe that this has any connection with my work.

"Anyway, regardless of who might be behind this, the agency isn't authorized to provide protection for me, and no one is going to put his career on the line to do it. It's outside their mandate. To put it plainly, they aren't allowed to function actively within the borders of the United States."

"They could ask the FBI—"

"No." Ransom's interruption was short, sharp. "Nobody can do a damn thing that Nate, Micah and I aren't already doing. It's not within the purview of any federal agency."

Mandy drew a deep breath, then another, wrestling with a sense of outrage. This man had worked for that damn agency for years, risking life and limb time and again, and now, when he needed help, he was *out in the cold?*

"Relax, Mandy. This is the way the game is played."

He seemed unperturbed by it, but she found it hard to believe that he could be. Surely he must feel some kind of resentment? If he did, though, she realized slowly, he wasn't going to admit it. This was the way things were done, men didn't grouse about the way things were. Of course not. He'd been playing by these rules for years, and he could hardly criticize them now.

"Surely they owe you something," she argued anyway. "After all you've done—"

"You don't know what I've done," he interrupted with sudden savagery. "Nobody owes me anything. But let me tell you something, Mandy, and remember this well. My list of possible suspects is very short."

"Short?"

"It's limited to the people who know I'm alive. I can rule out my family and Nate and Micah, but I can't rule out anybody else."

It took a moment, but shock trickled through her like ice water. "Your bosses . . ." she whispered in horror.

He didn't even bother to answer. No wonder, she thought. No wonder he wasn't twisting their arms and hollering at them over the phone.

My God.

Minutes ticked away in muffled, appalled silence.

And somehow, she realized abruptly, he had managed to turn the conversation away from her original area of concern: why was it so damn important to him to take her to the dance? Because, regardless of what he said, there was absolutely no way she could believe he merely wanted to dance with her. Heck, in the last three days he hadn't even *touched* her. Not even the most casual of touches. She was, in fact, beginning to feel a little like a pariah.

Which was just as well, she assured herself vigorously. She knew better than to get involved.

Right. That was why she kept catching herself staring at him, filling her eyes with him as if looking might finally satisfy the ache. She noticed everything, from the way his shirts stretched across his powerful shoulders to the way the denim of his new jeans was slowly beginning to mold his shape. She stared at him like a lovesick cow when he was outside and unaware that she was watching. She stored up everything in some hope chest of the mind, a place where she tucked precious memories for later, emptier days. And she was afraid, so very afraid, of that coming emptiness.

Some part of her argued that she should seize every moment now and store up a bundle of good memories against the days ahead. Another, saner part told her to hold herself aloof, because it would hurt less if she refused her feelings the room they needed to grow.

Still another part of her argued that there was no longer any way to avoid the pain. No way at all. Whether he left now, ten days from now, or a hundred years from now, she was going to hurt.

She was, in fact, trying to measure her pain in degrees, to limit her involvement to limit the pain. And wasn't that, she found herself thinking, merely an exercise in futility?

And none of this was getting her any closer to the truth he was withholding. She felt that if he was going to use her, she deserved to understand why. "Why don't you tell me the real reason you're so insistent on this dance, Ransom?"

He stared at her. "Why do you find it so hard to believe that I just want to dance with you?"

"Because you've been avoiding me like the plague since—for the last few days," she amended. She could feel her cheeks growing warm, but she refused to back down. Before their night together, the dance had seemed a gentle, stylized step in a slow courtship. Now it seemed more like a ridiculous pretense. As far as they had gone together, if Ransom really wanted anything further, he wouldn't have to wait to take her to the dance.

He continued to stare steadily at her. "I thought," he said finally, "that you wanted me to avoid you." And he *had* thought so. Her reluctance to get involved was the main impetus behind his own reluctance to trust her. How could you trust someone who might bolt in terror at any moment?

She didn't know how to answer him. Her heart began beating nervously as she wondered what the hell she was doing. She wanted the distance between them, didn't she? If so, why was she trying to provoke him into crossing it?

"The dance," she said finally, her hands clenched into fists on her lap. "What's so important about this damn dance?"

She was acting crazy, he thought, but then, so was he. When the hell had he ever been afraid to take what he wanted? Never. Never! So why the hell was he acting like a nervous virgin around her? "Micah's going to set a trap," he said after a moment. "You and I are going to be very much gone, and Micah and some of the off-duty deputies are going to stake out the house in the hope that the assassin will want to make the most of the opportunity. Everyone in the county knows I asked you to the dance, Mandy. Tom Preston and Marge Tate evidently saw to that."

"So you think someone might try to set another bomb or something?" The skin on her neck crawled at the thought.

"Or something."

Her brown eyes held such sorrowful fear when they rose to his. "They could destroy everything, Ransom. The house, the barn. Everything that means anything to me."

"The point behind the trap is to prevent precisely that," he pointed out. Superficially he was calm and in control, but inwardly the seething volcano was trying to bubble over. He hated to see this woman look so sad and afraid. He hated the thought that he was responsible for those feelings. He hated the fact that those feelings were standing between them. And yet, even if all this trouble went away, what did he have to offer her? What kind of promises could he make her?

She looked around as if seeking some means of escape. He ached for her, wished he could smash something to vent all the feelings that couldn't be unleashed. And then she amazed him.

"I guess I'd better take a backup copy of my book with me tonight. Just in case." Slowly, her eyes came back to him.

"That would be wise." A dozen rash promises sprang to his mind, but he didn't give voice to a single one of them.

The longer he lived with the awareness of what he was doing to her, the more determined he became to end it. And he *would* end it. As soon as the assassin was caught.

Until this evening, Ransom had seen Mandy wear only jeans and baggy shirts, except for the prim gray suit she wore to church on Sundays. Tonight she wore a full denim skirt with a flirtatious, lacy red underskirt, and a red silk blouse that instantly reminded him of the creamy curves beneath. In a second passion pushed past his every guard and swamped him. He wanted this quiet, mousy woman with a hunger that defied description.

Only she wasn't a quiet, mousy woman. When she smiled, she glowed with vitality and loveliness. When he made love to her, she blossomed like a rose. For him, she became beautiful. For him, she *was* beautiful.

He knew better. He knew to keep his hands to himself, to keep a proper distance. He knew the dangers of involvement, how quickly the heat between them could burst into conflagration. He knew how he loved to tempt and tease himself by touching her, kissing her, holding her and then pulling away. He knew the spell she cast on him.

All he knew, all his wisdom and caution, failed to stop him. Without a word he reached for her. Leaning back against the kitchen counter, he tugged her into the cleft between his legs until their bodies just barely brushed. Capturing her chin, he turned her face up and looked solemnly down into her wide, nervous brown eyes. Color rose in soft pink profusion to her cheeks.

"You look lovely tonight, Amanda Lynn." His voice was a husky caress. "Lovely enough to be irresistible."

Her breath caught and her pupils dilated. She was close enough to feel his muscular strength, close enough to feel the heat of his response to her. With a sigh that was almost a sob, she leaned into him and drank greedily of his aroma, his power, his warmth. Her hands slipped upward over his chambray-clad chest, testing strength and sinew, coming to rest finally in the golden silk of his hair. She felt the brush of his beard in the split second before his hot mouth settled on hers.

This was where she belonged. Her mind might deny it, but her emotions recognized it. Every cell in her body knew it. Oh God, it felt so good and so right to have his arms close around her, to feel his large hands stroking her back and sides with the intimacy of a lover. How was she ever, ever going to survive without this? Without him?

His tongue found hers in a demanding stroke that said he was out of patience. The touch reached every one of her nerve endings, igniting them, and she responded with an impatience that matched his. In those blinding moments nothing else mattered. Their bodies strained together; their tongues twined and their breaths mingled.

It was Ransom who found the strength to call a halt. He tore his mouth from hers with a deep, heartfelt groan and rested his chin on top of her head. Cradling her with strong hands that were suddenly gentle, he waited for sanity to return to both of them. One way or another, he found himself thinking crazily, this attraction was going to be the death of him. One way or another.

Mandy stepped back suddenly and turned away, thoroughly shaken by the moments just passed. Not because of the passion, but because she felt as if she were being compelled by some force to step outside her emotional fortress. It seemed to be beyond her ability to control, this urge to step into Ransom's embrace. Time and again she threw herself into his arms and gave herself up to him. She had lost control of herself. The realization was as terrifying as anything she had ever known.

The evening star hung bright in the western sky, while the sunset cast a green glow along the horizon.

"It's rare to see a sunset like that," Mandy remarked to Ransom as the pickup rattled along the dirt road.

"Yeah. I've only seen a couple that I can recall."

She was sitting too far away, he thought, conscious of the many reasons why she should. "Can I interest you in stopping at the drive-in for a hamburger before we go on to the dance?''

Mandy was surprised to feel the corners of her mouth lift while a bubble of helium seemed to burst in her stomach. The drive-in for a hamburger. It sounded so...young. So carefree. So like one of the many things she had missed in life. ''I'd love to.''

Half an hour later they were parked between other dusty pickups at the drive-in, munching burgers and listening to country music on the radio. For a few minutes it was possible to pretend that this was an ordinary date, that she was an ordinary young woman with every right to enjoy herself.

It wasn't an ordinary date, though, and she couldn't forget reality for long. There was a shadow lurking on the edge of this small bubble of happiness. There was always a shadow. She couldn't remember a time in her life when her horizons had seemed completely clear. No, that wasn't true. Briefly, during her marriage, just after she learned she was pregnant, everything had seemed perfect, everything had seemed possible. She had walked around in a haze of sheer joy for weeks.

''That was a heavy sigh,'' Ransom remarked. He had watched the shadows pass over her face and had a pretty good idea where her thoughts had strayed. She sighed again and looked at him. ''Worrying about evil wizards?'' he asked.

''I guess. It's hard not to when I think about why you want us away from the house tonight.''

He nodded slowly and shoved his trash into the bag. ''Yeah. I couldn't pass it up, Mandy. Everybody in the damn county is expecting to see me here, which means either the house is a great target or I am. Either way, something should happen, and we should get to the bottom of this. I want you to promise me one thing, though.''

She tilted her head, and he was momentarily distracted by the grace of her slender neck. ''Which is?'' she prompted.

''Promise you won't step outside the building or wander away from the dance floor on your own.''

Cold fingers ran along her spine. It had occurred to her before that she might be perceived as a tool to use against Ransom. He was suggesting nothing she hadn't already thought of, but hearing him allude to it made it seem much more real.

"Okay," she said, hoping he couldn't guess how frightened she suddenly felt. "That's easy enough to promise." She attempted to joke about it. "So you'll walk me to the ladies' room?"

His mouth quirked. "Sure. And set every tongue in the county wagging." He leaned toward her abruptly and nipped at her earlobe, sending a shiver of pleasure racing through her. "I don't intend to let you out of my sight, Amanda Lynn, and it isn't just because there might be danger."

"No?" Her breath caught on the word, and she felt suddenly as if she were swimming in the blue warmth of his eyes.

"No."

But it was a danger she couldn't afford to forget, she reminded herself a short time later as they drove to the high school gymnasium for the dance. She had suffered losses before in life, and she had no intention of living through them again. Parents, husband and child were all the losses any one person should be expected to endure. Only a complete masochist would set herself up for a second round.

But she could enjoy the passion, couldn't she? If she were very, very careful not to care too much?

All her reservations were soon forgotten in the excitement of the dance. She hadn't come to the Harvest Dance since John's death, and only now did she realize how many people she had lost touch with. Whenever she and Ransom agreed to sit out a dance, she found herself engaged in lively conversation with old friends who seemed to have a lot of news to share after four years. It was almost possible to forget that at every entrance to the room one of Nate's deputies was in evidence. They weren't being obtrusive, but they were there, a reminder she couldn't quite overlook.

But mostly she enjoyed dancing with Ransom. He was a very good dancer, good enough to turn her own relative inexperience into grace. And he held her as if she were precious to him, gently yet firmly. He also turned every dance into an experience so subtly erotic that her flush and breathlessness were only partly from exertion.

"Where did you learn to dance?" she asked him at one point, trying to get her mind off the way his hips kept brushing hers, a light, casual touch that seemed accidental yet occurred in a rhythm that was anything but. Her mind kept replaying the image of him as he had looked in the sunlight on her bed the morning after their lovemaking. So lean and powerful, so golden. So incredibly male and sexy. She got hot flashes just remembering.

"I took lessons years ago when I realized it was a lot less embarrassing to be able to dance than not to be able to. I was pretty surprised to realize that I liked it."

He liked it, all right, and he liked it better with Mandy than he ever had with anyone else. But then, he had never enjoyed sexual teasing the way he seemed to with Mandy, either. He had believed that at his age he pretty well knew himself, but he had learned a few things since finding her, and this was one of them. He enjoyed the teasing, the heightened awareness and the uncertainty about whether anything could come of it. With her, he enjoyed the anticipation as much as he had enjoyed the culmination with other women. He wondered if that would wear off with time, then realized he would never know.

The kindest thing he could do for Amanda Lynn Tierney was clear out of her life, and he couldn't even do that until this matter was settled. His only excuse was a poor one: he had never dreamed that he would bring so much trouble to her castle gate.

"Boy, I'm thirsty," Mandy said suddenly.

The double doors that led to the athletic field were open to the chilly night air, but the gymnasium had grown uncomfortably warm anyway. The floor was crowded with dancers, and it took several minutes for them to reach the bleachers, where Mandy gratefully sat down.

"My feet are killing me," she told Ransom ruefully. "It's probably shameful for a woman to admit it, but I haven't put on a pair of high heels in four years, and these are absolutely killing my feet."

He looked down at those dainty feet in their dainty red shoes with three-inch heels, then raised wickedly sparkling blue eyes. "I can think of a few things that would make those cute little feet feel a whole lot nicer."

Her heart skipped a beat. "I'll just bet you can," she heard herself say. "Are any of them legal?"

A crack of laughter escaped him. "All of them are, but what they lead to may not be. Relax here while I find you something to drink. I'll have Nate's deputies keep an eye on you."

She watched him wend his way around the edge of the dance floor, a broad-shouldered, narrow-hipped man with hair like liquid gold. Her heart skipped another series of beats as she thought about how she had held those hips to hers, how she had kissed and caressed every inch of that magnificent man. She could, she knew, touch him again. If she reached out, he would come to her. If she invited him, he would slide into her bed again and carry her to the mythical places he had showed her once before. He would claim her and make her his. He would sweep her up and carry her away on the whirlwind of his passion.

Oh, yes, and it would be so easy to let him. To ask him. To claim him for her own.

And so dangerous. It would never, never last.

"Is that golden-haired god yours?" asked a bright voice beside her.

Mandy turned, smiling, and found that another woman had joined her on the bench. The woman was blond and absolutely beautiful, Mandy saw, and she felt a twinge of insecurity and jealousy. Suddenly her coach had turned into a pumpkin again. Ransom, she found herself thinking, could never be interested for long in a plain brown mouse when women like this one were interested in him. "He's a friend," she managed to say pleasantly enough.

"Ransom Laird, right?" the blonde inquired, her eyes bright with curiosity.

"Yes." Mandy was tempted to turn away, but she couldn't bring herself to be so rude. There was something about this woman that she instinctively disliked, but she told herself it was merely jealousy that made her feel that way. Somehow, she wasn't quite convinced. "Do I know you? I'm sorry, but I can't place you." Lord, wasn't that catty?

But the blonde didn't take it amiss. "We've never met," she said, still smiling. "I'm visiting my cousin, Bernice Hadley. Do you know the Hadleys?"

"Vaguely," Mandy admitted. Very vaguely. She could recall having met them once.

"That's what Bernice said. You're Mandy Grant, right?"

Mandy nodded cautiously.

"Well, Bernice said she thought you might be sweet on this Laird guy, so I thought I'd better check it out first." Her smile broadened. "I'm not going to be here very long, so there's really no point in wrecking your life. Will I wreck your life if I ask him to dance?"

Mandy opened her mouth to say, "Of course not," but what came out was, "Actually, yes." Color rose to her face, so hot that it felt like a sunburn.

The blonde merely laughed. "Okay. No problem." She rose and started to turn away. "Say, do you know why the deputy at the door gave me such a hard time about who I was?"

Mandy shook her head, though she knew perfectly well why this woman had been required to identify herself. Nate had told his deputies to be on the lookout for strangers. "Maybe he was just curious about a pretty woman."

The blonde laughed. "I'd like to think so. Nice talking to you."

Moments later she had completely vanished into the crowd, and try though she might, Mandy couldn't pick her out again.

"Here you go." Ransom sat beside her and handed her a tall paper cup. "Diet cola. Hope that's okay."

"That's perfect." She knew they were serving beer from a keg in paper cups and was surprised Ransom hadn't gotten himself any. He liked beer, though he rarely drank more than a single can at lunchtime.

Of course, she thought suddenly, and the back of her neck prickled. Of course he wasn't drinking. He was on duty, or whatever you called it when you were an agent who was being hunted. He wouldn't want to cloud his senses or slow his reaction time.

"Damn," she whispered.

He looked at her. "Mandy?"

She shrugged. "Nothing."

"Nothing?" His eyes told her that he knew she was lying. "Ready to dance again?"

Mandy shook her head. "No, my feet still hurt. You go ahead and ask someone else if you want."

"Are you kidding?" His voice suddenly took on a husky note, and she found herself drowning in his eyes. "There are no other women here."

Her breathing speeded up. "There's a blonde. Bernice Hadley's cousin."

"A blonde? What blonde? I don't see any." He was teasing; his eyes never wavered from her face.

"She wanted to know if you belonged to me." Why was she telling him this? But the devil was driving her, she realized. She was a moth determined to soar toward the flame.

"And what did you say?" In the depths of his eyes, a smile was beginning to be born, and it was tugging ever so slightly at the corners of his mouth behind his beard.

Nobody but Mandy would even know he was smiling, but she knew, and it practically deprived her of breath. He was so close! She could smell him, his faint masculine aroma, so rich and musky, the shampoo in his hair and beard.

"I said you were a friend."

He placed his right hand over his heart. "I'm wounded."

The devil drove her on. "Then she asked if it would wreck my life if she asked you to dance."

His eyes sparkled. "And you said?"

"I said it would." As soon as the words were out, she wanted to snatch them back. It was such a bald admission, such a bold thing to say. He had, after all, never told her he wanted anything from her but sex. It might anger him that she had said such a thing. It might frighten him away. Men were notoriously scared of emotional involvement. It ought to scare *her* away.

"Did you?" He leaned closer, and his voice dropped until it was an intimate growl. "What do you say we blow this joint?"

She thought it was a great idea.

Yes, take her out of here, Ransom. Go find a quiet place and make love to her. Love her well. Love her completely. You're not going to get many more chances to love her or anyone else.

For now, old friend, I don't think you take my threats seriously enough. Maybe I need to remind you that I mean business. Yes, that might be a good idea. You're just not afraid enough yet, Ransom. Not nearly afraid enough.

Chapter 11

It was almost eleven when they left the dance. The moon had risen high, and stars spangled the dark sky. The Milky Way was a bright band of stardust, and it was possible to understand why the ancients had named it as they had. There was hardly a night sky anywhere to compare with that of Wyoming, Ransom thought as he helped Mandy into the truck. Only the desert had a better view.

He divided his attention equally between the road and the rearview mirror as they pulled out of town, then relaxed a hair when he saw their tail pick them up. Deputy Beauregard was doing his duty as planned.

Instead of heading straight home, Ransom pulled over in one of the picnic area turnouts that dotted the banks of Conard Creek and parked in the dark shadows beneath a tree. Without further ado he leaned back into the corner and pulled Mandy against him, so that she rested on his chest, her cheek tucked into the hollow of his shoulder.

Minutes passed in silence while he held her and watched out the back window in the direction of the road. Then, as arranged earlier, Deputy Beauregard, driving a pickup indistinguishable from Mandy's, passed up the road. If an ambush lay ahead, Beauregard and the two deputies in the bed of the pickup would flush it out.

For Mandy, who knew nothing about the second truck, it seemed as if Ransom wanted just to hold her and gently rub her shoulder, but presently he started talking in a quiet, thoughtful voice.

"Once upon a time, I was a kid," he said. "Ages and ages ago, before the dawn of civilization. At least, it seems nearly that long ago. It's almost embarrassing to remember how much planning and maneuvering it took to get hold of my dad's pickup for a date, and then to get the date, and then to get the date to agree to pull over someplace. I actually succeeded once."

Mandy smiled into the dark. "Was it worth it?"

"Naw. I didn't know what the hell to do once we parked. I had some ideas about kissing, but I'd never done it before, and I damn near panicked. I made a stab at it. It embarrasses me to remember how inept I was. It was a good thing Polly Perkins didn't have any more experience than I had. She seemed to think it was okay."

Mandy felt the craziest urge to cry a tear or two for the boy he must have been. Why did innocence always have to die?

"Anyhow," he continued, "I was just thinking how funny it is that you don't fully appreciate some things until you're almost too old for them. Like Polly and me sitting in my dad's '63 Chevy pickup, both of us hotter than Roman candles, because of our ages more than anything, and neither of us knowing worth a damn what to do about it." He laughed softly. "I sure hope Polly found somebody with the answers."

Mandy rubbed her cheek against him. "I'm sure she did."

His palm pressed against the side of her neck, warm against her soft skin. "I sure know what to do about it now, princess. And I'm old enough to appreciate that *who* I do it with matters more than what I do."

Her heartbeat grew loud in her ears.

"I'm hotter than a Roman candle for you, Amanda Lynn. I'm hot and hard and aching. I don't think I've been this hot or hard since I was sixteen." He caught her hand and drew it down to his groin.

She didn't resist. She stopped breathing, but she had no desire to resist. He was so frank. So honest about it. How could she be any less? She squeezed him and savored the groan that sounded as if it were torn from him. "Here?" she asked unsteadily. "Now?"

"God, Mandy! No, not here. I want you naked. I want you all over me and all around me. I want to be able to get my hands and mouth on every beautiful inch of you." Catching her chin, he turned her mouth up to his and showed her with his tongue just one of the many things he wanted to do with her.

Panting, desperate for air in a universe that had turned to flame, Mandy wrenched her mouth from his. "Let's go," she demanded breathlessly. Was that desperate-sounding voice really her own? She didn't care, and if anything happened to restore her common sense, she would lose her mind.

Ransom squeezed her so hard her ribs ached, and then he let her go so he could start the truck. Once they were back on the road, he tucked her under his arm and drove with one hand on the wheel, the other softly teasing her right breast. Back and forth his fingers brushed across her beaded nipple, and finally, wanting to give him some of his own medicine, Mandy placed her hand provocatively on his thigh. High on his thigh. She heard him catch his breath, felt his muscles flex and tense beneath her palm.

"Ah, lady, lady," he said raggedly. "You better watch that while I'm driving."

It was worse than ever, Mandy thought hazily. Now that she knew what making love with Ransom was like, she wanted him more than ever. Oh God, what was she going to do when he left? How was she ever going to bear the agony?

Almost as if he sensed the premonition of pain that threatened to shatter her mood, Ransom closed his hand fully over her soft breast and gently squeezed, sending another lance of longing straight to the center of her womanhood.

A soft whimper escaped her, and he heard it with such a sense of satisfaction that it defied description. This woman's hunger was more important to him than his own, her pleasure far more gratifying. Making her want him and satisfying her made him feel more like a man than he had ever felt in his life. He wondered how he could ever have mistaken anything else in his life for passion?

Damn! she made him feel alive. Alive in the way he had previously felt only when he was in mortal danger. Anger tried to rise in him, fury at the unfairness of life. Her past and his past were conspiring to deprive him once again. Damn it all to hell, hadn't he paid enough? Lost enough? Suffered enough?

Almost as soon as the angry thoughts burst through his guard, he clamped down on them. It served no useful purpose to think such things. Nothing changed. Life wasn't fair, a reality he had learned in the killing fields at the age of eighteen. Nor was he a whiner. He hated whiners. The anger sat like a cold lump of lead in his stomach, but he was so used to it by now that he hardly noticed it. He simply wouldn't allow it to control his mind or emotions.

Mandy, unaware of the seething fury in the man beside her, snuggled closer to his side and bit her lower lip when his fingers tightened almost painfully on her breast. Such a narrow line between pain and pleasure, she thought mistily. Maybe you couldn't have one without the other. Maybe there had to be pain so you could have pleasure.

She didn't ask any questions, Ransom noted as they pulled off the county road into her long, rutted driveway. He would have asked a million questions by now, but he was a trained agent. He was suspicious down to the last cell in his body. He would have wanted to know if they wouldn't disturb the trap by coming home. He would have demanded to know who would be guarding the house, who would be watching over their safety.

She asked none of those things, and he thanked heaven she was so trusting. He didn't want to tell her that they were still an integral part of the trap, that Micah was out there waiting for the stalker to make a move against them. That they were deliberately making it look as if Ransom were completely exposed. He was glad she didn't ask, because he didn't know if he could tell her a lie, and he knew in his gut that she wouldn't like the truth.

At the back door, he switched off the ignition, and the night was suddenly both silent and still. For a moment neither of them moved, and then Mandy tilted her head up, looking at him.

In the moon's pale, silvery light, his beard and hair were almost argent. She found herself thinking that he looked like a mythical, magical warrior from one of her stories. So magical that she almost feared touching him. Like a unicorn, he might vanish if the enchantment was disturbed.

He was listening intently, she realized, and his eyes were roving restlessly. Awareness trickled through her, driving back the heated feelings that had kept her distracted all the way here. They were in danger, and he hadn't for one moment forgotten it, even though she had.

"Amanda Lynn," he murmured, looking down at her, "I want to bury myself so deep in you that you won't know where you end and I begin."

Her breath caught and shattered in a puff as desire swamped her in waves of hot and cold that left her lightheaded. And then, like a fall into an icy stream, she heard the unspoken *but* in what he had said. He wanted to, but he wasn't going to. Cold swamped her fevered need, freezing it into something close to anger. Pulling away from him, she found the door handle and pressed it.

"Mandy?"

She refused to stop, refused to listen. How dare he treat her as if she were some kind of plaything, a kitten to be stroked into purring surrender and then set aside because it was inconvenient?

"Mandy!" He was trying to keep his voice down so it wouldn't reach beyond the yard, but she was stalking toward the kitchen door in a way that told him only Armageddon would slow her down. Swearing under his breath, he jumped out of the truck and caught up to her just as she reached the door.

"Wait!"

She couldn't have done anything else. He hauled her up against his side and nearly lifted her feet from the floor.

"Damn it, woman," he growled quietly, "you don't make a move without me tonight. Not a move."

And before he let her go beyond the kitchen, he checked out the entire ground floor of the house.

Later she would never be able to remember how they got upstairs, but suddenly they were there, in her room, swathed in the silver moonlight that poured through the sheers. Ransom cradled her cheeks gently in his rough hands and looked down at her with an expression both tender and wondering, an expression that made her throat ache.

This would be the last time, Mandy realized. Something in the way he was holding her and touching her told her that. Grief rose in her, bringing tears to her eyes. This was what she had feared. This was the loss she had dreaded and tried so hard to avoid, and now she found she wouldn't be able to avoid it after all. He was not to be hers, this warrior who had braved her castle walls and walked past all her defenses. He had made himself a place at the hearth of her heart, but he would not stay. Like a true warrior, he was merely pausing to rest between battles.

"Shh," he whispered as he saw the sparkle of an errant tear on her lash. "Shh..." His lips feathered kisses on her face, taking away tears, smoothing over satin flesh.

"Hold me," she begged. "Oh, please hold me...."

"I'll hold you," he promised. "All the night through I'll hold you, Amanda Lynn. No evil wizards, no malevolent spells, no wickedness, will reach you, I swear. I'll keep you safe through the night." Rash promises, he thought, when he understood that to ensure her well-being he must leave.

Rash promises, she thought tearily. Rash promises. He offered her a night's safety, not understanding that the knowledge of his impending departure brought the malevolence right into the bed between them.

He pulled the pins from her fine brown hair and combed his fingers through it until it settled around her shoulders like a soft cloud. All the while he murmured praise, murmured how she pleased him in every way. The moonlight blurred all the edges, gave an unreal cast to everything, and Ransom hated to draw the curtains. No one could possibly see in, he assured himself with a quick, intent look outside. Not even from the barn roof. Satisfied, he let the curtains be.

Because it was the last time, he undressed her as if it were the first time. Clothes yielded their secrets slowly, a whispering inch at a time, and as each new expanse of skin appeared, he worshiped it with his eyes and his mouth. By the time they stretched out together on her bed, bare skin to bare skin, Mandy was wrapped in a glowing, hazy languor. The dreamlike quality persisted as he trailed kisses over her breasts and thighs, as he touched and stroked and licked her to a fever. And then he brought her to culmination with the gentle, erotic stroking of his fingers. He gave, but he did not take, because he could not afford to lower his guard that much.

Afterward, because he would not take from her, she wept hurt tears, tears of impending grief, tears of unutterable loss. He cradled her tenderly and kissed her damp cheeks, then tightened his jaw against his own pain at having to deny her.

A sound woke Ransom while it was still dark. He roused from sleep with an image in his mind of something heavy falling, and for some reason was convinced that the sound had come from the far side of the barn, in the corral.

Mandy was curled up against him, and he covered her mouth gently with his, rousing her to full awareness without giving her the opportunity to make a betraying sound.

"I heard something from the barn," he whispered when she was fully awake. "I'm going to investigate. You get dressed and stay right here. Promise me you'll stay right here."

The last thing she wanted to do was wait here in the dark all by herself, wondering if Ransom was all right, but she realized that he needed her to make that promise. He would be unable to leave her to investigate unless he was sure she would be safe. In his place, she would want the same thing.

"I promise."

He dressed swiftly in the dark and was creeping from the bedroom before Mandy had even managed to find a pair of jeans. He wished he could be sure she would stay put. It wasn't that he thought anyone would want to harm her, but if she got in the way... If she made an easier target and they thought they could get to him through her...

Hell!

The moon had moved to the west and was hovering high over the mountains, but its light was still bright enough to see what needed seeing. Aware that quick, sudden movements were more apt to attract a watcher's attention, he slipped fluidly and slowly toward the corral, keeping as much as possible to the shadows.

It was cold, he thought with a small portion of his mind. They must have had the first frost, or at least come close to it. Irrelevant bits of information like that kept intruding into his mind, along with the bits that he was interested in, the bits that mattered. He could smell horses, hay, sage, grass, even a whiff of Mandy's marigolds, but he couldn't smell another man. Americans tended to have a distinctly sour odor as a result of the amount of meat they consumed, but there was no such subtle clue in the air, nor could he detect other bodily odors that would betray a watcher's presence.

Ergo, there was no one in the stable yard.

Uneasiness settled across his shoulders like a mantle. He had heard something. He had been in dangerous positions like this too often to believe that he had misinterpreted something in his dream for reality. No, he knew the difference. A sound had awakened him. A real sound.

So he must have misinterpreted the direction from which it came. Turning, he looked back toward the house. Nothing appeared to be amiss there. Besides, he couldn't believe that if he had really heard a noise from the vicinity of the house he would have interpreted it as coming from the corral. He might be rusty, but not that rusty.

No, he thought, looking at the barn, the sound had definitely come from somewhere around here. An owl, perhaps, that had miscalculated and bumped into something? Or maybe some small animal, a raccoon or even a rat.

Somehow he wasn't buying that, either. Each idea he tested didn't feel right, and he knew better than to doubt his instincts.

Every sense straining, he eased around the end of the barn. The horses were quiet, dozing undisturbed. Surely they would have been just a little uneasy if someone were prowling about? Not wanting to disturb them himself, because the noise they would make would cover the sounds he needed to hear, he eased back around the corner and decided to investigate the other end of the barnyard.

Ten minutes later he had explored all the way around the barn and found nothing. Just as he was ready to throw his hands up and conclude that he'd imagined the sound after all, something slammed with a deafening clang into the steel rain barrel not six feet away from him. Whirling, he saw water spewing from two sides of the barrel.

He needed no more than that. In an instant he was facedown on the ground and praying like mad that Mandy wouldn't venture out to see what was going on. Then, with the icy calm that had saved his neck more than once, he considered what he now knew: some kind of projectile, most likely a bullet, had passed through both sides of that steel barrel as well as through the water it held. He had failed to hear the telltale report of a gun, or even the soft pop of a silencer. Heavy caliber, no sound.

That meant sniper fire from a great distance, at least a half mile, possibly a full mile. That kind of distance told a tale. Crawling across the hard-packed ground on his belly, he got close enough to the barrel to see the size of the entry and exit holes. A .50 caliber round, he would bet, with a steel jacket. He was also willing to bet the rifle was a Haskins M500, a custom-made beauty that was a favorite of the

Special Forces. It was not a weapon just any Tom, Dick or Harry could get his hands on.

He had a burning desire just then to call his agency and see what they would do with that little bit of information. It was bound to interest the hell out of them, and they might even be grateful enough to let some information slip to Ransom, information such as who might be in this area that he should know about. Unfortunately, he wasn't sure who he could trust. Maybe Mark ...

But what interested him more at this point was his enemy's distance. At such a distance, Ransom was safe from anything except another .50 caliber slug fired from that rifle. He had a feeling that bullet hadn't missed him by chance. People who knew how to handle sniper rifles were seldom poor shots, and when all was said and done, that was a wide miss for a sniper.

Somebody was evidently still toying with him. Unleashing an infuriated growl, he began to crawl back toward the house. Mandy was probably out of her mind worrying, and he guessed it was time to bring out some of the arsenal Nate had managed to round up for him. Ransom suspected that Nate's contribution was one of those things the sheriff would prefer not to have anyone know about, so how was he going to explain things to Mandy? Things like a Heckler & Koch MP5K submachine gun, a sweet little number that could easily be hidden under a jacket. Maybe, this once, Mandy was going to have to settle for "None of your business."

He decided not to test his theory that the round had missed him on purpose. Instead he belly-crawled the entire way to the porch, then hunched over as he climbed the steps.

Inside, he straightened and stood at the door overlooking the yard. The sniper couldn't see him there, and he waited a few minutes to see if there would be another shot. He wondered if Micah and the other deputies had gotten wind of any of this and thought it unlikely. The four deputies were scattered to the points of the compass, stationed a couple of hundred yards away from the house and hidden in the terrain, but even so, the sniper was probably so far away that the deputies hadn't detected a thing. Sighing again, wondering what the hell he was going to do now, he locked the door and headed back upstairs.

This was frustrating as hell. Intolerable. This cat and mouse game could go on forever at this rate, and he didn't think his or Mandy's nerves could handle it. There had to be some means of smoking this character out. Maybe he ought to take Mandy away from here. Maybe if they could get this character to follow them, they could get wind of him.

Halfway up the stairs, he hesitated, then turned around, heading back down to the phone in the kitchen. There he dialed an old friend at home.

"Mark? This is King.... Yeah, I know, but I need something, and I figured you might want to trade. Just a small trade." He paused, listening, and then gave a soft laugh. "Well, how's a Haskins M500 with a .50 caliber round strike you?... Just now. Missed me by about six feet, which doesn't make me feel any better." Again he listened. "I know how rare they are. What I want to know is who out here might have one." He laughed. "Yeah, I know it's not much. How soon? Forty minutes? I'll be at this number." He rattled off Mandy's phone number. "Thanks."

He still had a few friends, he thought as he headed back up the stairs. There were still a few people willing to help him under the table.

He stepped into the bedroom, reassuring words already rising to his lips, and looked around.

Mandy was gone.

Micah was stationed in a stand of sage three hundred meters from the barn, about halfway to the county road. Stationed at similar intervals all around the Grant house and barn were three other deputies, all volunteers, all ready to do whatever was necessary to help John Grant's widow.

Mandy, Micah had realized sometime back, was something of a personage in this underpopulated county that, up until John Grant, hadn't lost a law officer in the line of duty since the big flood in '47. John Grant had been well-loved, his loss deeply mourned, and all those feelings had somehow focused on his widow. Consequently, three deputies were giving up an entire night's sleep to watch over her.

Micah was here for Ransom. Ransom had rescued him from a hole in the ground after he had been captured and badly beaten by the Vietcong, then carried him over his back to safety, some forty-five miles through enemy territory. Micah didn't forget even little favors, and often figured he owed Ransom more than life would ever give him a chance to repay.

He heard a clang from the barnyard, clear in the cold night air, and instantly slipped from a state of open awareness to an intense alertness that brought every sound, every shadow, every movement, into crystal clarity.

Minutes dragged by in unbroken silence, and gradually he began to relax into the state of open awareness again, a state where he stilled and listened, simply letting everything wash through him until something caught his attention. A horse had probably bumped up against something. A million things could have made that sound, and he saw nothing suspicious.

And then, close to twenty minutes later, he heard a shout, the sound of a man in mortal pain. He stiffened, thinking it sounded like a bobcat, but not quite. Not quite. He began to creep toward the house, wondering if he would hear it again.

Instead, less than a minute later, he heard a single rifle report on the still, cold air. It was the signal that the trap had been sprung.

Micah found Ransom in the yard, pacing like a caged tiger, rifle in hand. As soon as he saw Micah, Ransom halted and looked at him.

"They got Mandy."

"Well, hell!" Disgusted, Micah looked around and made out Tom Watson and Ed Dewhurst coming in from their posts. That left Charlie Huskins, who had been watching the northwest side of the property, the most rugged terrain. It might take him a few minutes longer to show up.

"I didn't hear or see a damn thing, Micah," Ransom was saying tautly. "I heard something and came out to investigate it. When I'd just about given up, somebody took a potshot at me with a .50 caliber round." He pointed at the rain barrel.

"Hell, I heard the impact of the bullet, but I sure didn't hear a shot." Micah looked at the other two deputies, who also shook their heads. "So the sniper was quite a ways away. Maybe 800 meters or more."

Ransom nodded. "Must've been, if none of you heard anything. Anyhow, they were successful in distracting me. I figure I was away from Mandy for thirty minutes, and I never heard a thing. I should've heard something." He closed his eyes for a moment. "There must be at least two of them. One to fire the rifle from a distance while the other kidnapped Mandy."

"Well, hell," Micah said again.

"I figure they knocked her out," Ransom said. "I smelled something like ether in the bedroom."

"That makes sense, considering you didn't hear anything. Damn it, where's Charlie? He oughta be here. Ed, you know where he's at?"

"Yeah. I'll go check it out, Micah."

"No, wait." Ransom grabbed Ed Dewhurst's arm. "Where was Charlie stationed?"

Micah pointed away to the northwest.

"That's the direction the sniper fire came from," Ransom told him. Little by little, he was piecing things together. Throwing his head back, he stared off toward the northwest, his nostrils flaring like a predator catching wind of its prey. Internally, he was calm. Too calm. It was the calm of a man who knew that everything depended on his ability not to feel anything at all.

"Okay," he said after a moment. "I think it's a foregone conclusion that they want me, not Mandy. Taking her like this is obviously an attempt to draw me out, to get me to come after them. They want to use her against me." He didn't want to think about how. "And that means they're not going to try to make a clean getaway. They want me to find them. Just me."

He looked at Micah. "You do whatever you have to do as a lawman, but you give me a clear field, Micah."

Micah returned the look steadily. "They won't leave the county."

"Fine. I'm going after them. You just keep clear."

"We got a little problem, man. I realize you can't track these bastards until there's enough light, but I can't wait that long to go after Charlie."

Ransom didn't even hesitate. He knew perfectly well that if he and Micah went looking for Charlie Huskins before sunrise, they might mess up tracks that would lead them to Mandy, but he also knew Charlie's life might well depend on immediate medical help. He also knew that if they messed up, whoever had taken Mandy would find a way to leave another trail.

"We'll find Charlie together, Micah."

Micah nodded. "Tom, you go call Nate and tell him what's going down. Me and Ransom here are going for a little hike."

Ransom stopped Tom. "I'm expecting a phone call from a guy called Mark. He'll ask for King. When he does, just say one word—castled."

"Castled?"

"Right. Then he'll give you some information. Probably just a name. Write it down. It may be the name of our kidnapper." Turning, he looked at Micah.

Micah nodded, and without another word the two of them headed out, rifles in hand, to discover what had happened to Charlie Huskins.

Some things were never forgotten, and it sometimes amazed Ransom how fast he could slip back into the habits of the hunter. In an instant it all felt perfectly familiar and natural, and it happened more easily than changing clothes.

Micah was a slightly better tracker and he knew where Charlie was supposed to be, so he led. The ground near the buildings was hard, the vegetation sparse from lack of water. There would be few signs here to guide them.

Bringing up the rear, Ransom took the job of protecting them both while Micah's attention was completely focused on looking for signs. In his hands he held a simple deer rifle, but under his jacket, tucked beneath his arm, was the MP5K submachine gun. Just over twelve inches in length, it was completely hidden. He hoped that when he encountered the kidnappers they would assume his only weapon was the rifle. Certainly they would have no reason to imagine he carried the so-called "room broom" under his arm. Law-abiding citizens didn't have such weapons.

In this direction the terrain roughened rapidly into rocky outcroppings and began to ascend, an early precursor of the mountains to the west. The light was getting worse by the minute, too, as the moon settled in the west and only the very first pale tendrils of dawn stretched over the eastern horizon. It was actually darker now than it had been all night. Depth and perspective were lost. Everything became flat and colorless. If Micah hadn't already had some idea where Charlie should be, there would have been no point in continuing until sunrise. But Micah knew, and he kept moving forward slowly, very slowly, studying every blade of grass and smear of dirt that he could see.

Suddenly Micah held out a hand and squatted. Ransom immediately scanned the area, looking for any sign of danger. When he saw none, he moved closer to Micah.

Low-voiced, he asked, "What is it?"

Micah touched the ground and raised a finger to his nose, sniffing. "Blood."

At once Ransom scanned the area, looking for signs of a scuffle, signs of what might have happened to Charlie. "There," he said suddenly to Micah. "To the left. I'll go."

"No, you cover me. Charlie'll know me. He might not recognize you if he's hurt."

He was hurt all right, Ransom thought as he shadowed Micah. The further they moved into the cleft between two outcroppings, the stronger the smell of blood became. He knew what they were going to find even before Micah swore an oath that Ransom had never heard him use, even under the worst conditions.

"Micah?"

"He's alive. Damn it, Ransom, he's still alive. I can't believe . . ."

Ransom scanned the area, reluctant to take his attention from the clefts and heights that could hide attackers. "Do you need help?"

"No, just keep watching my back. There's only one wound, and the bleeding's pretty much stopped."

Pivoting slowly, Ransom kept watch and tried not to let his fears for Mandy surface. Charlie's injury was a confirmation, a statement that these folks, whoever they were, were willing to kill to achieve their ends. The cat and mouse game was over. Now came the hurting and maybe the killing. Son of a bitch!

Hard, harder than he'd ever had to in his entire life, he clamped down on his feelings. He had never, ever, feared for himself the way he feared for Mandy. Lurking just beyond the barriers that he placed between himself and his feelings was a chaos of pain and fear that would craze him if he let it through. He couldn't afford to let that happen. He couldn't afford to let anything affect the clarity of his mind or the objectivity of his thinking. Drawing a deep breath, he squeezed his eyes shut for a second. Just a second.

"Ransom."

He looked over at Micah. The sky was beginning to lighten at last. In another few minutes the hunt would begin in earnest. "Yeah."

"I've got to carry Charlie back. You go on. I can manage."

Ransom nodded. "First I want you out of this gorge. It's too good a place for an ambush."

He helped steady Micah as the deputy pulled Charlie over his shoulders and straightened to his feet. "Let's go," Micah said.

Ransom grabbed Micah's rifle from the ground and followed him out of the cleft. Only when they reached open ground did he halt. Micah stopped, too, turning to look at him. On his shoulders, Charlie groaned.

"I won't be far behind you," Micah said.

"Don't. Don't follow me. I don't want these people desperate or cornered."

Micah shook his head. "Hey, it's me you're talking to, man. You know better. They'll never know I'm behind you, and now that I'm heading back with Charlie, they'll probably never even look."

"Micah—"

"Forget it, Ransom. You know Nate and me better than that." Shifting Charlie's weight a little, Micah headed back toward the house. In the distance, Ransom could see the dusty beige of Nate's Blazer pulling up at the house, and behind it there was an ambulance.

The eastern sky was pink now. Turning his back on the distant house, Ransom looked up at the rocky terrain.

It was time.

Chapter 12

Several times Mandy had started to rouse, aware that something was terribly wrong, and then a sweet smelling rag was clamped over her mouth, sending her back to a dreamless sleep. Somewhere in a dark tunnel that trapped her, she vomited while a voice cursed savagely and something clamped her head; then she sank again into the smothering black velvet.

She heard a bird. It was nearby, bright, cheerful. Hearing it, she felt reassured and let herself drift away again, this time without the aid of the rag.

What finally dredged her back to the world were thirst and cold. Blinking, she looked up into the bright blue Wyoming sky. Early morning, she thought groggily, maybe nine or ten. What was she doing outside? Sighing, she tried to turn over into a more comfortable position and realized that she couldn't move. Not a muscle.

Panic brought her fully awake, and she lifted her head, trying to see what was wrong. She was tied up. She was spread-eagled on a rock and tied hand and foot like some kind of offering.

Like a goat set out to attract a lion.

Like bait for a trap.

And no matter where she looked, there wasn't another soul in sight. She would never even know who had done this to her, or what they meant to do to Ransom when he came for her.

Because he would come for her. He was that kind of man, and it didn't matter one whit whether he cared for her or not. Even if she were a total stranger, he would still come for her, because he was one of those damn-fool decent men who would risk everything for a principle. An unbearable pressure gripped her chest as she tried to deny the coming horror.

Oh, God, there had to be something she could do! Nausea welled in her stomach, the aftereffect of whatever drug they had given her. She closed her eyes and tried to calm herself by taking slow, deep breaths. If she vomited while lying on her back like this, she would probably choke. By forcing herself to keep breathing slowly and regularly, she gradually regained her self-control.

And then she cried. There just wasn't any way to stop the tears. They came hot and hard, running down the sides of her head from the corners of her eyes, but not once did she sob aloud. She would not give her captors that satisfaction.

And she struggled. She struggled past the point of reason, hoping she could loosen even one bond. She tugged and pulled at her bindings until her ankles and wrists were raw and sore, and still she pulled, because a single seductive hope kept rearing its head—maybe if she pulled just one more time. Maybe if she yanked just one more time. Maybe with just one more tug she would find freedom. And each time she told herself to stop, that it was obviously hopeless, the hope crept back into her mind until it nagged her into tugging just one more time. Because maybe that one more time would do the trick.

Minutes dragged by, uncounted and countless. Time lost meaning in her endless, unending misery. Whether she wanted to or not, she had time to think about some things, and in the process she made a couple of discoveries that surprised her. She was astonished to discover just how much she loved life, just how much she wanted to live. And she was totally confounded to realize that however much life meant to her, Ransom's life meant even more.

A whole lot more.

Not that he would care, she thought unhappily. If there had ever been even a remote chance that he could come to care for her, she had surely destroyed it with her on-again-off-again craziness.

It suddenly seemed like a good time to make a few resolutions. After all, she would probably be dead before the day was over. This might be her last opportunity ever to promise herself that she would be stronger and braver. It was hard at the moment to try to promise herself that she would try living rather than hiding, because if she could have hidden at the moment, she would have done so in a heartbeat. But she promised herself anyway. If she survived this, she would take a few chances. She would be less of a mouse. She would make love to Ransom until he begged for mercy and then she'd ...

Oh, hell, she thought as another flood of hot tears blinded her. Who was she kidding? She was never going to get out of this alive. If only there was some way to keep Ransom from sticking his head into the noose along with her!

Ransom moved over the rocky terrain slowly, scanning the area constantly for any sign that could guide him. The past few years seemed to have vanished. He had slipped easily into the intense, single-minded awareness and concentration necessary to the task. He had sunk with hardly a thought into the mind-set of the hunter. Each step he took, he took with thought and deliberation, well aware that he was not only the hunter, but the hunted, as well. A trap lay ahead for him, a trap in which Mandy was also caught. One careless move could be the end for both of them.

Fury carried him tirelessly forward. Some corner of his mind noted that he was in a killing rage, something he had rarely felt. He was not a vengeful man by nature. Vengeance had always struck him as a wasted effort, because it solved nothing. It certainly didn't erase whatever had already happened.

That was just as true now as it had ever been, but now he thirsted for vengeance. He lusted after it. They had taken Mandy. They had scared her and possibly hurt her, and they very likely intended to kill her after they killed him. This time he wanted vengeance. This time, by hell, he would take it.

The enemy had chosen their ground well. This corner of Mandy's ranch was rugged and grew more rugged with each passing yard. Frequent outcroppings made tracking next to impossible. Vegetation was sparse, making it difficult to find signs. With little more than occasional broken blades of grass to guide him, he had to move slowly, and his slowness was to the advantage of the enemy. It also made Ransom even madder with every step, because every minute was another minute of suffering and terror for Mandy.

The thought of what she might be enduring at this very moment clamped around him like a burning vise, squeezing all the anger in the world into a hard knot in Ransom's gut, a knot so hard that it hurt. A knot so small that it became a black hole, sucking everything into it. He could almost hear the whipping, whistling wind in the empty corridors of his mind as anger consumed everything else and left him empty of everything save blood lust.

Once again he saw signs of disturbed ground, and he bent, measuring out a new direction and the passage of time. Before he straightened, he left a signal of his own. Behind him, in the endless trail back to the ranch, were markers that only Micah and Nate would recognize, each one an invisible signpost.

They would come. He never doubted it. He had to trust them to leave him free to act as necessary, trust them to pick up on clues as to his intentions, trust them to be a help, not a hindrance. He couldn't think of two men on earth he would trust more, but Nate was far removed from the realities of this kind of operation, and Micah—well, Micah had been in the Special Forces group in the army until his retirement. At the very least, he was fresher than Nate. But however in or out of practice they were, he had to trust their minds. He had to trust the instinctive understanding that had once been so much a part of them in Southeast Asia. There had been times when he could have sworn that he, Nate and Micah were one mind in three bodies. He spared a hope that that hadn't completely changed.

Pausing, Ransom straightened and looked upward over the rough slope he had been steadily climbing. Turning his head a little, he saw a path through the scrubby pines that clustered ahead of him, leading to the top of the hill he had been climbing for the last several hours. And suddenly he saw the trap.

Hunkering down, he stared up at the bald top of the hill and considered. In his gut he knew Mandy was up there and her captors were waiting for him. Right up there.

All he had to do was figure out how to ransom her. How to exchange himself for her. Otherwise, she would be dead right alongside him.

Motionless, as if carved from stone, he stared upward and pondered. There had to be a way. There was *always* a way.

The path was obvious before him, deceptively clear of obstacles. It was almost as if the forest had opened up for him, like the parting of the Red Sea. The last time he had seen a path like that had been the day he walked away from the prison camp.

And suddenly he was there again. The crisp Wyoming autumn day and pines gave way to steaming heat and thick jungle growth. The path had been before him then, too. Clear. Unobstructed. He had looked at it and realized it had been there all along. This time there had been a difference.

The difference had been inside him. Before, he had always nurtured a flicker of hope. Before, there had been a spark in him that had wanted to live. Whatever degradation he suffered, whatever dehumanizing torture and humiliation, there had been a part of him, just a small, stubborn flame, that refused to quit. That morning the flame had died. That morning there had been one blow too many. One curse too many. One humiliation too many. He had ceased to care. Death offered his only hope.

So he had looked down that path and taken it, expecting to die.

And now he looked down another path, and once again he ceased to care. Death would be a welcome solution to an awful lot of his problems, and fear of it would not hold him back. If anything happened to Mandy, though, he would cut his own throat without a moment's regret. How could he possibly care what awaited him along that path if walking down it might help Mandy? He had seen the worst. There wasn't a thing anyone could do to him that hadn't been done before. There wasn't a pain or a wound or an abuse he didn't know. There was nothing on God's earth left to frighten him.

Except what might happen to Mandy.

It was that possibility that held him still, that launched his mind into a whirlwind of calculations. Before he could move, he needed to convince himself that he had considered every probability, every potentiality. For himself he would have plunged ahead and trusted his instincts and experience to carry him through whatever was waiting. For himself, he didn't care. For Mandy, he cared more than he had ever cared for anything in his life.

So he would go up there and try to exchange himself for her, and he thought he knew an argument that might be persuasive. Even so, he would be up there, and while he tried to keep the enemy busy talking, he would be able to evaluate the situation, locate the people involved so he could eliminate them, and try to get Mandy free. And then, if he survived, he would face the fact that he was the kind of crud who could bring this sort of trouble to her gates.

Once he had held high ideals; Mandy had come closer than she probably guessed when she likened him to a knight. But then, Mandy saw more than she ever let on. She saw past the webs of illusion to the realities behind, and that was probably why she was so terrified of her own vulnerability. Other people sailed through their days viewing everything through the distorted mirrors of their minds, believing with blind faith that everything was going to be okay and refusing to consider that it all ended in the grave eventually, anyway. Mandy knew better. She knew that the piper always had to be paid. She knew that caring meant loss, and loving meant pain, and that each day was a maze of potential cruelties and suffering.

Could he really blame her for keeping her drawbridges up? Could he condemn her because she saw the truth and avoided the rain and the storms, the floods and disasters? That would be like saying she was crazy because she refused to build her house on the San Andreas Fault. No, he couldn't condemn her, and that was why he was going to get the hell out of her life just as soon as he gave her life back to her.

It was ironic, though, that this woman who refused life had brought him back to life. Because he had been dead for a long time. He realized it only in his resurrection, understood that somewhere along the way his ideals had passed away, his ability to care had atrophied, and that even in his joy at the prospect of fatherhood he had been little more than a zombie, a living dead man. His decay had all been internal, and he had been careful not to let it show. To all the world he appeared to be the Ransom Laird he had always been. He had thought of his return from captivity as Lazarus rising from the dead, but now he knew better. He had been resurrected in Mandy's care, and only because of Mandy.

He swallowed hard as he squatted in the rapidly warming morning light, staring up at the path to life or death, heaven or hell, and he remembered. He remembered how she had taken his shirt from his back and smoothed her palms like healing balm over the ridges of scar tissue. He remembered how his throat had tightened then, too, and how his awakening in those moments had been one of the most painful experiences in his life. He hadn't wanted to feel, but she had made him feel, and it was just like being born. Agonizing.

And losing her would be death, eternity in hell, a cold bleakness forever without end. Amen.

He didn't dare close his eyes now, hardly dared blink, and he couldn't breathe around the lump in his throat. He wanted to scream from the pain of impending loss, but he was the hunter and the hunted, and the hunt was drawing to its inevitable close. Cradling the deer rifle almost casually in one arm, he straightened and stared at the top of the hill.

They were up there, and so was Mandy. He could feel her like a tug under his breastbone, an ache in his heart, a fire in his soul. How could he have been so smug, thinking she needed to understand that you couldn't have pleasure without pain? How could he have thought he knew some mystical secret of life that she failed to perceive?

Damn, she had *known.* She had felt this pain in her chest, this ache in her heart, this fire in her soul, and she had lost John Grant, a loss so great that Ransom was only just now beginning to really understand how she had suffered. Because this was the first time in his life that he had ever loved another person more than himself. He had judged Mandy Grant from ignorance, and he would have squirmed with shame if he hadn't been hurting with the same awful depth that had taught him his lesson. *This,* then, was the price of caring. She had *known.* He had not.

Now that he understood, he knew he would never, ever, ask her to face this pain again.

Never.

A yellow deerfly, growing energetic in the morning warmth, landed on Mandy's nose. Frantically she wiggled her head, trying to shake the fly away, but the huge, ugly thing clung stubbornly. Sticking out her lower lip, she blew a sharp puff of air upward, and the fly moved on.

Not far, though. This time it settled on her hand, and this time it bit. She jerked at the sharp, stinging bite and wondered almost hysterically if she was going to live long enough to watch her hand swell to twice its normal size. Long enough to cuss because she wouldn't be able to type until the allergic reaction passed.

Long enough. Suddenly there wasn't long enough in the entire universe, in all of eternity. Suddenly she wanted to weep, not for what might never be, but for all she had never let come to be. For all the squandered days and nights, for all the ignored opportunities, for all the friendships never formed, for all the love never shared.

For all the *waste.*

And that was what her entire life had been, she thought desperately now, as her throat ached and a huge weight of grief settled on her chest. She had let reality slip through her fingers in favor of the safety of her dreams and fantasies. Except for the too-brief time with John, she had given nothing of herself to anyone, and that was all that mattered, wasn't it? In the end, an end such as she had come to, when there were no more opportunities of any kind, all that mattered was what she had given, and she had given next to nothing.

She had taken little and given nothing, and nothing, absolutely nothing, had been made better because she had existed.

Lord, she couldn't even lie here and think over all the things she had done, because she had done so little. She might as well never have lived, and that was a hell of a sorry epitaph. Damn, it wasn't even as if she had written a great novel that would move men to tears and laughter in centuries to come. No, she hadn't even achieved that, though she had always longed to. She had just never had the guts to put herself on the line that way—to risk the rejection of something so personal, so much a part of her inner self.

And if... And if she could have just one more chance to do something, to give something, it would be to tell Ransom that she loved him. She had loved him from the moment he had held her beneath the cottonwood and shared her grief. Maybe even from the moment he had tramped up her driveway, appearing like some disreputable golden god. Why had she refused to face it? Why had she run from what had already happened? Damn, couldn't she even face up to what *was?*

Overhead a hawk circled lazily, a black speck in a flawless blue sky, a symbol of utter freedom. Not that she was suited to freedom, she thought sadly as she swallowed more tears. She might as well have spent her life in prison for all the good she had made of her opportunities and freedom.

If... What a vain word. But *if* she could have another chance, she would reach for it all. No matter how frightened she grew, no matter how her knees knocked or her heart quailed, she would risk it. She would love with every ounce of feeling she was capable of. She would give herself, her caring, her time, her concern, to anyone willing to accept it. Maybe... maybe she would even try again to have a child. That thought really made her heart quail. John's death had brought her to her knees, but Mary's loss had filled her with mortal anguish. It was as if she had lost John a second time, and even more completely and totally. With Mary's loss, she had known herself to be truly alone.

A blackbird squawked from a nearby tree, a sound that, at some subliminal level, she recognized as a territorial warning. She was not alone in these woods or on this hilltop. Someone had disturbed that bird. Ransom? Her heart thudded sharply and then began a rapid, heavy pounding. The waiting was almost over. Even the air seemed expectant.

Micah had long since disappeared into the rugged terrain, but Nate had remained behind. They had both agreed that Nate was too far out of practice and might be a hindrance. So Nate stayed at the house, practically sitting on top of the radio like a hen sitting on her egg, waiting for Micah's call. Around him hovered all of his off-duty deputies and a couple of the on-duty ones, as well. Conard County was a little low on routine law enforcement this morning, but he was damned if he cared. If the voters wanted to get cranky about it, Nate was willing to return to full-time ranching. Hell, he was getting too old for this kind of excitement, anyway. His two best friends in the world were up in those hills somewhere, along with a woman who meant as much to him as any of his daughters, and he'd never felt so damn helpless in all his days.

Glancing around at his men, good men to the last, he wondered vaguely if Micah and Mandy realized how many friends they both had in this county. They were both outsiders, yet both had managed to become an integral part of the fabric of Conard County. Damn it, nothing better happen to them, or Ransom, either. Ransom was another one who would probably fit in around here like a long-lost son, if only he would settle down long enough. Nate swore again, savagely, and a couple of his deputies smothered reluctant smiles.

He wished he had some idea what Ransom was up against. From what Micah had told him, there had to be at least two people out there, one to shoot the sniper rifle and one to kidnap Mandy. That was a minimum, but he doubted there were any more than that. As much as somebody evidently hated Ransom, it didn't seem likely that they would bring half an army to deal with him. No, one person and an accomplice would be about all anybody would want on an operation like this.

But two could be enough. Enough to deal with Ransom if Micah didn't get there in time. Certainly enough to have already hurt Mandy. That thought kept zinging him like a bee's stinger. What if she was already dead? They only needed the possibility that she might be alive to draw Ransom out. They didn't need to *keep* her alive.

He muttered another curse and wished he knew something about whoever was out there. Ransom's friend had called back, but his information had been next to useless, for Nate anyway. Who the hell was *Mantis,* anyhow? The name might tell Ransom something, but to Nate it was meaningless. The guy on the other end of the phone had evidently dragged some information out of Tom, though. Damn, he would have to teach that boy not to spill his guts to everybody who asked. But Tom had told the caller about Mandy's abduction, about Charlie being wounded, about Ransom going off into the hills with nothing but a deer rifle, and Micah going off after him. Hell, what if the caller wasn't a friend? What if Tom had spilled all that stuff to an enemy of Ransom's?

Nate swore yet again and hunted through his glove box for antacids. Too damn old for this, yes sir.

Well, thank God for small favors, he thought suddenly as he heard the familiar sound of a helicopter. He'd sent for the chopper at first light, but there had been some mechanical problem or other. That chopper was the pride of the Conard County Sheriff's Department, a big old army Huey they had refurbished for rescue missions. Aboard her were two of the best emergency medical technicians in the state, and some of the best life-saving equipment made.

The chopper sounded just the same now as its brothers had twenty years ago, Nate thought as he watched the dust-colored chopper settle into the yard. They had called them Dustoffs back then in Nam, the medevac choppers. The sound of those rotors still sent chills dancing along his spine. God, he prayed suddenly, don't let us need the EMTs. Don't let anyone else get hurt.

When the hammering engines were turned off, the side door on the helicopter rolled back, not to disgorge the familiar technicians, but to allow six total strangers to disembark.

"What the hell is going on here?" Nate demanded as two men in dark suits and four men in camouflage approached him. "Where are my paramedics?"

"Sheriff Tate?" said one of the suited men, a tall, thin type with expressionless eyes. "I'm Special Agent Wade Gentry, Central Intelligence Operations. I understand you've got a situation here involving one of our agents."

"Involving *three* of my *friends*," Nate growled. "One of them *used* to be one of your agents, which hasn't seemed to interest anybody very much of late."

Something flickered in Gentry's dark eyes. "It never stopped interesting some of us," he said after a moment. "They've finally untied our hands."

Seconds ticked by in silence before Nate relented with a nod. "Okay. So how did you find out what's going on?"

"A man named Mark, a mutual friend of mine and Ransom," Gentry said. "He phoned me this morning to tell me about a curious call he'd had from Ransom and what he'd learned from one of your deputies."

Nate rubbed his chin. "That was an awful fast flight from D.C."

"I've been in Casper all along, just waiting for the go-ahead. I've been sitting on my hands waiting for the word ever since the windshield in Mrs. Grant's truck was shot out."

Nate stuck his chin out. "Why do I find that hard to believe?"

Gentry shrugged. "Probably because the agency left Ransom thinking nobody gave a damn. But they couldn't promise him assistance until they were sure they could provide it, and they weren't sure. We're not authorized to act within the country, Sheriff. I think you know that."

"I do. So what the hell are you doing here now?"

"There's a little mess we need to clean up. A certain double agent. We've gotten permission. Finally."

"This double agent wouldn't be somebody code-named Mantis, would he?"

Gentry was silent for a moment. "I guess Mark told you that. And I guess he didn't tell you who Mantis is."

"I'm dying to find out."

Gentry sighed. "I'm afraid I can't tell you, Sheriff."

Nate considered several possible reactions to that, most of them enough to get him arrested.

Then Gentry spoke again. "The praying mantis has an interesting peculiarity, Sheriff."

"Yeah?"

"As soon as she's impregnated, the female devours her mate."

Hell, Nate thought, fury twisting through him like a cyclone. Hell. If only there was some way to warn Ransom! "Just what are you planning to do with all this muscle you brought along, Gentry? If you think I'm going to let you go up there and mess things up, you've got another think coming. Ransom was pretty definite about nobody following him."

"I believe one of your deputies went after him," Gentry observed.

Nate sighed and damned Tom yet again. "Micah Parish. He's an exception to a lot of rules. Army Special Operations and a good friend of Ransom. And Ransom didn't even want him. I don't know anything about you, Gentry, or about these guys with you, so don't think I'm going to let you go stomping around out there and possibly cause more trouble. If you doubt me, consider this, I didn't go myself."

Again Gentry was silent for a while. His dark eyes seemed to take Nate's measure, and then they moved to the rugged terrain behind the house. "How long have they been out there, Tate? Four hours? Don't you think by now it's too late to change things? By now he must have found her."

"Maybe."

"And if he has, Mantis is pretty occupied right now."

"Mantis has help. At least one other person, maybe more."

Gentry shook his head. "Just one other person. Mantis prefers working alone."

"Well, thank God for that," Nate said gruffly. "Ransom and Micah won't have any trouble dealing with that. I just hope to God Mandy's okay."

He stared up at the rough, rocky hills and came to a decision. Ransom probably *had* located Mandy by now. "I guess you're right, Gentry. We can't do much to make it worse, not now. Let's go."

It was a little like walking down a tunnel, Ransom thought absently as he climbed toward the hill's bald peak. The rocky shoulder was almost completely free of growth, except for the occasional hardy bush that grew in the dirt the wind had blown into the rocky cracks. On either side rose the tall, proud cones of elderly pines, giving the sense of walls, though they were hardly impenetrable.

It went against his grain to approach so openly like this, but they were waiting for him, and there was no way he could approach that peak completely undetected. No, they would be sure that he had followed their track—there was no other way he could find them—and that made it likely they had watched for him. Trying to conceal himself now would only prolong things.

It was an unaccustomed creepy feeling, though, to walk openly and deliberately into the maw of a trap. There had been a couple of times in his career when he had been in similar situations, but never so completely exposed, never so completely alone. His skin crawled with awareness, and the muscles of his neck and shoulders tightened almost into knots, as if they could harden into a bullet-proof vest. With each step he anticipated an attack, and with each step he was vaguely surprised it didn't come.

He wished he knew who was waiting for him. It was so important to know your opponent, and this time he didn't have even a hazy idea of who he might be up against. That made it harder. It was always much easier when you knew the parameters of a problem. They had taken Mandy to drag him up here, but anyone could have done that. There was nothing revealing in their actions that would tell him what he needed to beware of.

So he walked blindly into the trap, hating it every step of the way. His eyes roved restlessly, seeking any sign; his ears strained for any betraying sound. Any clue would help, but he had none. And for the life of him, he couldn't imagine who might want him dead after all this time? He had crossed all kinds of people over the years, but most of the people in his business saw it as a deadly serious game that was played according to certain rules. Not too many would waste their time coming after him so much later. Most of them realized, as he did, that revenge was wasted effort.

So who the hell was it?

Mandy saw Ransom approach. He was walking toward her as casually as if he were out for a morning stroll. Nothing about him indicated that he felt any tension, that he was aware he was hunted. Nothing except the way his eyes roamed, refusing to settle, even on her.

Her throat tightened until the pain was almost unbearable. Dear God, she loved him, and now he was walking into an obvious trap without a bit of hesitation. Walking with the pride, decision and determination of the warrior he was. Coming to her rescue. Oh God!

Wildly she struggled at her bonds, knowing only that she had to escape so he wouldn't need to come any deeper into the trap.

"Go back," she begged in a tear-thickened voice. "Oh, God, go back!"

But he just kept coming, walking steadily and surely toward whatever awaited him. Tears burned in her eyes, blinding her briefly before she blinked them away. The sun turned his hair to golden fire, and he looked so...so... Oh God, how she loved him!

They had tied her, trussed her like a sacrifice on that boulder, he saw. Rage rose like bile in his throat, scorching him. For this, he would kill. For this, he would take revenge. Whoever had done this to her was going to pay, if he had to reach beyond the grave to do it.

He reached her side and looked down at her. He was beyond speech, and so was she. The table of rock she lay on was at his chest height, and he was able to see with disturbing clarity what her escape attempts had done to her wrists. Without a word, he pulled out his pocketknife and slashed at the first rope. He didn't care if an army surrounded them and pointed their rifles at him, he was going to free her wrists from any more agony.

After he released the first rope, he walked around the boulder, reaching for the second. Just as he touched the blade to the rope, a shot rang out, sending up flakes of granite from the boulder on which Mandy lay. Ransom froze, not moving a muscle except for the fingers of his hand. He tucked the knife into Mandy's hand and closed her fingers over it. A glance at her wet eyes told him she understood.

It also nearly killed him to see the love there. He had done that to her. He had made her care again. He deserved everything that was coming to him and then some. He had breached her castle walls and brought her to this. Yes, he ought to be shot.

"Back away from her, Ransom," came a familiar voice from the trees. "Back away or I'll shoot her right now. I know you, Ransom. You'd rather keep her alive on the off-

chance you can rescue her. So drop that rifle and back
away."

For an instant he didn't move. He *couldn't* move. Everything inside him froze as a fist of understanding grabbed
his stomach and twisted it into a painful knot. And then
slowly, very slowly, he dropped the rifle and backed up. If
he got far enough away from the rock, maybe he could keep
attention away from Mandy so she would have a chance to
use the knife.

He backed up another step, then another.

"Hold it right there, Ransom. There are two rifles trained
on you right now. One of them's a nice M500, and it's
loaded with an explosive round. Your girlfriend will be raw
stew."

Ransom held his arms out, away from his body, and
turned slowly toward the voice. Tilting his head back, he
looked up into the trees. Then, quite calmly, he said,
"Hello, Karen. I thought you'd been terminated."

Chapter 13

Mandy stiffened in shock, understanding at once. Ransom's wife. The woman who had betrayed him and sent him into terrible captivity. The woman who had aborted his child. Anger rose in her, anger and pain for Ransom. At that moment, for the first time in her life, she felt honestly capable of murder.

"Not quite dead, darling," came the mocking answer. "It's all your fault that I might well be, though."

"I don't quite see it that way, Karen," Ransom answered while his mind worked frantically, thinking at light speed, considering and rejecting ideas.

"No, of course you don't, darling. But it *was* your fault. All of it. You were a target of opportunity, as they say. If you hadn't pursued me quite so diligently, I wouldn't have been ordered to make use of you. I wouldn't have been ordered to get pregnant. God! The entire idea sickened me. Breeding! Worse, breeding *your* child. You can't conceive how thrilled I was when I learned you couldn't get out of that mission."

"I'm beginning to imagine," Ransom said coldly, turning his head a little so he could see Mandy from the corner of his eye and still keep Karen in sight. A shaft of relief pierced his concentration when he realized that Mandy was cautiously sawing at the rope with the knife he had left in her bound hand. The angle was awkward, and her activity was further limited by the need not to draw attention, but she was working at it. Good girl!

"No, I don't think you *can* imagine!" Karen said bitterly. "You should have died in that labor camp! If you had, everything would have been all right!"

"Why is that?" He was deliberately playing dumb in a bid for time, not that he really knew what the devil he was going to be able to do, but time would at least give him the opportunity to come up with something. He needed Mandy free before he attempted anything, but even more, he needed to know exactly where Karen's accomplice was located. That was now the wild card in the deck. Until he knew where her friend was, he didn't dare do anything.

"Why? *Why?* Did the beatings dull your mind, Ransom?"

"Maybe. It just seems to me that if you could escape the sanction—which you so obviously have—it would have been an even simpler matter to skip the country and start a new life somewhere else. Obviously you have other masters who could help you out." Keep her talking, keep her talking. Restlessly, his eyes scanned the surrounding trees and brush, seeking the other person.

"But I don't. Not anymore, darling, and that's your fault."

"How so?" From the corner of his eye he watched Mandy ease slowly onto her side so she could work at the rope better. He moved again, trying to make it impossible for Karen to watch both him and Mandy at the same time.

"Don't move, Ransom," Karen said sharply. "Your little friend can saw at that rope all she wants. She's not going anywhere alive."

Mandy's hands trembled visibly at that announcement, but she never stopped sawing. It was all she could do at the moment, so she would do it. After she was free there might be an opportunity to do something else, but unless she was free she couldn't do anything at all. And unless she was free, Ransom's options would be seriously limited. Damn, it wouldn't have been any harder to saw through steel!

"Why not let her go?" Ransom asked, keeping his tone carefully neutral as he once again edged away from Mandy. "She can't possibly hurt you now, Karen."

"No, but she can certainly be useful, darling. You're besotted with her. It was written all over your face at the dance last night. And she's besotted with you. She made no secret of the fact."

Mandy's stomach lurched sharply. So Karen had been the woman at the dance! She had actually talked to her!

"So, darling," Karen continued, "she's very useful. She'll do anything to protect you, and I can easily imagine any number of things I could make her do that would drive you utterly crazy."

Now it was Ransom's stomach that lurched, and he had to battle with the horror that rushed through him in sickening waves. He had never imagined such depravity, but he knew Karen was capable of it. Hadn't she condemned him to that prison? If she could do that...

He edged a little farther away from Mandy and scanned the trees, seeking Karen's accomplice. This was not the time to react emotionally, and he clamped down savagely on the feelings Karen was stirring up. At last, he was able to speak coolly.

"I don't see how I can have much to do with your present problems," he said. "If you hadn't betrayed me, everything would have been fine for you. I would have stayed home and raised the child you didn't want, and you could have gone your own way."

"You really are surprisingly obtuse," Karen said sharply. "They had no intention of letting you retire, Ransom. No, they planned to use your child as a hostage to keep you working, but as a double agent." She gave a brittle laugh. "Never thought of that, did you? I might almost have enjoyed watching you squirm, but I couldn't stand the thought of having a child. Do you really think I want my body disfigured that way? That I want to go through the positively animal experience of giving birth? No, thank you! I needed to get rid of that child, and they wouldn't let me, so I had to get rid of *you*. Once I was rid of you, the child didn't matter. I didn't have to have it. And having it was the whole problem.''

"And you did get rid of me. That should have been the end of it.''

"Except that you came back, darling. You came back and betrayed me. You not only let *your* masters know that I'd betrayed you, but it became obvious to *my* superiors that I must have been responsible. Once they realized I had defied their orders, they had no further use for me.'' She laughed harshly. "So you see, my darling ex-husband, there's no place on earth for me to hide. But at least I'm going to have the satisfaction of knowing you have paid. And believe me, you *will* pay. Dearly. Starting with that woman.''

The knife at last cut through the rope and Mandy's left wrist was free. Heedless of the danger, she sat up and started working on the ropes confining her ankles. She heard what Karen was threatening and was convinced that her imagination probably couldn't begin to conceive of the horrible things the other woman was dreaming up. Which was just as well, because she really didn't need to be any more frightened than she already was.

And she made up her mind that no matter what Karen threatened, no matter how much they hurt her, she would not do anything they told her to do. No matter what the price, she wouldn't allow herself to be used against Ransom.

"Erik, darling,'' Karen's voice suddenly sang out, "why don't you enjoy yourself before the bitch gets free?''

Mandy jerked and looked up, her stomach climbing into her throat as she saw a huge, hideous man emerge from the trees. He looked exactly the way Hollywood had always depicted thugs, she thought hysterically. And she knew what he intended to do. It was there in the smile on his lips, the look in his eyes. She bit her lip hard to stifle an instinctive protest and quickly lowered her gaze to the rope she was sawing at. Maybe, just maybe... The hope was vain, but there was no other.

It was precisely the moment Ransom was waiting for. Now he knew where both of them were. Reaching up, he grabbed at his jacket collar as if he were having trouble breathing and managed to rip open all the snaps. Now he could get to the machine gun, but Mandy was between him and Erik. Also, Erik and Karen were so far separated that it would be difficult to get them both fast enough. If Erik reached Mandy and was able to use her as a shield...

"Mandy, lie down. Now!"

She wasn't used to taking orders, and for an instant the command didn't compute. In that instant Erik leapt forward and Karen leveled her gun at Ransom.

Oh God, thought Ransom, it was over. That bastard would get Mandy.

And then, with a bloodcurdling howl that would have pleased his ancestors, Micah hurtled out of the trees toward Karen. At the same instant Mandy came to her senses and lay down flat, giving Ransom a clear shot at Erik. He never hesitated. He whipped out the machine gun and sprayed fully sixty rounds at the huge man. Accuracy didn't matter with this weapon. Mandy closed her eyes, sickened by the sight.

Just before Micah reached her, Karen's gun fired, getting off a well-aimed round at Ransom. The impact of the bullet spun him around and threw him back against the boulder. Mandy heard his grunt as he hit and sat up immediately, just catching sight of him as he sank to the ground. Oh God, he'd been shot! He'd been shot! Grabbing the knife, she sawed frantically at her bonds again, desperate to get to Ransom, while Micah wrestled on the hard ground with Karen.

Suddenly the clearing was filled with a deafening whop-whop sound, and Mandy looked up to see the medevac chopper fly in over the treetops. Oh, thank God, thank God. Sobs began to choke her as she sawed at her bonds. They never would have gotten Ransom down the hill without help. Thank God for Micah. She was going to kiss him until his cheeks turned red.

A cry drew her attention toward Karen just in time to see Micah get his arm under her chin and grab her around the neck. After a few seconds the woman sank quietly to the ground, as limp as an empty rag doll. Micah saw Mandy's horrified gaze.

"I just pinched her carotid artery," he said, bending to handcuff Karen. "She'll wake up in no time. Unfortunately."

"If I had a gun, I'd shoot her," Mandy said hoarsely. "Honest to God, Micah, I'd kill her."

"Yeah, it tempts me, too." He clapped a second set of cuffs around Karen's ankles, then hurried over to Ransom as the chopper settled cautiously on the rocky hilltop.

"How is he?" Mandy demanded, unable to see anything at all except Micah's dark head as he bent over Ransom. Once before she had felt this frightened. She remembered it vividly. She had been standing by John's grave, listening to the minister intone a prayer, and had suddenly realized that she was in labor and it was too soon. She felt just as helpless now. "Micah? Is he—is he—?"

"No. No. He's alive." Slowly he looked up over the edge of the boulder at her. "He's alive, Mandy."

"Is it . . . bad?" She bit her lip until she tasted the coppery tang of blood. She didn't want to hear this. She didn't think she could stand it.

"It's not good."

Nor did it get any better. Her last sight of Ransom was as he was lifted aboard the chopper in a basket stretcher. He was unconscious, and even his lips were white. Mandy couldn't bring herself to glance at the bloody mess that had been his chest.

"He'll get the best medical care available, Mrs. Grant," said a tall, thin man in a dark suit. "I promise you, he'll get the best."

Then he climbed into the helicopter with Ransom, Karen and another man in a suit, and they took off. Mandy was left in the clearing with Nate, Micah and four strangers in camouflage. And the bloody corpse that had been Erik.

"It'll be okay, sweet pea," Nate said to her. "Honey, I swear, he'll make it. That sumbitch will make it or I'll kill him."

She couldn't even cry. For the second time in her life, she hurt too badly to weep. "Where are they taking him?"

"I don't know. I'll find out, but right now, I don't know."

It was as if Ransom had vanished from the face of the earth. He was taken initially to the hospital in Casper, but as soon as his condition was stabilized, he was whisked away on Gentry's orders. Nate tried everything he could think of to discover where he'd been taken, but all trails were dead ends.

"I'm sorry, sweet face," he told Mandy after a week. "We're not going to find him until he wants us to find him."

Mandy regarded him from bleak, dry eyes. "I would just like to know if he's alive."

"Yeah. Me too."

Never before had she felt quite like this, Mandy thought as she moved mechanically through her days. John's loss had been different, a sharper spike of pain that had to be surmounted. This felt . . . endless. As if she had fallen into a pit and was now wandering in darkness over a featureless terrain.

She wrote, but she found little satisfaction in it. A heavy frost killed her marigolds at last, and she cleared the dead plants from the garden, unable to take her usual pleasure in the seasonal task. The freshly turned earth was barren, as barren as her soul.

There was plenty of time for regrets, plenty of time to consider her own foolishness. She had felt Ransom's farewell that last night and had only herself to thank for not having said something, done something, to let him know she wanted him to stay. She couldn't blame anyone else for her craziness, for her inability to reach out, for her emotional cowardice. She felt like that old joke, because she had looked into her mirror and found her own worst enemy: herself.

Autumn deepened, growing colder at night, warming less by day. In the mornings now she needed to break the ice that formed on the watering trough. The horses were welcome work, however. They kept her hands busy and her body tired so the emptiness wasn't quite as noticeable.

It would have been easy, she thought, to fall once again into the belief that if she held herself aloof she couldn't be hurt, but this time she didn't fall back into her familiar patterns. She refused to. This time, she promised herself, whatever happened, she would be a participant, not an unwilling victim.

She began to feel sick in the mornings, and after a couple of weeks she knew why. Hope blossomed, just a frail little tinge of color to her days. Maybe this, at least, would last this time. Maybe, just once in her life, she wouldn't lose. Maybe she could be allowed just one person to care for. Maybe this time her arms wouldn't be left empty, her heart would be filled. Determined, she went to the doctor and began to follow his every instruction.

The days became cold, though snow did not fall, and she spent less and less time outdoors. She liked, though, to stand at the storm door that had replaced the screen door in the kitchen and catch the late afternoon sun. The rays slanted beneath the roof of the narrow porch and poured golden light through the glass, and they felt so warm and bright that it was almost a caress.

She was standing there one afternoon, absorbing the heat and the light, when a shiny red Blazer pulled up into the yard and halted. The sun was behind the driver, concealing his identity in shadow, and all she could see was the outline of a cowboy hat. Nate, she thought, or Micah. One of them must have bought a new car and wanted to show it off. These days she saw Micah quite often. They had become friends.

The driver climbed out and came around the front of the vehicle toward her. Time stood still, and her heart stopped beating. That walk, with its slight hesitation, was as familar to her as her own face. That shape, a little too lean again, was one her body recognized every line of. His golden beard was a little longer, and when he swept the hat from his head he was shocked to see much more gray among the gold.

Ransom. Her lips formed his name, but no sound merged. Instinctively, one hand rose to her heart, the other settling protectively over her stomach. He was alive! Her heart began rejoicing, even as her mind issued warnings. He hadn't called, he hadn't written, in all this time. If he wanted her, if he cared for her, surely he would have called? Or written? Dread and joy warred within her.

He opened the storm door, and she stepped back to permit him to enter. Blue eyes, eyes exactly the color of the Conard County sky, searched her face as if he were hungry for the sight of her. But she didn't dare believe that. Not even now, when he stood right before her, did she have the guts to believe in happiness. Not yet.

"I told myself," he said presently, in a voice grown rusty with feelings, "that you were better off without me. I told myself that you were right, if you didn't care you couldn't be hurt. I told myself that I had been unforgivably smug, that I had hurt you by battering at your castle walls, and that if I was half the knight you believed me to be I would walk away before you got hurt any more or any worse. I told myself that I had spent such a short time in your life that you would get over me fast." He drew a long ragged breath. 'I told myself I had no right."

Things inside her, old walls, old barriers, old defenses, began crumbling painfully. This was going to hurt like hell, she realized. Regardless of what he said, of what happened next, regardless of the outcome, she was about to shed her protective skin, and it was going to hurt.

"I was sure," he said, "that you wanted me gone. I believed you wanted me to go away before I made you any more vulnerable than I already had. I was convinced you wanted your old life back. And I know I'm not worthy of you."

"Ransom—" The cracks were widening, the dams were crumbling, and she reached out instinctively toward him.

"Shh. Let me finish. I need . . . I need to explain."

Blinking back the threatening tears, she managed a nod

"I had plenty of time to think about a lot of things whil
I was stuck in that damn hospital bed. I really got all woun
up about what was best for you. And then I realized some
thing else. I realized that I was afraid to trust you. I real
ized that all the things I was thinking were based on that. I
suddenly occurred to me that I had to stop trying to do wha
was best for you, that I had to trust *you* to know what wa
best for you. Damn it, am I making any sense?" His eye.
scoured her face for understanding.

"I think you're making perfect sense," Mandy answered
around the pain in her throat. Why wouldn't he take her int
his arms? All she needed, all she wanted, was to be in hi
arms, to feel his warmth and strength and know that he wa
still *alive*. Oh, God, why had she needed to come so close t
losing him just so she could appreciate him?

"Well," he said after a moment, "that was kind of scary
After . . . after all that's happened, it isn't the easiest thing fo
me to trust, I guess."

"I guess," she murmured, understanding.

"So I went off on another tangent, telling myself that yo
probably hated me by now, because I hadn't even calle
you."

"Hate isn't what I was feeling." The thought had neve
occurred to her.

"No?" The question held hope. "Well, I was convince
you couldn't feel anything else. That lasted a few days."

When he remained silent, she prompted him, still seek
ing the words that would allow her to throw herself into hi
arms. "And then?"

"And then . . ." He drew another deep, ragged breath
"And then I realized I can't live without you, that life isn'
worth a damn if you aren't there to share it with me, and
said to hell with pride and rationalization and what was bes
and whether you hate me. I'm here, Amanda Lynn, and I'l
be damned if I'll go away again, unless you tell me to. If yo
tell me to go, I'll go and never come back, but otherwis
you're stuck with me."

Stuck with him? As a handyman? As a lover? As a live-in boyfriend? Wild emotions were rising in her, pouring through all the cracks in her defenses, and she had to battle an urge to shake him. She would, she realized with a pang, take whatever he was giving and count herself lucky, but some last vestige of pride and need kept her silent about the baby. He had married once for the sake of a child, and she knew he would do so again. But if it were possible, she wanted him to want her, just her, enough to commit himself. Please, God, I want to have my cake and eat it, too, just once. Just this once, *please*.

And then it struck her that she had to take a step herself. He had spoken of his doubts and reservations, of all the things he feared and worried about, and now it was up to her to reassure him enough to take another step. She *owed* it to him to step toward him just as he was stepping toward her.

"I would *never* ask you to leave," she said hoarsely. "Never."

That word *never* might have been a magic incantation, because suddenly her bleak, gray world blossomed in all the colors of the rainbow; all the sharp edges softened, and pain spun away dizzily as those strong, beloved arms closed around her and lifted her high. Dimly, she realized that he was carrying her upstairs, and her insides clenched pleasurably in anticipation, but mostly she just knew that at long last she had found her place and her identity and her home.

"I love you, Amanda Lynn," he whispered as fiercely as the warrior he was. He lowered her with infinite care to her narrow bed and came down beside her with an expression of wonder in his eyes. "I love you more than life, more than hope. More than I thought it was possible to love."

He didn't wait for an answer, and in truth he hardly needed it. She had told him that she would never ask him to leave, and from this woman that was the most important declaration of all. She had asked him into her castle, past all her moats and drawbridges. She had made a place for him beside her hearth, and she had said she would never ask him to leave.

Gently he kissed away her tears of joy, and gently he claimed her with his body. She wore denim and cotton, bu it might have been lace and silk as it whispered away in the waning light. He wore denim and wool, but it might have been shining armor as he cast it impatiently aside. Wha mattered, the only thing that mattered, was the way their flesh melded, banishing solitude and loneliness, sorrow and yearning. Gently he moved in her, and gently she rose to meet him. Gently. Gently.

"Ah, princess," he whispered, "I've missed you. The light was gone from my soul, and my heart never stopped aching. I felt lost in ways I've never felt before. And all the while I was telling myself to let you go, I was dying because you're part of me. You make me whole."

She wrapped her arms tightly around his broad shoulders and spread her soft palms against the ridged scars on his back. "I love you," she whispered. "I love you. You're my home. My family. You make me belong."

He rose on his elbows and moved harder, his body demanding her response. "You're mine. Mine."

"Yes . . ."

"You'll marry me." He thrust harder.

"Yes." She gasped.

"We'll grow old . . . and gray . . . and . . ." He groaned deeply "Together. Oh, God, Mandy . . . Mandy . . . Mandy . . ."

They catapulted together beyond thought, soaring upward on wings of passion until they melted in the heat of the sun.

Later, he pulled the comforter over them and tucked her close into the curve of his hard body. "I have to insist on a bigger bed," he told her, a smile evident in the words.

"Of course. King-size." She rubbed her nose against his cheek and inhaled the wonderful scent that clung to his beard. "I thought . . . I thought you were never coming back, that I had driven you away."

"It wasn't exactly that you drove me away, princess. It was that I was suddenly afraid I was pushing you into pain. I began to feel like a man who was pushing somebody out of an airplane without knowing if their parachute was working. I don't know how better to put it. I just suddenly became very aware that I could cause you a great deal of suffering. So I thought it would be best for you if I left."

She tunneled her fingers into the golden hair that covered his newly healed chest. "I sort of felt that way myself. It wasn't easy for me to face the fact that I'd gotten involved in spite of myself."

"And now?" He tilted her face up and tried to read her expression in the dusk. "How do you feel about that now?"

"Glad. Thrilled. Ecstatic." She kissed his neck. "Oh, God, I love you so much, I don't care what it costs." For a long moment she hugged him as tightly as she could. And then she asked the question that had plagued her for weeks. "You haven't told me how badly you were hurt when Karen shot you. And what happened to Karen?"

"Karen's been taken care of," he said grimly. "She was handed over to the opposition, and they're a lot less finicky about how they handle traitors. You don't have to worry about her."

If Ransom felt anything at all about that, she couldn't tell. It was a subject, she decided, that should be buried forever, right now. "And you?" Her hand touched the new, red scar tissue on his side.

"The wound was pretty bad," he admitted. "I'm short a few more parts now."

"What parts?"

"My spleen and a few ribs. They managed to save my whole lung, though."

She shivered and tried not to think how he must have hurt, how close he must have been to death. She might have to face that eventually, but she refused to let it shadow her joy right now.

For his part, Ransom was feeling exposed again, raw and vulnerable, as only Mandy could make him feel. This time, however, he felt no urge to run and hide. This time, as he held her close, that vulnerability seemed a small price to pay for the warmth this woman gave him. Many times, out of necessity, he had trusted others with his life, but never before had he trusted anyone with his heart—not even Karen when she had carried his child. Entrusting his heart to Mandy was suddenly an easy thing to do. She made him feel . . . welcome. Loved. Whole. At peace.

"Mandy? You did say you'd marry me? I didn't dream that?"

She laughed. He had never heard her laugh quite that way before, a joyously free sound. A truly happy unshadowed sound. "You didn't dream it."

"You don't want to sort everything out first?" It suddenly occurred to him that this woman had made a hell of a commitment when she accepted his proposal. She hadn't asked a thing, not where they would live or whether he would continue as an agent. She had given herself without reservation. His throat suddenly tightened, and his eyes burned with a flood tide of feeling for her. "No reservations?" he asked hoarsely. "No doubts?"

"Well . . ." she said, feeling suddenly more confident and sure of what she was doing than ever before in her life. How could she feel anything else when this golden warrior looked at her as if she were the answer to his every dream and prayer? "There's just one thing you should know first."

"What's that?" The look in her eyes kept him from getting too worried about what she might say. Those eyes weren't about to wound him. No way. They held his with glowing warmth.

Mandy took his hand and guided it down to her stomach, the as-yet flat place where her gift to him was nestled. Feeling suddenly incredibly shy, she leaned up and whispered her news in his ear.

For an instant Ransom didn't move. For just an instant she feared that perhaps he didn't want . . .

"Really?" The word was husky as it escaped him. "Really?" He pressed his hand more firmly against her satiny abdomen and closed his eyes. "Mandy . . . Mandy, are you sure? I know how you felt about Mary, how you hurt over losing her, and I wouldn't put you through that again for the world."

"Everything's going to be fine this time," she said bravely. "I want—I want so badly to give you a baby."

He kissed her with every bit of the love he felt for her, b. he couldn't quite relax. "It isn't necessary, sweetheart. I'm thrilled with the thought of a baby, but I don't think I could stand to see the light go out of your eyes. I don't think I could stand to see you turn into the Mandy Grant I first met, so sad. Oh God, you were so sad!" He wrapped her in his arms and squeezed her as close as he could get her. He would do anything, anything, to spare her further sorrow.

"I'm sure," she said bravely, hugging him back, sensing his pain and wanting to ease it. "I want to do this. I *need* to do this. For both of us."

After a short while he released a reluctant laugh. "Someday I may figure out how to say no to you. Okay, princess, but this means we aren't going to hang around for a June wedding."

The smile returned to her eyes and face when she saw the smile in his. "No? When do you suggest?"

"I figure Friday will do just fine, mostly because I figure I can't swing it any sooner." He dropped a kiss on the tip of her nose. "Of course, if you want a big shindig—"

"No. No. All I want is you. Just you."

He spent the next hour showing her that he felt exactly the same way. Much, much later, as she was dozing gently beside him, she heard him say, "If it's a girl, I want to name her Lynn."

Without opening her eyes, she smiled. "Okay. And a boy?"

"I'll leave that up to you, Amanda Lynn. Just as long as it's not Ransom."

That opened her eyes. "Why? It's a beautiful name!"

"It's a miserable name for a kid. People made jokes and puns out of it all my life. Nope, no Ransom, junior. No kid of mine is going to have to put up with that kind of teasing."

Hiding a smile, she snuggled closer. "If you insist. But I wouldn't mind being 'ransomed' again, if you've got a minute or two."

He groaned. "Now don't you start it!" But he rolled her gently onto her back and leaned over her, a glint in his blue es. "I'm going to be 'ransoming' you for the rest of your life, princess, and don't you forget it."

Forget it? Not likely! "Then how about starting with a king's ransom?" she purred suggestively. "A princess is surely worth that much."

"She's worth a hell of a lot more, Amanda Lynn," he said, his voice gone completely husky. "One hell of a lot more. And don't you ever forget that, either."

* * * * *

It's Opening Night in October—
and you're invited!
Take a look at romance with a
brand-new twist, as the stars
of tomorrow make their
debut today!
It's LOVE:
an age-old story—
now, with
*WORLD PREMIERE
APPEARANCES* by:

Patricia Thayer—Silhouette Romance #895
JUST MAGGIE—Meet the Texas rancher who wins this pretty
teacher's heart...and lose your own heart, too!

Anne Marie Winston—Silhouette Desire #742
BEST KEPT SECRETS—Join old lovers reunited and see what
secret wonders have been hiding...beneath the flames!

Sierra Rydell—Silhouette Special Edition #772
ON MIDDLE GROUND—Drift toward Twilight, Alaska, with this
widowed mother and collide—heart first—into body heat
enough to melt the frozen tundra!

Kate Carlton—Silhouette Intimate Moments #454
KIDNAPPED!—Dare to look on as a timid wallflower blos-
soms and falls in fearless love—with her gruff, mysterious
kidnapper!

**Don't miss the classics of tomorrow—
premiering today—only from**

PREM

Take 4 bestselling love stories FREE

Plus get a FREE surprise gift!

TAKE A WALK ON THE DARK SIDE OF LOVE

October is the shivery season, when chill winds blow and shadows walk the night. Come along with us into a haunting world where love and danger go hand in hand, where passions will thrill you and dangers will chill you. Come with us to

In this newest short story collection from Sihouette Books, three of your favorite authors tell tales just perfect for a spooky autumn night. Let Anne Stuart introduce you to "The Monster in the Closet," Helen R. Myers bewitch you with "Seawitch," and Heather Graham Pozzessere entice you with "Wilde Imaginings."

Silhouette Shadows™
Haunting a store near you this October.